Lock Down Publications and Ca$h
Presents

I0679417

FOR MY ENEMY'S SAKE

WHEN THE STREETS SAY SO

Written By

IRA B.

FOR MY ENEMY'S SAKE | IRA B.

First Edition 2025

Printed in the United States of America

Lock Down Publications
P.O. Box 944
Stockbridge, GA 30281
www.lockdownpublications.com

Like our page on Facebook: Lock Down Publications
www.facebook.com/lockdownpublications.ldp

Stay Connected with Us!

Text **LOCKDOWN** to 22828 to stay up-to-date with new releases, sneak peaks, contests and more…

Like our page on Facebook:
Lock Down Publications

Join Lock Down Publications/The New Era Reading Group

Visit our website:
www.lockdownpublications.com

Follow us on Instagram:
Lock Down Publications

Email Us: We want to hear from you!

PROLOGUE

Harlem, New York

'I can't let this nigga catch me,' he thought tiredly. In the process of running for his life, Roe risked a glance over his shoulder, and to his discomfort, General was no more than twelve yards behind and letting his Glock 40 bang with a vengeance. There was no way Roe was gonna die tonight, especially not at the hands of a childhood friend who was not an archenemy.

General, who had been chasing Roe for nearly two blocks now, lifted his arm again and let off two more rounds in rapid succession. Then he cursed under his breath when neither round hit its target.

Suddenly, Roe shot across the street, zigzagging to throw General's aim off more, as he searched for a possible route to escape his enemy's wrath. He leapt onto the sidewalk and, with his pistol in hand, squeezed the trigger, letting off four wild rounds in General's direction.

Blocka! Blocka! Blocka! Blocka!

Returning gunfire, General shot across the street, barely missing the front fender of a passing car by inches, but his focus was on the chase. Only Roe was in his line of vision. If only he could catch him!

In the surrounding area, innocent bystanders ducked and ran for cover in the darkness of the night as automatic rounds rang out in violent explosions.

As he ran as hard as he could, Roe could feel himself cramping up from lack of physical training, and he was growing tired by the second. The fear of dying would keep him going, no matter how badly his unconditioned body threatened to shut down. Being the smoker he was, his wind was falling short, but his adrenaline surged through him to a dizzying effect. That was when the unexpected happened.

Blocka! Blocka!

"Fuck!" General fumed when, again, neither round did the damage he wished them to do. He, too, was growing tired of chasing the nigga, for Roe should have already been dead by now, and he needed to get back to Baby Thad—wherever he had happened to go when the shit hit the fan. Vega too.

Before Roe even knew what was happening, a police cruiser pulled out from one of the dark alleyways out of nowhere. Because he was running at full speed and couldn't prevent colliding into the driver's door of the cruiser with a vicious bang, he did so and unfortunately lost his grip on his gun from the wicked impact. It literally fell and skidded beneath the car, out of reach.

General took advantage of the situation. This time, when he lifted the gun, he dumped six rounds from the Glock, shattering the driver's side window, causing Roe to cry out in sudden agony. Now he had Roe where he wanted him, advancing upon him with nothing less than murder in his eyes. He stepped a foot away from his enemy. Oblivious to the dead cop behind the wheel of the cruiser with her brains blown out, General's mind was in a dark place where only destruction lay.

"I told you, nigga."

Roe winced, struggling against the side of the car to keep himself upright. He'd been shot through the back of his right shoulder, which he now held with his free hand. "I didn't have shit to do with that!"

Sirens blared from a distance.

General looked down upon him. "It's too late for that shit now, nigga," he said and aimed the gun at Roe's head. "You done fucked with the wrong nigga, son."

Click! Click!

The Glock was as empty as a bottle of Hennessy

'Shit,' thought General. 'Just when I had this nigga!' He looked down at the gun with a murderous glare. All of a sudden, another police cruiser turned onto the street up ahead. Its siren was shrilling loudly, the lights atop it flickering into the night, illuminating the darkened sky with its unwanted presence.

As General cast a glance over his shoulder, he couldn't believe his luck. They were coming fast.

Tucking the Glock at his waist to secure it, General reached down to snatch Roe up to his feet. "It ain't gonna be that easy, nigga. Come on!" he sneered, shoving Roe away toward the belly of the alley. Together, they disappeared into the night, followed by a chain of events that would put the whole city under siege through perilous actions. It was now past the point of no return. It was on and poppin'.

Chapter 1

Ten minutes prior

Old Man Crow bolted from where he had been in a slumber on his sofa. The sound of gunshots rang out just outside his front door, and his blood surged as he focused to remain calm despite being rudely awakened after fighting himself to sleep thirty minutes before. As the TV glowed in the dark living room of his Harlem residence at a modest volume, Crow, who was paralyzed from the waist down, wondered just what was going on out there.

From his trained ear, Crow detected several weapons shooting at once, having served as an army veteran for nearly thirty years. He knew a way when he heard it, and he knew there was a war going on outside his front door.

"Damn it!" Crow grumbled at the realization that he'd left his own .32 ACP Browning automatic pistol back in the bedroom inside the nightstand.

Having been captain of the 19th Armored Field Artillery for two decades, Crow knew guns and kept them lying around the house in close reach. To his dismay, the closest one was across the damn living room, beneath the pillow of his recliner that sat next to the fireplace. That was his .455 Webley revolver. The M1 Garand .30-06 rifle was hanging above the mantelpiece, his 9mm Luger was inside the kitchen counter drawer, and the old .38 caliber Smith & Wesson revolver was beneath the bathroom sink. Old Man Crow was well armed but couldn't get to either one of them as fast as he wanted to, thanks to the vehicle accident three years ago that left him adjusting to a life in a fuckin' wheelchair.

Just when he had made up his mind to crawl over to the recliner for his gun, he was brought to a halt immediately at the sound just outside his front door. Then it burst open, startling the old man half to death. Crow had the fleeting thought that he was in great danger from some unknown enemy until he recognized who it was.

Gun clutched in his hand tightly, Baby Thad entered the house and banged the broken door shut behind him. He backed himself up in the nearest corner next to the door with his gun at ready, as if waiting for the enemy to burst through it next, and then he was gonna light his ass up like a blunt of sour Kush.

More shooting was heard in the distance outside. Baby Thad willed his pounding heart to cease its violent battering within his chest.

From where he sat, observing the scene, Crow could see the desperation in the young man's eyes. He knew that look very well. It was the look of fear of death and survival and the look of a darkness only known by one who had witnessed some very cruel things. Baby Thad looked like a cat trapped in a corner, surrounded by a pack of pit bulls, with no other choice but to fight to the death. Yeah, Crow berated attentively. He was in that same position hundreds of times. He had the scars to prove it.

Once Baby Thad sensed the immediate danger had passed, he stepped out of the corner and approached the nearest window. He wondered where his homie Vega had run to.

"Back away from the windows, son! You're putting yourself more at risk by being seen if someone was to be on the other side looking in," said Crow in that commanding tone he'd yet to retire.

Startled by the voice, Baby Thad whirled around on the old man, ready to squeeze on him. He held steady after seeing exactly who the owner of the voice was.

"Settle down, youngin'."

"I left my boy out there," said Thad.

Crow hit the power button on the TV to shut it off, placing them both in darkness. "If he has any sense, he'll get outta the situation he's in just as you had. Now, go over there and grab my gun from under the cushion of that recliner. Better to have extra firepower just in case whoever's after you come lookin' for you here.

Hesitantly, Thad looked in the direction where the shadowed hand of the old man was pointing. Then he approached the chair and retrieved the gun, reluctantly handing it over to Crow as though unsure of doing so.

"Thank you," Crow replied gratefully. "Now, tell me what the devil you've gotten yourself into, Thad."

Taken aback by the mention of his name, Thad regarded the old man through the obscured living room attentively. Then he thought the old man only knew him by name because he served on the corner just beside his house daily. Baby Thad's name was well known in the streets as a result of his hustling and music. Therefore, it shouldn't have come as a surprise when the old man called him by name for the first time since moving to Harlem several years ago. Baby Thad rang bells in the streets.

With an aggravated sigh, Thad perched himself on the arm of the couch next to Crow's. That same instant, a lighter struck as Crow lit what appeared to be a pipe, and the whiff of weed smoke caressed Thad's sense of smell. That was all the encouragement Thad needed to reach for the pack of Newports in his Eviso jeans.

"It's not me them niggas was after…" Thad explained the situation.

Vega was still running after seeing Baby Thad break off, leaving him in the middle of a war zone. Whoever was shooting behind him appeared to be devoted to the chase, refusing to give up. Vega ran with all his might and bent the next corner up ahead.

Blocka!

"Muthafucka!" muttered Vega after hearing the bullet soar just above his head before entering something solid at his near left.

A moment later, Trel was rounding the corner behind him in chase. He was determined to catch Vega for what he did to Man-Man. The moment Trel and his crew ran down on General and his homies on some beef shit, Vega killed Man-Man off top before his gun jammed. Now he was left without any protection at all, running for his life like never before.

Up ahead, Vega saw an old Baptist church and ran straight for it, giving all he had. He was running like he had a pack of wolves behind him.

Trel let off several more rounds in his direction, grazing his target beneath his right lower rib cage.

"Shit!" Vega groaned and instantly ducked off behind the big church, chest hurting with his pounding heart. The burning sensation in his side made it clear that he needed to do something or die trying.

Approaching footsteps were heard just around the corner. Vega waited.

Knowing that he must get to Vega or regret it later, because Vega definitely wasn't one to sleep on, Trel convinced himself, tonight, Vega would die. The second he turned the corner around the side of the church, a wicked blow sent him lying flat on his back. The gun flew in another direction, several feet away, as Trel fought to stop on point through the dazed effect.

Vega damn near cried out in pain as a result of how hard he had hit him. His hand was sure to be broken from the impact of Trel's hard head.

Shaking the pain away from his hand to no avail, Vega scanned his immediate proximity for where the gun had fallen. A few seconds later, his eyes landed on the weapon, and the first step he made for it, Trel tackled his legs with vicious intent. Vega went down hard, and through the struggle, they fought one another while trying to get closer to the gun.

These niggas did everything from biting to trying to poke the other's eyes out. After a minute of wrestling and whatever it took to get leverage, Trel got himself out of the situation and went for the fallen gun. Vega was right behind him.

Blocka!

The gun exploded the instant Trel wrapped his hand and finger around the trigger. But Vega was on him like a tick on a dirty crackhead, now fighting for control of the gun.

Blocka! Blocka!

Two more shots rang out during their battle for controlled possession, shattering glass nearby.

From Vega's standpoint, he was having major difficulty due to his broken right hand. He knew that one slip-up could cost him his life, and the way things were going at that moment, he feared it might just happen. Vega did the unthinkable.

Just when Trel thought he had full control of the gun, Vega latched onto his neck savagely, biting down into his throat like a champion-fighting pit bull.

Trel, reduced to begging for release, felt Vega clamp down harder onto his jugular. Vega's teeth viciously sank into his flesh. He tasted the warm, salty blood gushing into his mouth, as the desperation to survive caused the animalistic beastiality to overtake his conscious state of mind. Before he knew what was going on, a large chunk of Trel's throat was ripped from his body. It was a horrific scene.

Snarling down at what was left of Trel, he spat his enemy's flesh aside. Vega bent down to retrieve the gun from Trel's lifeless hand. Without so much as a flicker of remorse,

Vega dumped the rest of the four rounds from the clip into his face.

"Bitch ass nigga!" Vega growled before turning away from the corpse, disappearing into the night.

He couldn't wait to see Baby Thad. For leaving his side to go through what he just gone through, Vega had dark animosity for his childhood homie.

Just several yards away, lying beneath a bench in the church's courtyard, a pair of half-drunken eyes had witnessed the whole thing.

The night was far from over; it had just begun.

After taking a few more drags from his third cigarette in less than ten minutes, Thad stubbed it out in the glass-leaf ashtray before him on the low coffee table. He had just explained to Old Man Crow what was going on.

Thad got up to peek out the window. There was a lot of commotion outside as people gathered near the crime scene where Man-Man lay murdered in the middle of the street. Police were all over the place, the flashing lights creating a colorful, glow-in-the-dark sky, and two ambulances were on standby. It was a circus out there.

Neither General nor Vega had yet to answer their muthafuckin' phones when Thad called, or maybe General's phone was still on the dashboard, which was still parked at the corner across the street. That was the last place Thad remembered seeing it just before Trel and his crew walked up and strapped up on some beef shit. Now Trel could only hope the best had come out of the whole situation with his niggas.

"I don't understand you youngin's nowadays," said Crow with a shake of his head. He was very disappointed. "You go to war over some of the dumbest shit in the world. And what makes it so bad is y'all are going against your own damn people!"

Thad didn't respond, so Crow continued. "I mean, damn. Y'all grew up together in this neighborhood from babies, and here y'all are, killing up one another as if—"

"The ones closest to you could be your worst enemies," said Thad with mild aggression.

"And that's true, Thad. I agree with you on that."

Stepping away from the window, Thad reclaimed his perch on the arm of the chair. "Like I said, them niggas brought that shit to us, so we gave 'em what they wanted."

"How did you know they didn't come to reason?"

"With guns out?" Thad retorted.

Crow said, "You got a point there, youngin'."

During the explanation, Thad told Crow the essence behind the whole situation, omitting details that didn't need to be uttered. It all started a long time ago, in reference to General's and Roe's fathers. One was a district attorney, the other a criminal lawyer. The real beef originated between the fathers, who were once close friends as well at one point in time.

As a result of their father's beef in the courtroom, both General and Roe created their own in the streets. Both were hustlers who ran with two different circles, but it was Roe who really disliked General. He had gone as far as going out of his way to make it known, but General was too much of a hustler to acknowledge Roe's unnecessary behavior. He was more about his money. Though Roe was as well, he was still on some shotty shit.

This had been going on for ten years now.

Both arch enemies grew up fighting each other and fighting for one another, a bond long broken and traded in for a cold, hard hatred that couldn't be avoided. At times, the two would find themselves competing against one another on a variety of levels, but a recent incident brought the two at odds once again—this time, to a-whole-nother degree. It had been a long time coming.

General and Roe were out for blood now. Death was in the air.

A few days before, General's father, Melvin Whitaker, helped represent a high-profile case, which was won after two years of fighting. It was evident Roe's father, District Attorney Robert Hunt, was royally pissed to the point he and Melvin went into a shoving match outside the courtroom. Robert Hunt threatened Melvin in front of many, accusing Melvin of having a conflict of interest with the aforementioned defendant. That accusation fell on deaf ears with Melvin.

Then the fool Robert was seen conferring with a young hoodlum, the day before Melvin was mugged in the parking lot of his office building, who fit the hoodlum's physical description. That was all General needed to know to believe the same hoodlum came from Roe's circle.

Just when General and his crew were planning to see about Roe about the matter, Roe and his crew showed up on the set. Then all hell broke loose.

"So, what's next, Thad?" Crow asked curiously.

Before Thad could answer, his cell phone shrilled with life. He fished the phone from his pocket and checked the number. It was a number he didn't recognize, but he answered it anyway.

"What's up?" he answered.

There was a brief pause. "You know what's up, bitch! You leave a nigga out in the water like that?" asked Vega's hoarse but menacing tone. "I'ma leave your bitch ass in blood, nigga. When you see me, you better duck, 'cause I'ma—"

"Vee, what the fuck you talkin' about?"

Crow looked up at him.

"I'm war ready!" Vega hissed like a venomous cobra. "That's what I'm talkin' about, son."

The click of the dial tone was the next thing Thad heard. Almost speechless, Thad could not believe what he had just heard.

"The fuck's wrong with him?" he whispered, not feeling so good about the situation.

Stuffing his pipe with more weed, Crow finally said, "I got a serious question for you, son."

Thad called the number back, only to get a busy signal. "Fuck!"

"Thad?" Crow spoke up again.

When Baby Thad finally looked up at the old man, he saw a grave expression on Crow's face. Even through the dimly lit room, he could see the man's eyes, which reflected the moonlight from the nearby window. What he saw in them were tears, a sight that could not be resisted but beheld greatly.

"Yeah?" Thad belatedly replied.

"What do you know about war, son?" asked Crow. Seeing the answer in Thad's eyes without the verbal response he intended to hear, Crow told his story.

Chapter 2

Muttering vulgar expletives under her breath at whoever was banging on her door like the fuckin' feds, Lisa couldn't wait to see who it was so she could give them a piece of her mind. Ma wasn't feeling this shit at all, and as she made her way to the door, she wondered if she may need her razor just in case she had to cut a bitch.

The banging continued. Lisa halted before the front door and demanded to know who the fuck it was.

"Lisa, open the muthafuckin' door!" the voice said aggressively from the other side.

Recognizing General's voice, she wasted no time unlocking the door and opening it for her bro. What she got instead startled her and made her panic, stifling a shriek that could have probably been heard all the way to Queens. Suddenly, Roe's bloody form was shoved through the door, nearly colliding with Lisa, but instead tumbled onto the floor of the foyer in an agonizing heap.

General stepped over the threshold into the entrance hall, looking like something out of an urban horror film. His Coogi attire was drenched in blood, and the look in his eyes was menacing enough to make the devil himself cringe with caution.

"Oh, shit!" Lisa gasped loudly, looking down at Roe's fallen body before her on the freshly scrubbed floor.

General shut the door behind him and locked it, then grabbed hold of Roe's shirt collar, and dragged him down the hall into the kitchen doorway. By now, Lisa was out of her mind with dread.

"Where your phone at, ma?"

"What happened to him?" Lisa questioned instead, dropping her knees alongside Roe. It was obvious she knew Roe well and wanted to help him, and she snatched down the dry dish towel from the handle of the oven to place against his wound.

"Fuck that chump!" General ignored Lisa's attempt to tend to the wound of his enemy. Then he went in search of the phone, wondering why he hadn't murdered Roe by now.

General needed to call and check up on his little homies.

A cry of intense and excruciating pain bellowed from twenty-eight-year-old Roe from inside the kitchen, causing Lisa to cry out apologetically for hurting him more.

Inside the living room, General paused instantly when he saw movement from the corner of his eye. He spun in that direction, frowning in response at who he saw standing there in front of him. He went for his Glock and moved in Dred's direction with wicked intentions, rushing him fast and placing the gun to his head.

"What the fuck you doin' here, nigga!" General snarled as he glared into Dred's green eyes.

Dred, who was Lisa's former boyfriend, according to what General had heard, was from the South Bronx and was known in the streets of New York for selling the best weed in the city. Also, Dred was a fool when it came to gunplay, but his circle was small when it came to having a team to back him up. All he had was his brother, Mango, and his right-hand man, Cuda, who also was pure hell and feared in the streets by many.

At that moment, General didn't five a fuck how many niggas feared Dred or his people.

"Yo, son," Dred said, unafraid but cautious. He, too, knew of General's street caliber. "It ain't even that serious, man. You need to get that gun outta my—"

Whop!

With an open hand, General damn near slapped the skeleton out of that nigga. Since he didn't have any bullets left in his gun, the only pressure he could apply was physical. Besides, he didn't like the nigga anyway.

"Whatcha gonna do, nigga? Huh? Jump bad and get your ass dealt with right here?" asked General.

Of course, Dred wasn't stupid enough to test him when he had the upper hand, especially while still dressed in his boxer shorts and tank top. There was no way he would go up against General at the movement.

"I told you to stay easy from my people one time, Dred," said a fuming General. "But you couldn't respect my call, and now you gotta deal with me—"

"That bitch called me over here, homeboy!" Dred said with aggression in his voice.

"Then she called you to your death, nigga." With that said, General began pistol-whipping him right there in the living room, shattering Dred's jaw from the vicious blows he rained down on him with the big Glock 40.

Dred had to die tonight, too. General knew he had to kill the nigga after this. To keep Dred alive would be one of the most foolish decisions General could ever make. Death was around the corner of every muthafucka who crossed his path after tonight. Shit was crucial.

"General, stop! Stop!" Lisa screamed, pulling him by the arm to prevent more damage General was causing.

Bolting to his feet, General shoved her aside and rushed down the nearby hallway toward Lisa's bedroom. This was cause for immediate action, and General did not doubt in his mind that wherever Dred's pants were, his gun was close by. If the nigga didn't have it on him, there was only one other place it could be. Being the type of nigga he was, Dred stayed strapped with a pistol, and to catch him without it was very rare.

Unfortunately for Dred, he was caught without it, and now he had to pay the piper.

Vega quietly slipped out the back door of his house, not to wake his mama and baby sister, Tiera. In his hand was a heavy-duty garbage bag containing his bloody clothes and a can of lighter fluid. He walked into the backyard toward the fire barrel his mother set out to burn trash in, and he dumped the bag of bloody clothes, drenching it with lighter fluid, then set it ablaze.

Vega watched it burn for a few minutes and spun on his heels, trekking alongside his house en route to his next intended destination.

At nineteen years old, Vega had been through some dark things since he jumped off the porch ten years before. He'd done some things that disturbed his sleep many nights, but what he went through tonight took the cake. Vega saw his life flash before his eyes for the very first time.

Now he was a walking time bomb. His hand swollen twice the normal size, two pistols tucked at his waist, and blood in his eyes, Vega was mad. Minutes later, Vega was making his way toward the murder scene, observing his surroundings and looking for anything to give him reason to snap. He was a loose cannon. Vega could explode on some Kamikaze-type shit. The nigga wanted to destroy something badly. Luckily, Thad wasn't anywhere around.

Vega watched as they loaded Man-Man's body on a gurney and into the back of an ambulance. There was blood all over the pavement, which indicated that Man-Man suffered before going to meet his maker.

"You sure you wanna be out here right now, cuz?" a voice asked at Vega's right.

When Vega turned, he was looking into the eyes of Rhonda, one of the many dopeheads of Harlem. Word on the streets was Rhonda used to hustle hard back in the day before victimizing herself with her own supply. Now she was barely getting by, having to trick or steal or whatever it was to get by and earn the money to support her habit.

It was blatantly obvious that Rhonda knew it was he who had killed Man-Man earlier.

Shrugging, Vega turned away from her without a word.

"Watch yo' back, cuz," Rhonda called out after him, dressed in a pair of Levi jeans, men's Stacy Adams, and a skimpy tank top revealing her slightly bulging stomach.

Vega stepped onto the southbound sidewalk of the shadowy street, headed in the opposite direction from the bloody crime scene. Moments later, the ambulance was shooting past him along the street, followed by a police cruiser.

Soon afterward, Vega was tramping across the front lawn of Thad's mama's house. He climbed the porch steps and raised his fist to knock on the front door.

"I should kick this bitch in and..." Vega's sudden dark thoughts were interrupted by the opening of the front door, and to his surprise, it was Thad's mama standing there in the doorway before him.

"Troy," she said, calling Vega by his real name. "Where is my boy?" she asked with great concern.

Refusing to meet the eyes of the woman he'd grown to love and respect as a second mother, Vega replied, "That's who I'm lookin' for."

"He ain't here, baby. I thought y'all was together." Mama Doll looked at Vega closely and sensed something strangely odd about her son's best friend. "What's going on, Troy? What happened up the street?"

Vega shrugged. "That's what I'm tryna find out, too." He turned away from her and headed for the steps.

"Troy!"

He halted, looking over his shoulder at her.

"You can lie to me all you want to, but just bring my baby home to me when you see him. Whatever is going on, son, I want both of y'all to watch each other's backs. It's crazy out there. I love you, baby, and find Thad if you can," she stated with emotion, backing away from the door.

Vega didn't respond. He just turned and walked away with a heavy heart. Mama Doll had just fucked him up.

As he distanced himself from the door, a lone tear escaped his angry, brown eyes. He wasn't sure if he could honor Mama Doll's request, for the awakening demons within him starved for something more atrocious. Keeping Thad alive was a hard pill to swallow.

Once inside Lisa's bedroom, the scent of weed, smoke, and sex assaulted General's nose. That didn't stop him from searching the room for Dred's gun while still clutching his bloody wound. Big homie was on a mission, and nothing was going to stop him from accomplishing it. General wanted blood and demanded it.

"Bingo!" said General after finding Dred's 9mm beneath his pair of Red Monkey jeans on the floor at the foot of the queen-sized bed. He unlocked the safety, checked the magazine, and slapped that bitch back in with a sigh of mere satisfaction. Now it was back to the business at hand— murder business.

Exiting the bedroom, General lifted the gun and let off a warning shot in Roe's direction, causing his enemy to halt in the middle of the foyer.

The nigga was trying to make a run for it!

"Where the fuck you think you going, nigga!" General went across the back of Roe's head with the gun, and Roe dropped to the floor, groaning in absolute pain. Why couldn't he just kill the muthafucka and be done with the nigga?

"Man, if you gonna kill me, then do it, nigga! Quit bullshittin' and—"

Whop! Whop!

General went upside his head twice more with two wicked blows. "Shut the fuck up!"

"Kill me, bitch ass nigga!" Roe spat.

"Oh yeah?" General aimed the 9mm at Roe's head and applied pressure on the trigger.

The second the gun exploded, Lisa knocked General's aim off, sending the bullet grazing Roe just along his left temple. Roe cursed angrily, bringing his good hand up to touch his new wound and pulling back bloody fingers.

"Stop this bullshit in my house, Jarrod!" Lisa snapped and shoved him hard in the chest. "You done lost yo' goddamn mind, nigga!?"

Forcing himself not to blow her muthafuckin' brains out too, General said, "You got one minute to tie that nigga ass up, or I'm killin' everybody in this muthafucka! Now take me for a joke if you want to, sis."

Lisa had no doubt in her mind he was serious. She looked down at Roe with great concern, knowing better than to test General at this particular stage.

To General's astonishment, Dred still lay on the living room floor, writhing in pain, staring up at him through one of his good eyes. His whole face had swollen to the point he was unrecognizable. The only way one would know it was Dred was his signature shoulder-length dreadlocks, high-yellow complexion, and the Jamaican flag tattooed on the right side of his neck. The nigga wasn't even from Jamaica! Dred's father was half-Jamaican, and his mother was Black and Mexican, but it didn't stop him from fronting like he truly was.

If the nigga didn't have a thing for beating on Lisa and just loved and respected her enough, he wouldn't be in the predicament he was in, and due to the fact Lisa and General grew up together, calling each other brother and sister from another mother, General felt it was his responsibility to protect her as if she were his very own biological sibling. If that meant crushing a nigga's soul for hurting her, then a muthafucka had to get it.

"You picked your own poison, son," said General, using an expression he borrowed from A1, his aunt Wanda's husband. "Now you gotta die, nigga."

Instead of putting a bullet in Dred's forehead, General stepped over and crushed his windpipe with three deadly kicks to his throat. Dred struggled but died an agonizing death without putting up a fight. It was eerie as hell.

'Soon,' thought General, 'I'ma have to end up killin' that nigga Mango, and Cuda too."

"You did it, didn't you?"

Turning around at the sound of Lisa's voice behind him, General couldn't ignore the pain in her eyes. "It was either him or me, sis. What the fuck else was I supposed to do about the nigga? You can't sleep on a nigga like that, ma, so he had to get dealt with," he replied.

She was silent.

Shaking her head sadly, Lisa said, "Now my baby gotta grow up without a daddy. That's messed up, Jarrod," she whispered and stomped down the hallway.

"Lisa!"

"Fuck you, nigga!" she retorted just before slamming her bedroom door behind her. A second later, General heard something crash and break loudly from beyond the bedroom door inside her room. Ma was hurt, having just blown General's mind with her admittance. *Baby?*

General glared down at Dred's lifeless body and kicked him again. "See what the fuck you made me do!"

23

Chapter 3

The scene was as bleak and gaudy as a goddamned carnival. It was going on 11:20 P.M. The coroner's car, the mobile crime lab, and an unmarked Crown Vic were parked near the mouth of the alleyway, along with several patrol units with red-and-blue car lights flashing, radios squawking insistently between static spurts. Three uniformed officials stood in a huddle, conversing, while a small crowd of spectators waited anxiously on the other side of the yellow crime scene tape.

Nearly an hour and a half had passed since the death of Officer Yolanda Dovolani, a young, beautiful twenty-five-year-old who was fresh out of the academy. She hadn't been on the force for four months and was already a casualty.

People straggled from nowhere and stood in clusters, conferring in subdued and fragmentary bursts, attempting to get a better view of the body. They didn't know the trouble that would follow in the dead officer's wake—a whole new meaning of trouble that the state of New York would not be ready for.

Officer Yolanda Dovolani was the only child of the sister of a well-respected and feared capo of the Italian mob based in Chicago, Illinois. All it took was one phone call, which would be the spark to burn that muthafucka down to the ground, so yeah, they'd better get prepared.

At some point, Melvin appeared, roaring toward the scene in his big Dodge Ram with purpose-filled eyes as a patrol officer turned to look in his direction and directed the notorious criminal attorney to a more appropriate and available parking area.

In the meantime, Investigator Rita Brown exited her car and decided to meet the lawyer halfway. In passing, Rita spotted two minicam crews on set. A redhead reporter from one of them was already picking up film clips and interviews for the six o'clock news in the morning. She didn't spot any other reporters, but they were doubtlessly in the vicinity. It was going to be a long night.

"What do you got for me, Brown?" Melvin asked the second they were in one another's presence.

Rita gestured for him to step aside and away from the curious eyes and ears. She explained the situation, and Melvin listened intently without interruption, but the effect her words had on the lawyer with every moment that passed was evident.

"And what's the extent of this investigation?" he asked.

"Sir, you know damn well what the extent of it is. We have several witnesses stating that your son, Jarrod, had a shootout two blocks away from here earlier with Rolando, whom, I'm quite sure, you know. The shooting was led in this direction, and what we gathered so far is a gun with Rolando's prints all over it, and—"

Melvin interjected, "What do you have on my boy, Brown?"

"Nothing solid, but you, knowing how the NYPD is going to take this matter," she replied, "they're gonna find what they find and build a case against him whether what they have is solid or not. You know how they play, especially now that one of their own was killed in the process."

"And I'll see that whatever they try to pull is ripped to fuckin' pieces!" he said with a growl.

"I'm pretty sure you would, sir."

The Uncle-Phil-looking lawyer from The *Fresh Prince of Bel-Air* regarded her attentively. She was the daughter of a good friend of his, a retired federal judge Melvin went to school with back in the day. Rita had been a great asset since she joined the force. However, she was doing her own thing, but she did her job. Melvin had no clue she was on General's payroll and probably wouldn't give a damn even if he did.

Despite his dislike for General's way of life, the lawyer would do whatever it took to see that his son was protected and secured for all he was worth.

"This is bad, Melvin. Do you have any idea who that cop was that was killed?" Rita spoke again.

"I'm sure you'll enlighten me."

"Yolando Dovolani is the daughter of Patricia Napoli. Does that name ring a bell?"

Melvin thought for a moment and paused. "Patricia Napoli," said Melvin, looking over at her oddly. "The sister of Mario Napoli? That mafia guy who—"

"Who allegedly ordered the murder of her Italian husband a few years ago, right in the middle of your courtroom? Sir, that's exactly who I am talking about."

Rumors said that Joseph Dovolani, owner of Dovolani's Luxury Jewels Corporation and the father of the dead cop, knew too much about Mario Napoli's illegal street dealings. He became a liability after being apprehended for drug activity and money laundering through his company, so he was savagely murdered right there in front of the judge and multiple witnesses before his killer was shot down. Then it so happened that Joey Dovalani was tied in with the Chicago-based Italian Mob of the Napoli Family. People were still talking about the incident to this very day, and not a damn thing was done about it.

"Oh shit," muttered Melvin when reality of how severe the situation was set in.

"My point exactly, sir."

Suddenly, there was commotion coming from the southeast of the scene, on the other side of the crowd of spectators. Two officers made their way in that direction, but

26

not before the source of the commotion burst from the crowd. To Melvin's discontent, it was D.A. Robert Hunt, dressed in khakis and a button-down, his face a mask of fury.

"Here we go." Rita sighed with awakening aggravation.

Both officers stopped Robert short and pulled him aside to talk to him.

While observing, Melvin watched as the D.A.'s face transformed to a series of expressions beneath the streetlight while patiently listening. He cast a glance in Melvin's direction, held the man's gaze long and hard, and pushed away from the officers moving in his direction. Robert Hunt wanted trouble.

Melvin stood where he was, a big bear of a man.

"I'm just about tired of his ass," said Rita.

A moment later, Robert, with one of the two officers in tow, came to a halt before Melvin. Standing five-nine, weighing a little over two hundred pounds solid, Robert definitely wasn't a slouch either. Now they were face-to-face, Melvin towering over him by four inches.

"What the hell your boy do to my son, Whitaker!" Robert snapped, his tone laden with accusation.

Melvin shrugged his big shoulders. "You got one second to get your hand out of my face."

"Or what?"

Whop!

One quick jab to Robert's chin knocked the D.A. off his feet and into the arms of the officer behind him.

"Self-defense," said Melvin. "Next time, you won't get it that easy." He walked away, back toward his truck, while Robert blinked stars away from his consciousness. He hopped into his truck and brought it to life.

As he took his leave, roaring away down the street and out of sight, the D.A. rubbed his sore chin with evil in his eyes. Then he, too, turned away and headed for his vehicle, fishing for his cell phone to make an important call.

"This is crazy," said the officer.

"Sure is," Rita Brown added. "And it is about to get even crazier in a minute."

Crazy wasn't the word. Madness.

It was muthafuckin' madness!

Chapter 4

"I gotta get outta here," said Baby Thad, standing up and stretching his limbs.

Crow remained where he sat. It wasn't like he could just get up and walk Thad to the door like he used to do to those who visited his home, although Thad didn't come for a visit and just bombarded in that muthafucka uninvited, seeking a place to hide and lay low for a while.

They'd just had a very serious talk about life and war, Crow giving him the game from a true warrior's perspective.

"Remember what I said, son," Crow said. "Never feel that you have nothing to lose, because then you move out of desperation—"

"And desperation is the worst motivation for action," Thad completed the jewel of wisdom Crown had dropped on him earlier.

The old man nodded encouragingly. "And come back to fix my damn door too, youngin'."

"I will," promised Thad. Without another word, Thad headed for the front door and was brought to a sudden halt.

"You forgot something, son."

When Thad glanced back over his shoulder at Crow, he noticed the old man had his arm outstretched before him.

"I ain't too old not to be shown some love," Crow said from the couch.

With a smirk, Thad doubled back to give the old man a pound with his fist, showing some love. "Thanks, Crow."

29

"No, son, thank you."

"For what?"

Crow said, "It's not often I get any company these days. Despite the situation, I enjoyed your stay. You're a smart, young man. Thad, I like your style. Utilize the long life you got ahead of you to the best of your ability.

"I will."

"Now, get the hell out so I can get some rest."

Chuckling to himself, Thad found his way out of the door after making sure it was closed shut. Indeed, he would be back to fix the old man's door, maybe even buy him a new one instead. He definitely owed Crow for accepting him into his home during his time of need.

'That old dude is pretty damn cool,' thought Thad as he descended the porch steps. 'But, damn, he done been through a whole fuckin' lot too.'

Outside, fewer people were crawling about the street now that the body was gone, so the excitement had died off. Only a few crackheads were noticeable, a lone police cruiser parked out before Mr. Jones' house across the street as a cop finished up his interview, and some little niggas up to no good. Thad went in the opposite direction of his corner, where Man-Man's body had lain, away from General's car, which was a 2014 Cadillac ELR he'd bought several months ago. There was no telling whether that was the officer's purpose for staying back or not, to keep an eye out on the car to see who might come back to get it. The NYPD was slicker than a can of grease.

'Perhaps Lisa would get word and come pick it up since it was in her name,' Thad thought. Little did he know, Lisa's place was exactly where his big homie was.

"Yo, Thad!" one of the little niggas called out.

There were four of them in all, as Thad recognized them all from his side of the field. Lil' Beezo, Worm, Taye, and Quint, all of whom were starving for a street reputation, but it was Taye that Thad favored the most. The young sixteen-

30

year-old hoodlum reminded Thad so much of himself growing up. Worm was the leader of the pack, a young, vicious seventeen-year-old lil' nigga. Word on the streets was he already had a couple of bodies under his belt.

"What's crackin', homie?" asked Lil' Beezo, the chubby one with the designer braids and Jordan slippers.

Thad gave them all a pound, casting a quick glance over at the black cop exiting Mr. Jones' houses several houses down. "What it do, y'all?"

"Peanut," said Worm.

'Peanut?' thought Thad. "What about him?"

"Don't try to play us, Thad!" said Worm, a little, skinny ass, jet-black nigga with two gold teeth in the front. "You know he was down with that shit earlier."

"And we got him over in the path right now," said Taye.

"Yep." Quint coughed into his hand.

Taye added, "We been waitin' on you to come back out from being with the old man."

Now Thad was faced with yet another problem, and he contemplated his decision. The person they were talking about was from the other side, one of Roe's street lieutenants, and come to think of it, Peanut was with those niggas when the shit popped off, including two other niggas he couldn't quite put a name to. Roe had come with a team, but if these young niggas got Peanut, where had those other two muthafuckas run off to?

Who were them niggas, anyway? Those fools had hoodies on, which prevented easy detection.

It was in that moment Thad allowed what Taye said to register. They had seen when he sought Crow's house for safety after looking over his shoulder and seeing two niggas chasing him with their guns blazing.

Who the fuck were they?

Luckily, Thad had escaped their wrath when he ducked behind Ms. Rose's house, which was the closest and darkest spot he could find, and Crow's house was next door.

"What's up, cuz?" Worm was growing impatient.

Thad knew he had to prove to these little niggas he was down with the hit. Plus, Peanut had to get dealt with accordingly for bringing that bullshit to their side.

A car door slammed shut, and the black cop started his car. A minute later, the patrol cruiser drove by them and turned out of sight at the next stop sign.

"You ready?" asked Taye.

"Let's go," Thad said, grudgingly.

They all moved as one unit toward the path behind crackhead Tootsie's house. The path had seen some gruesome things.

"If you ain't gonna kill me, nigga, at least lemme—" Roe was saying before he howled in blinding pain when General punched him on his bullet wound.

General said, "I told you to shut the fuck up, nigga."

"Kill me then!"

"Yeah," said General after tying Roe's hands behind his back with an extension cord. "But I'ma torture yo' bitch ass before I do."

"I didn't have shit to do with that."

"Even if you didn't, it's about time I do you in anyway. Should've did this shit a long time ago."

"But you couldn't!" Roe winced as he spoke.

There was no response from General.

"You still got love for a nigga! I'm your muthafuckin' brother, nigga!"

General kicked him hard in the stomach, causing Roe to double over in more pain.

"We ain't shit, son! Brother? Nigga, you a goddamn dead man!" snapped General, turning away from the piercing gaze of Roe's effective eyes. There was something he saw in them that greatly disturbed General.

Minutes later, General was inside the kitchen and punching away at Lisa's house phone. He figured he would call to check up on his homies later and contact Rita. That way, he could get the four-one-one on the night's event and try to start some type of dialogue he could build from.

"Brown," spoke a sharp but feminine voice on the fourth ring.

General leaned against the kitchen counter. "I'm listening, ma," he responded with no further words.

"Boy." She sighed. "What in the hell have you gotten yourself into now?" Then she briefly gave him a rundown.

As he listened, General, thinking about the dead body in the living room, a barely conscious Roe lying in the foyer, a brokenhearted Lisa in the bedroom, crying and shit, and then the troubling facts of what he was being told, on top of everything else, was enough to make a weak muthafucka fold.

What had he gotten himself into? Rita saying the word 'mafia' brought him up short.

"What did you just say?"

"What I'd rather discuss with you in person and no longer on this phone."

"What did you just say about the mafia?"

"Where are you, boy?"

He snapped, "Tell me what the fuck did you say, RiRi, and stop bullshittin' with me!"

"Curse at me all you want. Where are you?"

This was really getting on General's fuckin' nerves. Being the stubborn bitch she was, he knew he couldn't win with her under such conditions as the present, and of course, her integrity and loyalty wasn't to be questioned for no reason, for Rita could be trusted with even the darkest of secrets.

She said something about the dead cop he'd mistakenly killed being connected with the mafia. General's mind had been going a million miles per hour with all kinds of shit.

"I'm listening." She borrowed his words of expression.

Casting a glance toward the hallway, where Roe lay to its right and Dred just across the hall in the living room, he couldn't summon her there. Rita would probably freak the fuck out. Then again…

"Call me back when you get your mind right, boy."

Click.

Rita was gone. The bitch hung up, and General was heated.

The sound of a door opening down the hallway made him turn in that direction. Suddenly, Lisa appeared in the kitchen doorway, clutching her famous blade, looking like she wanted some major problems.

"What's up, sis?"

"Get them niggas outta my house," she said gravely, eyes as hard and cold as a polar bear's toenails. "Or, nigga, I'ma make you kill me next. And I put that on Chinx, bro." She had to be serious when she mentioned her dead cousin, a recently murdered local rap artist who was signed under French Montana's *Coke Boyz* label.

With that said, Lisa disappeared from the kitchen doorway. The front door closed shut behind Lisa moments later, leaving General to wonder where the hell she was going. Then he accepted the fact he had really hurt her immensely when it had always been his mission to prevent it from happening. She called Baby Thad, hoping his little homie was all right and would be able to come help him clean up because he surely didn't want to have to kill Lisa, too.

***

Six-year-old Jamia was emotionally relieved when she heard her mama's car pull up outside. For the past two hours, she'd been scared out of her mind. She thought her heart would burst from absolute fear.

'Thank God.' She put her baby brother, VJ, back to sleep, or else his little ass would still be hollering now probably.

The gunshots had frightened him just as they had her. Jamia waited for her mama at the front door.

Angie, who was a thirty-three-year-old scandalous bitch with one of the baddest bodies in the city and had thing for young niggas was a poor excuse for a mama. For two hours, she neglected her children to trick for a little of nothing and a bomb of Mollys to support her drug habit. The bitch was a straight up hoe! If it weren't for her food stamp card, her monthly child support, and her trickin' side hustle with boosting fake purses, Angie wouldn't have a damn thing.

When she opened her front door, she was startled by Jamia's unexpected presence, already rolling high off Molly.

"Damn, girl! Why you ain't in the bed?"

"I almost got shot, Mama!" Jamia told her animatedly.

"What!"

Then the child took her by the hand. "Come look, Mama!"

"Girl, if you don't get your ass back to bed—"

"Come see!" insisted Jamia.

Something about her daughter's behavior worried her. High as a kite, Angie allowed her beautiful little girl to drag her down the hallway toward her bedroom. Upon entering the bedroom, the first thing she saw in the dimly lit room was her twenty-two-month-old son lying in Jamia's bed instead of his own, sleeping.

After turning the light on, Jamia ran over to the window across the room and pointed to the left, about nineteen inches down from the top. Then the child said, "See, Mama?" and spun around on her heels, pointing at the far wall next to the little twin bed. That was when Angie panicked.

"What the fuck?" Angie circled the hole in the wall by the bedroom window with a manicured finger. She knew a bullet hole when she saw one. Hell, she had one in her damned leg from seven years ago. Then she turned to inspect the other wall.

"They was behind the church, Mama," said Jamia. "See, Mama! He still out there!"

Plucking the embedded bullet from the far wall and examining it carefully in the palm of her hand, Angie moved over next to her daughter.

"Mama?" VJ's small, groggy voice came as he sat up in bed.

Angie was out of her element, staring out of the bedroom window with her mouth agape in bewilderment. What she now saw sobered her up fast. About ten yards away, outside the window, behind the large church, beneath the glow of the moonlight, lay a still form. There was no mistake, the still form was the corpse of Trel, but Angie didn't know that. What she did know was that whoever it was, they were dead. She could feel it in her heart.

"Oh, shit! Oh, shit!" Angie grabbed her daughter and backed away from the window.

"You see him, Mama?" asked Jamia.

VJ began cutting the fool when he saw that neither of them was paying him the slightest attention. The stubborn child was ranting and raving, demanding attention.

Looking around the room as if searching for an escape route from the wicked images of a dead body outside her daughter's bedroom window, Angie spoke up.

"We gotta go, baby. We gotta go!" said Angie, her high blown for the moment.

Angie gathered up her children and some chosen belongings to take with her and left the house for her sister's. If the killer even suspected her daughter had seen anything, he would have to go through hell to catch up to them. Hopefully, by morning, he would be long gone, dead, or anywhere else in mind other than Jamia witnessing the murder.

Angie needed to pop another Molly bad!

Chapter 5

By the time the five homies made it to the path, Baby Thad was surprised to see his little cousin Marc sitting down on a red crate, smoking a Black & Mild. At Marc's feet lay Peanut, and next to Peanut was Murda, a massively built, tiger-striped pit bull who stood up at their approach.

Thad didn't step any closer to Murda for no reason, as he could have sworn the monstrous dog's eyes were glowing red in the dark, and Peanut was unconscious, having been knocked across the head earlier with a red brick by Quint.

The tension on the path was thick as a King of Diamonds stripper on a good night.

Drawing his weapon, Thad looked at Taye. "Wake his ass up!" he ordered.

It was Marc who did so, slapping Peanut several times across the face. "Wake up, chump!"

Murda stood guard like the champion fighter that he was. If DoughBoy, who was Marc's uncle and the owner of Murda, knew he had his dog out there, there would be hell to pay. DoughBoy was a fool about his dogs, Murda especially, having won abundantly from his fights.

Groaning, Peanut slowly climbed back to consciousness. Despite the fact Peanut was the brother of the chick Baby Thad used to fuck when growing up, he had no remorse for what was about to happen to him. Thad squatted down next to Peanut's head. "You can make it easy on yo'self, nigga.

You tell me who them two cats was in the hoodies that was with you tonight, and I'll let you live," he reasoned.

It was a good thing Murda knew Thad, or his ass would've been gas. The dog was trained to go, and when he went, he went hard! He was a killer.

"You gonna kill me anyway, B," Peanut said.

"I gave you my word."

"Your word ain't shit, and you know it!" Peanut had already accepted his fate when Taye and his crew jumped him in the path.

Thad stood back up and cocked his gun back, chambering a round.

"You got one more chance, Peanut."

"I know what'll make him talk." Marco jerked the thick chain, and Murda released a deep, menacing growl.

Both Worm and Lil' Beezo stepped back cautiously, aware of how destructive Murda could get. Peanut was perspiring nervously as he looked up into the eyes of the beast of a dog standing over his head. When Murda locked his jaws, it was a done deal. Peanut had witnessed the dog fight several times to know and had even bet with the champion fighter once before. Murda was highly respected in the pit ring.

"Who were they, nigga!" Marco demanded to know.

Scared out of his mind, Peanut said, "Twin and Forty."

"What?" Quint froze instantly at the mention of his brother's name, and all eyes were on him.

Sensing danger now, Quint drew his pistol, and before he could do anything, Taye stole him with a mean right hook. Instinct made Worm move, and he went for Quint's gun and, without much difficulty, wrenched it away before he did some serious damage.

"He's lying!" Quint screamed angrily. "That muthafucka lying on Forty! He wouldn't do no shit like that!" He was lying on the ground, looking up at them all.

This situation was beginning to get crazy.

"You tellin' the truth, Peanut? Don't make me—" Thad was saying before Peanut cut in.

"I swear, on my mama, them niggas was down with it!

Quint shot across the ground of the path and attacked Peanut. This excited Murda to the point he wanted to jump into the action. No one intervened while Quint and Peanut fought one another in the dark path. The niggas were going at it hard, as if they had something to prove.

When Thad exchanged a glance with Worm, a deep, silent communication transpired between the two. Somebody was about to die. Then, without further hesitation, Worm stepped up and shot Quint in the back of the head, splattering brains and skull all over the place. Worm had just murdered a childhood friend.

"God damn!" Lil' Beezo's heart squeezed with emotions at the sight of his dead homie. He looked over at Worm with total disbelief on his face. "You didn't have to kill him."

"What?" Worm replied.

Lil' Beezo just shook his head sadly.

"You thought that nigga was gonna stand there and let us get at his own brother for what he did? Hell fuckin' no! It is what it is, cuz." Worm was coldhearted.

Now, Peanut didn't know what to do. After seeing Worm kill Quint, he knew it was over for him.

Taye and Marc were stunned speechless.

"You got it on your heart, B?" Worm challenged Lil' Beezo.

Lil' Beezo said, "Leave me alone, Worm."

When Worm made a move toward his friend with that look in his eyes, Thad stepped in between them.

"It's over, bro," said Thad, laying a hand on Worm's shoulder. "We gotta go."

Holding Lil' Beezo's gaze for a long moment, Worm hurried away from him and shot Peanut twice in the chest.

"Bitch!" Murda barked once to punctuate his feelings toward the matter. He was amped up.

"Don't worry about them niggas, cuz," Marc spoke up as he looked at Thad. "We'll handle them," he assured his cousin.

Thad's cell phone rang. It was General. It was time to put in some work.

***

Eight minutes after twelve, Melvin pulled into the driveway of his Brooklyn residence. The glass-and-cellar structure was about forty-five feet wide and three stories high, each floor positioned strategically to keep the neighboring houses out of sight.

To the right, a closed, three-car garage sheltered his wife's champagne-colored 2015 Chrysler 200 and a new, silver Mazda MX 5 Miata with a vanity license plate that read *ROSIE*. The end slot was where the Dodge Ram belonged, but it was parked just outside of it.

The back of the large house was austere, a windowless wall of weathering wood. It was Rosie's dream house. Rosie was General's stepmother whom he couldn't go a day without wishing she were anything or anywhere other than in his life. He couldn't stand the conceited bitch. She tried so hard to compete with his mama, but the bitch would never stand next to the essence of his world. There could only be one.

Melvin got out and trudged across the gravel to the entrance door and let himself in.

"I was wondering when you were coming back home." Rosie uncrossed her shapely legs and rose to her feet from the expensive leather sofa. She was a beautiful woman in her mid-fifties, a former journalist who had committed herself to writing true crime and fantasy novels to stay busy and relevant.

"Pack your bags," said Melvin. "You're going to stay with Mary for a little while. I've already spoken with her, and she's expecting you before morning."

"What?"

"You heard exactly what I said."

Rosie wasn't trying to hear that shit. She demanded an explanation. "You can't just walk up in my house and tell me to pack my things and expect me to just do it. Have you lost your damn mind, Melvin?"

Forcing himself to remain calm, Melvin explained the current situation and hoped against hope that Rosie surrendered to his demand.

"I can't believe this!" Rosie was heated now. "I knew this would happen. I just knew it!" she cried out.

He watched his wife of fifteen years stomp out of the spacious living room with an attitude. Melvin released a sigh of relief and left the room next. He went straight to his home study office and shut the door, locking it behind him.

Inside the office, Melvin marched over to his massive desk and stepped behind it, reaching up the far wall to remove the large African painting he'd wasted ten thousand dollars on. Behind the painting was a large wall safe. He wasted no time punching in the six-digit code to open it.

The phone on his desk rang and startled him, causing Melvin to whirl around with a start.

"What?" he answered on the second ring.

"Is that how you answer the phone now, Mellie?" a woman's voice replied, hinting that she was just as tempered as him.

"Lynn." Melvin swallowed.

Lynn was General's mama, who had obviously heard the news and was calling to check up on things. This was the monarch of their creation, the gangster of a son that had brought them together once again.

This was Melvin's first love and General's only love, the queen of both their existences.

The weaponry stared back at him from inside the private safe, and Melvin already knew what he had to do before it even left Lynn's mouth.

"Save my baby," she said, meaning it more than anything.

"I will," Melvin promised her, and that was all that needed to be said.

Now it was really on.

***

With every blow from the butt of the 40 Caliber to Ranny's face, blood splattered in every direction. The crackhead was nearly unconscious as he groaned in pain with every wicked impact. The instant Vega laid eyes on Ranny, he remembered the crackhead owed him twenty dollars. He lured him into the neighborhood park and decided to get it out of him in blood.

Vega had snapped, no longer the same person he had been three hours prior. He couldn't be paid to crack a joke now.

The incident with Trel had changed him. He was a monster, demonic.

Something from the corner of his eye stole his attention. Rising from his sitting position on Ranny's chest, Vega regarded the person walking down the sidewalk across the street from the park, and that person was Lisa. She was on her way to her cousin Peaches' house to crash until morning, giving General his peace to take care of his business.

Vega snarled darkly as he looked in her direction. Then he noticed something shiny in her hand as she walked past under the streetlight. Lisa looked straight ahead, but her eyes wandered cautiously around her proximity.

As he watched her journey down the sidewalk quietly while clutching her blade, Vega thought about all the times she'd shot him down when he tried to put the mack down. He'd been wanting to hit that fine ass for years, and at the moment, he felt like poking the pussy, show her what she'd been missing, and give her that pound game he'd only fantasized about. What made Vega think twice was General and knowing that was his big homies' people. Under different circumstances, he would've had to have Lisa once and for all.

A gunshot rang out in the distance, causing them both to pause instinctively. Lisa observed her immediate surroundings while looking in the direction from which the blast came. A second blast rang out, and Vega reached for his second gun. Now clutching both of his pistols with deadly intentions, Vega was oblivious to the fate Peanut and Quint had just been served on a cold platter.

Lisa pressed on more urgently now. Up ahead, Lisa spotted General's car parked at the curb of Main Street and found herself running to it.

Stepping out from the shadows, Vega watched Lisa dash for the car at the end of the street. Without hesitation, she opened the door and slid in behind the wheel. At that same instant, another vehicle turned onto the street at Vega's right, creeping slowly as if one were about to pull a drive-by. Suddenly, the car turned into the nearby driveway, and he recognized Mr. Clive's Impala. He was one of the few righteous men who lived in the neighborhood.

A faint groaning came from behind Vega as he looked over his shoulder to find crackhead Ranny still lying there with a stray dog now licking his bloody wounds.

Screeching away from the recently bloodied scene in the expensive Cadillac, Lisa drove right past her cousin Peaches' crib with no intended destination in mind.

'Lucky bitch,' thought Vega as he stepped away from the park's curb. She was lucky indeed because not only her sexuality but her life had just been spared in respect for his big homie General. Vega would have liked to break her off something proper, goon-style. Back on the hunt for more blood, he went, unaware that Thad was just one street over.

That was the same direction in which he was headed right now.

Chapter 6

They were quiet as they walked along the side of the street beside one another, both maintaining their thoughts about the situation to themselves. This was the moment Marc thought it would be best to confide in Thad, but a flicker of fear of doing so stopped him.

At seventeen, Marc was starting to see the street life for what it was. Growing up just around the corner from his big cousin Thad, he had always been in the house and was never allowed to venture beyond his front yard too much. Having been raised by a God-fearing mama who was so strict he couldn't stand her at times, Marc only perceived life for what it was through his bedroom window.

Two and a half years ago, Marc's mama died from a ten-car pile-up over in the Soho one weekend. From that moment on, Marc threw caution to the wind and jumped headfirst into the street life. After hooking up with Lil' Beezo and Taye, joining their team, Marc never looked back for any reason.

Now that Marc was making a name for himself in the streets of Harlem as a young hellraiser, he was destined to die in those same streets his mama had prohibited him from.

Thad, puffing on a Newport as he walked next to his cousin, noticed something he hadn't seen until now. In Marc's back right pocket was a red bandana hanging, suddenly bringing Thad to a halt as he regarded him attentively. Murda looked up at Thad oddly.

"What?" Marc questioned him curiously.

Thad held his gaze for a moment. "So you gangbang now, cuz?" he asked in that dead-serious tone.

Unconsciously, Marc reached back to check and see if his red flag was still there.

"G-Mack," said Marc with a shrug.

"So, you Blood?"

Marc nodded.

The punch to Marc's chest came so fast he was too slow to see it coming. Then Thad shoved him hard, willing himself not to smash his little cousin right there.

Murda growled up at Thad. Thad drew his pistol and cocked it back, daring Murda to try his luck and get blasted on.

"The fuck's wong with you, cuz?"

"Nah, nigga, what the fuck is wrong with you, Marc? How can you rep the same shit that murdered your old boy?"

Marc dropped his head.

"Answer me, nigga!" Thad demanded angrily.

"I had no choice."

"You had no choice?" Thad demanded angrily.

"I have no choice."

"You have a choice." Thad looked at him as if Marc had taken leave of his senses.

There was silence.

"I should kill your stupid ass right now, cuz. You may as well should've slit your old boy's throat yo'self!" Thad didn't have anything against Bloods. Hell, some of his closest homies were affiliated with the organization. A group of them had been the cause of his uncle Pookie's death ten years ago, his mama's baby brother. Now it turned out his baby cousin was claiming the same set that killed his father, who ignorantly had no clue what he was getting himself involved with. Thad was so heated he had to walk away before he harmed Marc.

"Cuz!" Marc called out, but Thad kept it moving along.

Now, Marc was really worried.

Stopping in his tracks, Thad turned around and approached his cousin with a grim expression on his face. Marc's heart was thudding crazily. When Thad came to a halt, inches away from Marc's face in the middle of the street, he spoke low, with a menacing tone that couldn't be denied.

"Who is your big homie, cuz?"

Marc hesitated.

Whop!

Another punch to the chest sent Marc backpedaling while keeping a tight grip on the dog chain because the dog tried to get to Thad. Thad aimed the big pistol at Murda, and the dog ceased his vicious threats, seeming to comprehend the consequences if he didn't. "Don't make me ask you again, nigga."

A pair of headlights turned onto the street at Thad's left, headed in their direction. From a nearby house sat two hood niggas sharing a blunt of Kush. They were witnessing the whole thing from the front porch. They spoke amongst themselves about the situation before them, understanding exactly what was going on between the two cousins.

The whole hood knew how protective Thad was about his baby cousin, and for Marc to join a Blood set after what was done to Pookie, it angered him to a-whole-nother degree. One of the homies on the porch was Blood also.

"Big Man," said Marc

"Big Man, huh?" Thad knew exactly who Big Man was. Although he respected the big homie, and the respect was mutual, Thad still felt tried because Big Man knew better. He knew what had happened to Pookie, and he knew how much it meant to Thad. "Lemme have that flag, Marc," he said, holding out his hand.

Marc took a step back. "I can't let you do that, cuz. You ain't gonna take my flag."

"It's like that?"

Marc didn't respond, but Thad knew all he needed to know through his cousin's eyes.

"That's cool." Thad nodded solemnly. "It's all good."

A moment later, General's all-white Cadillac pulled up to a stop behind Thad. He turned around and looked at the car in great surprise as the passenger window rolled down, revealing Lisa at the wheel. Without Lisa giving a second glance at Marc, he opened the door and slid inside the car.

"What's up, lil brotha?" she asked.

"Get me away from here before I end up killin' his ass," Thad muttered as he stared ahead, refusing to look at the pitiful expression Marc was presenting.

***

Seconds after Melvin hung up the phone, Rosie did the same thing, hanging up the phone upstairs, and she sat there on the edge of the bed in a silent rage—the calm before the storm. She had just heard the ending of the brief conversation between Melvin and Lynn. Her heart squeezed with dread and loathing as she shook from the boiling rage brewing within her. The talk about how to keep their son safe and secure was all good, but hearing Melvin tell Lynn he loved her before ending the call stung.

Rosie was steaming hot! Her husband had just told another woman he loved her, and there was no way he could deny it, nor could she.

Bolting up from the bed, Rosie finished the task of packing her things, adding another suitcase to the bunch. She had no intention of going to her sister Mary's house in Queens. She was about to make Melvin wish the only person or woman he would ever love was his mama because she was about to crush his muthafuckin' spirit.

Afterward, Rosie carried her things down to the corridor. Once that was done, she found Melvin in his office, sipping

Scotch from his personal collection. He was hanging up the phone again the second she stepped through the door.

Melvin looked up at his wife. "You're done?" he asked.

"I most certainly am."

He rose from his throne chair behind the massive desk. "Good. I will drive you—"

"That won't be necessary, Melvin. I'm not going to Mary's," she cut in with direct contact. Before he could even demand an explanation, she spoke up again. "I will find a hotel for the night and catch the first thing smoking to Jersey in the morning. I can't deal with your bullshit right now."

"Bullshit?"

"Yes!" She shut her eyes for a moment to gather some self-control. "Look, Melvin." Her tone was soft and calm. "I heard you on the phone with her, and you told her you loved her. Then maybe that's who you need to be with if you love her that much, Melvin. I'm not gonna crowd you. Go right ahead."

"Is that all?" His tone had taken her aback. "Rosie." Melvin sighed. "I told you from the beginning that I'll always love Lynn, and you said you understood. Now, all of a sudden, you hear me tell her, you wanna throw what we have away? Stop acting like you don't know where my heart and love truly stands, dear."

She held up a patient hand when Melvin attempted to approach her. "That's the problem, Melvin. I don't know what I know anymore."

"Now that's the bullshit, Rosie."

"Call it what you want."

No sooner than the words left her mouth did a loud bang reverberate throughout the house. Rosie jumped, startled by the unexpected explosion, and Melvin rushed to her the instant the second blast erupted. Then came the sound of the front door being kicked in, and running footsteps entered the house.

49

"Quick! Behind the desk! Hurry!" Melvin shut off the light and the thick study door carefully, shoving Rosie toward the back of the desk in the dark room.

Behind the large desk, Melvin hit the hidden button beneath it to activate the hidden passage behind the tall bookshelf to its right. He quickly pulled the secret passage door open wide enough to push Rosie inside.

"Don't leave me!" she argued.

"I must for now, dear." Melvin shoved her further inside and shut it, hoping she would take the passage down where it would lead to safety beyond the pool house out back.

Listening intently, Melvin figured there were two or three intruders inside the house by the sound of their footfalls on the marble floor outside the office door. Having already removed the weapons from the safe, Melvin didn't hesitate to arm himself with a twin set of Colt 45s in both hands, fully loaded. He waited behind the protective shield of the desk, his eyes trained on the door.

"Come on, bastards," he whispered anxiously.

And came, they did, bursting through the office study door with guns drawn, and Melvin gave the first muthafucka a shot through the dome.

The element of surprise stunned the second gunman behind the first, and brains splattered his face, knocking him off balance for a second, and Melvin pumped three rapid slugs into his chest, damn near sending him airborne from the vicious impact.

"Shit!" Melvin heard the gunman say after realizing he was protected by a bulletproof vest.

'Another headshot will do it,' thought Melvin the instant a third gunman rounded the corner of the doorway, armed with a pump-action shotgun. He ducked quickly the moment he saw fire spit from the barrel of the big gun. The explosion alone was enough to destroy some shit, but it was the impact it had on the massive desk Melvin feared wouldn't last long before it was blown away, which meant he needed to do something, or else he was a dead man.

Suddenly, machine gun fire erupted in harmony with the deafening shotgun blast, tearing the desk apart. Now, Melvin knew he needed to do something, and that something was the button to unlock the secret passage again. He belly crawled through, away from harm. Rosie was no longer there and had found her way through and down the passage. He followed, hoping to catch up with her before she did something stupid.

"Damn," Melvin grumbled sharply. "I'ma kill that fuckin' Robert if it's the last thing I do!" He knew no one else sent those goons after him but Robert Hunt, and for that, Melvin was gonna hit him where it hurt. Showtime.

***

"What's the deal with you?" Lisa asked Thad, breaking the silence between them.

Instead of answering, Thad fired up another cigarette.

Lisa continued. "Well, yo' boy done really fucked me up for the night." She told him about what happened, from the moment she answered the front door for General until that very instant, growing emotionally disturbed by the minute. "Now I'm at the point where I really wanna cut his fuckin' head off!"

"Drop me off at the corner."

With a glance in his direction, Lisa sensed something about Thad that made her weary. This, too, was like a brother to her. Mama Doll loved her as though she had brought Lisa into this world herself, but there was a sadness she sensed about him, on top of a dark aura from where she had no clue it originated.

Although Baby Thad had earned his stripes in the streets, growing up with misguided intelligence and the desire to always prove himself, he also manned up. Still a young gangster, no doubt, Thad had begun focusing his dreams on being a music artist. He was one of the few in General's circle who wanted to venture out from the street life to explore other potential desires. Thad's desire to create music was top priority, though he still maintained his everyday hustle of selling dope on the block.

After General saw how raw and serious he was about his music career, he decided to encourage and assist Thad in his endeavors. From investing in Thad's music career and hustle game, General believed Thad's voice would be his ticket out of the game, and that was exactly what Lisa was stressing about now, having thought Thad had put away his gun for the microphone instead.

The nigga had big dreams of being a rapper—big dreams—and looking at him now, Lisa wondered if what General had going on could shatter those dreams if Thad wasn't careful. People only lived once, and life happened now, and she was afraid her little brother was beyond caring at that moment.

"I'm pregnant, Thad," Lisa confessed.

That damned sure got his attention. Thad turned to look at her, glancing down at her flat stomach. "What?"

She sucked her teeth stubbornly, rolling her eyes. "I didn't even get a chance to explain the situation before all hell broke loose. You know how that boy gets," she said.

Thad had to fire up another Newport with that one.

"Now that fool done killed Dred and—"

"How far are you?"

"Three weeks."

"So you gonna keep it—"

She snapped. "I wish you would ask me some dumb ass shit like that! Hell yeah, I'm keeping my child., and since General wanna go and do some shit like that, his ass will—"

"He gonna help you take care of it anyway, so don't even waste your breath. You family, and that's all that matters."

"Whatever."

They pulled up to the corner, several houses down from where Lisa lived.

"Go put this crap up, sis. Don't want nobody thinkin' you brah and try to get at you. Shit's crazy right now, so be careful, ma," Thad warned her before getting out of the car.

"I'll be at Peaches' house."

"Word."

Thad got out, retrieving his cell phone to hit General up. "I'm outside, brah."

"Come 'round back," General replied.

Behind Thad, the Cadillac made a U-turn and disappeared in the opposite direction, leaving him to journey alone where a crucial task awaited him.

Chapter 7

By 3:30 A.M., Dred was taken to Brooklyn and left behind an old, abandoned building where he would eventually be found. General had called Crazy Ray to borrow his old, beat-up Plymouth to handle the mission, paying the dopehead handsomely for his services. The drop-off was in a secluded area with not much traffic, except for that of a few winos and homeless squatters. It was an area where Dred wasn't wanted.

As for Roe, he had been hogtied and left down in the basement of Lisa's house. General wasn't sure what he really wanted to do with the nigga, maybe use him as insurance for his own personal gain or something. He wasn't gonna die just yet. The question 'why?' had run through Thad's head a hundred thousand times by now. He just couldn't see what General would get out of keeping Roe alive.

General said he would handle it; then so be it.

A fleeting thought of the matter crossed Thad's mind. He saw something in General's behavior earlier that indicated he didn't have the heart to kill Roe now that he was of a clearer head. The two had been inseparable from birth, having come up in the same playpen and sandbox until they were seventeen, which was the beginning of their troubles. Both General and Roe shared a bond, a deep brotherly love, and that was what Thad felt kept General from really killing him.

Was General truly his brother's keeper?

Was it even worth it?

There had been many times when General told him old stories of his and Roe's growing up. For someone who undoubtedly hated the other so much, he sure held onto the memories. There was no telling what General was up to, now that he was alone with Roe to do whatever he pleased. Thad wouldn't know, because he was entering his house at the moment, having been assured that his presence wasn't needed anymore.

Thad also knew that General didn't really want him involved, but who else was there he could trust? He couldn't reach Vega, wherever the hell he was. Speaking of which, General couldn't wait to see about his little homie and get to the bottom of this animosity he had for Thad now.

There was another issue Thad had a heavy heart for. He and Vega were closer than he and General would ever be, but it was hard to forget the venom Thad heard in his friend's voice when Vega spoke of his intentions to harm him. That had him more hurt than confused, and Vega definitely wasn't the one to be taken lightly.

"That's you, baby?" Thad heard his mama's voice call out from the front of the house. "Thad?"

"Yeah, Mama!" Thad shut the back door and trudged down the hallway toward the living room.

The house was as quiet as a cemetery.

Once he made it to the living room, Thad found himself standing face to face with his mama. Without a word, Mama Doll looked her son up and down, quietly inspecting him as though he could probably be anything but her son, but then she hugged him.

"What's up, mama?" Thad asked.

"You could've at least called to tell me you was alright, baby. I was so scared. I didn't know what to do. Did Troy tell you what I said?" she asked, looking relieved now that he'd come home.

"Troy?"

55

"He stopped by here looking for you earlier."

That didn't sit right with Thad at all. First, Vega called and threatened him, then came to his house looking for him? Or was it the other way around? However it had gone down, Thad wasn't feeling that shit one bit.

'What if Vega was angry enough to…' Thad didn't even want to complete that thought.

Sensing her son's discomfort, Mama Doll looked into his eyes. "Is something wrong with Troy, baby? What happened? Please tell me Troy is alright, Thad," she pleaded.

Seeing the deep worry in his mama's face about the nigga who threatened to do him harm angered Thad. He wanted so badly to tell her the truth about what happened, but Thad knew there was no way he could do such a thing. The truth would only worry her more. Plus, he wasn't sure what happened to Vega that night. Whatever it was, it wasn't good for Vega to come at him salty and shit, but there was no questioning that something did happen to Vega, and now he was blaming Thad for it.

He needed to see Vega for himself.

"He's good, Mama. I talked to him earlier, too," he lied.

"Baby, why are you lying to me?" Mama Doll knew him too well for him to stand there and lie to her face.

"He's good, Doll." Thad kissed her cheek.

Shaking her head, Mama Doll decided to leave it be. Besides, she'd already been enlightened on what went down. The whole hood knew. Before she allowed him to leave her sight, she had one more question for Thad. "And have you talked to Jarrod?" she asked. "How is he?"

"I just left him a few minutes ago. He's good, Mama. Everything is alright now."

"But it isn't alright, and you know it!"

"Get some sleep, Mama. You got work in the morning."

Sighing, Mama Doll said, "And you need to take a bath. You smell like death all over." Then she stepped around him and headed to her bedroom without a backward glance. Her baby was home, and that was all that mattered.

Thad went to take that bath. He had Dred all over him indeed.

***

The second General entered the house again, he heard Roe faintly calling out to him from the basement. He kicked himself mentally for not gagging the nigga's mouth shut when he had the chance. Roe was getting on his last damn nerve.

Grudgingly, General went down to the basement to see what the hell he wanted, but halfway down the stairs, he paused instantly when there was a knock at the front door. Looking over his shoulder at the basement door, General wondered who it could be at that time of night.

"General!" Roe called out to him in his raspy voice. "Jarrod? I know that's you, nigga!" he added.

Ignoring Roe's aggravating voice, General rushed down the basement stairs with the intent of gagging the nigga's mouth. To answer the door, he had to, or else Roe was gonna ring the alarm with suspicion for whoever it was that was out there.

"Bro, you ain't' gonna kill a nigga. Call my man Doc for me."

More knocking sounded off.

Roe continued. "Doc will patch me up. Whatcha doing, son?" he asked.

Snatching both of the nigga's shoes off, then his socks, General went for his mouth to stuff it for him.

"Hell no!" Roe protested, clenching his mouth shut.

General slapped fire from him with a backhand and squeezed the muthafucka's jaws to force the sock down in his mouth. As quickly as he could, he tied the second sock around the nigga's head as best he could. Roe put up a struggle but lost in the end.

The knocking ceased, but that didn't stop General from bounding for the stairs.

"Bitch ass nigga!" Roe said the second General's foot hit the first step. The gag had loosened and came out, making General boil with rage. Roe let out a disturbing laugh, groaning and grunting in the process. That shit sounded weird as fuck.

He said, "I saved you. Now spare me, bro." That made General pause. "Yeah, you heard me. Remember when I saved your ass from drowning in the pool that night? Huh!"

General felt something awaken inside him, but before he allowed it to affect him, he ran up the stairs. By the time he made it upstairs to the nearest window where he could take a peek outside, he was taken aback at the sight of Mango's Denali parked in the front of the house. Dred's little brother had finally come to check up on his sibling.

"Shit," General muttered with disdain. There was gonna be a whole lot of it when it hit the fan.

***

For the past two hours, Mango has been trying to reach his brother, to no avail. Now, as he tried Dred's number again for the millionth time, a dark wave of unspoken fear washed over him. The tide was pulling him under the current to the point it was hard for him to breathe under his control. Mango had a premonition that his brother was in danger, but where was he?

For Dred to miss an important meeting with their Philly connect was unusual, and it bothered Mango greatly, and Dred would never ignore his call for no reason.

From the passenger seat, Cuda could see how much the situation was affecting Mango, who was on the verge of hysteria at any moment. He knew it was a problem when

Mango brought him along to meet with Knowledge, the Philly connect, when it had always been Mango and Dred. Although he was honored to be present, Cuda couldn't help but be worried about this big homie, too.

"I swear, Cuda"—said Mango, a heavyset, high-yellow cat with a shiny, bald head, dripping in platinum jewels—"if something happened to my brotha, I'ma set the city on fire!" he raved.

"When you last talked to him, he was here, right? Then he gotta be up in there," said Cuda. He was also a light-skinned cat who resembled the rapper Webby but with shoulder-length braids to the back. He was one of them pretty-boy ass niggas but ruthless. The nigga was a straight-up killer but humble, and far more dangerous than Dred had ever been.

"He ain't up there, or else he woulda been—"

Cuda chimed in. "Yeah, I know."

There was a moment of silence.

The phone in Mango's lap shrilled to life, and he answered it with haste. "Yeah?"

Cuda lit up a freshly rolled blunt.

"What it do, kid!" the voice on the other end of the phone said.

Fila thought Mango recognized his voice.

"Shit, son. Lookin' for that brotha of mines."

"That's who I'm lookin' for too! He told me to hit him up after I closed the club down tonight." Fila owned Club Virgo, a Yonkers-based strip joint. He was one of the brothers' most loyal and reliable customers.

"I haven't heard from him in several hours."

"That's not good."

"Damn right, it's not good!" Mango snapped.

Dred had promised Fila four kilos of coke, and he was holding him to his promise. The two had always had a good system going, and now, all of a sudden, Dred couldn't be found.

"Maybe he's laid up with one of them bitches he keeps on standby," said a now doubtful Fila.

"Not when there's business involved."

Cuda passed Mango the fat blunt in rotation.

"You checked Lisa?" Everybody knew about Dred and Lisa.

"That's where I'm at right now."

"That's where he called me from earlier." Fila sounded very disappointed. "Or maybe he's laying low after that murder went down over in your area."

"Murder?"

"Yeah." Fila gave him a brief on the situation.

Now, Mango was really worried as he listened to Fila's account of what had gone down. Mango was unaware of the situation, having just arrived back in the city from Philly. Hearing what Fila was telling him made Mango's heart pound with surging adrenaline as what he had thought several minutes ago came rushing back to him at once. Was Dred really in danger?

"Alright, Fila, I'm gonna look into that. I'll hit you back as soon as everything's in order," said Mango.

"You do that, kid."

"One."

"One." Fila hung up, cursing under his breath in response to what he'd just heard.

Mango pulled on the blunt, pensive. Then he reached beneath his seat to retrieve the pistol there, sitting it in his lap as he inhaled more weed smoke into his lungs.

"What's the deal?" Cuda finally spoke up, so Mango told him. The instant Mango stopped talking to hit the blunt again, Cuda said, "You know what that means."

"General had to come here to lay low."

"What if Dred was here when or if he did?"

That was another thing. Mango was very much aware of his brother and General's dislike for each other, regarding Lisa. It never got to the point where violence was involved, but it could very well have been if they'd bumped heads that night. It definitely would have been a major scene if they had, in which Mango figured his brother couldn't have been present if General had shown up.

Or could he?

As if reading his thoughts, Cuda said, "His car ain't here, so Dred gotta be somewhere else."

"But why would he miss the meeting?"

Cuda just shrugged.

Silence passed between them for a long moment.

Mango reached over to start the truck. "If I don't hear from that nigga by sunrise, it's on and poppin'! And this is the first place I'ma burn to the muthafuckin' ground," he said and put the truck in gear.

"And I'm right there beside you, Mango."

"I know," Mango assured him. "That's why I fuck with you, son." Then he pulled off down the street, wondering where the fuck his bother could be right now.

From inside the house, General released a relieving sigh as he watched Mango's Denali drive off. Clutching his pistol tightly, he knew they would definitely be back, but he wouldn't be there next time, for it was time to make a move, and he knew just the place to go.

Chapter 8

Baby Thad shuddered awake at once. A terrible dream clung to him. He bolted from the bed to shake it off, and as soon as he was on his feet, he realized he'd only been dreaming. It was more of a nightmare than anything.

Thad looked over at the clock on the dresser, and it read eight minutes after eight the next morning. 'Damn,' he thought with a frown. He didn't get any rest at all after nearly tossing and turning most of the night.

Five minutes later, Thad exited the bathroom and made his way into the kitchen. As he grabbed himself something to drink, images of the crazy night before invaded his consciousness.

Mama Doll left him a note describing what she'd seen on the six o'clock news this morning, before going to work at Harlem Hospital as a registered nurse. She promised to call him later, and Thad could see the urgency in her handwriting, having known her longhand to be remarkably neat. Thad didn't like her to worry so much, but it was something beyond his control.

At twenty-three, Thad has caused the woman more worry to last her a lifetime.

Then the telephone rang.

Thad stepped into the living room and picked up the cordless phone, switching on the TV, and grabbed the remote to find the news channel.

"Hey, bae," said a very feminine voice.

Dropping down onto the sofa as he prepared to converse with his girl, Ciera, Thad flipped through the channels for something interesting. "What's up, ma?"

"You," she said smartly. "What's going on, Thaddaeus Birkett?"

"Whatcha mean?" He knew she was serious when she called him by his full name.

"Now you wanna play dumb." She sucked her teeth.

"Cee?"

"What, nigga!"

Ciera was from Harlem originally but grew up in the Bronx, living with her grandparents after her mom went to prison for vehicular homicide. Two years his senior, she was now a bartender at the 40/40 club and a single mother herself from a previous relationship, but this was Thad's boo, the bitch with whom he had been committed to for the past sixteen months.

Ciera told him what she knew, telling him what he already knew himself.

"But do you know they're charging Roe with the murder of that police officer? It was on the news this morning. They said he's armed and dangerous and all that kinda stuff. And they said that you was involved in that shootin' last night too." Ciera struck a nerve.

"Who the fuck is 'they'?" he asked.

"The streets, bae. My girl Tangi said—"

"I told you about that scandalous bitch, Cee," Thad replied and looked up when a shadow passed by the front window. He jumped to his feet and rushed over to the window, his adrenaline surging immediately with excitement. To his surprise, it was Taye and Marc walking across his front lawn toward the front door of the house.

"Thad!"

"Yeah?" he replied absentmindedly.

"You ain't even listening to shit I'm sayin', nigga! What're you doing?"

"Ma, I'ma have to hit you back. Something just came up and—" he was cut off, as expected.

"Whatever, nigga. You always throwin' a bitch on the backburner like I'm not important!"

"You are."

"Then act like it!"

Thad had to set her straight. "What's more important is me staying alive and on point, and I can't do that with you buggin' me right now, ma. Shit is serious, and I can't afford to slip."

"I am not buggin' you," she retorted.

"Then let me take care of my business, and I'll hit you back up later. I need to get in them guts soon anyway. You been dodging a nigga lately."

"It's wet right now."

"I'll see," Thad replied and ended the call, making his way over to the front door the second there was a knock. Without further ado, he opened the door to allow them entry.

Both Taye and Marc greeted him in turn, Thad glaring at his cousin before turning away. They all filed inside the living room, and Taye sparked up a pre-rolled blunt.

"Them fools was missing in action last night," said Taye as he passed Thad the blunt. He was referring to Forty and Twin, the two niggas Peanut gave up. "We checked all them niggas' spots. I ain't been to sleep yet!"

Nodding in acknowledgement, Thad said, "They'll pop up soon."

Marc was silent for some reason.

"They found them niggas Peanut and Que this morning, too. They still 'round there now."

A straight-faced Thad grudgingly passed the blunt to Marc, who took it without a word spoken.

Taye continued. "That's what's gonna force Forty out when he find out about Que."

"And that's when he's gonna get the business," said Marc, finally finding his voice in the conversation.

Thad figured it wouldn't be long before Peanut and Quint's bodies were found in the path. It wasn't unusual that the path was the quickest way to the nearest convenience store, a block away, where people might pass through on their way to work or school every morning. Perhaps it was Mr. Bruce's neighborhood-watching ass who might have wandered out there this morning to inspect the scene in regards to the gunshots he'd heard the night before. That was crackhead Tootsie's old-ass daddy, the same muthafucka who'd try to extort a nigga on every corner.

"Say, what's the game plan?" asked Taye.

"Yeah," Marc said.

Thad leaned forward, and at that moment, he thought back on the discussion he'd had with Crow last night about war and trust. Then he said, "Never act like you don't have nothing to lose, because then you move out of desperation, and desperation is the worst motivation for action. You got that?"

Both Taye and Marc nodded in unison.

"Now, listen up…" Thad continued and gave them the game.

***

Robert put his hand on the butt of his revolver as he drove down through the valley.

A police cruiser turned onto the same street and stayed with him. He waited for the cop to hit the lights and sound the alarm. The car followed him onto Livermore. He turned left onto North Second and peered into the rearview mirror. The police cruiser kept moving in a straight line on Livermore. He had to lose them quickly.

On Mufford Street, Robert turned right and rode past rows of houses on a quiet street. Finally, he came to North Eighth and turned down toward a friend's house. Three blocks away, he put the car in cruise control and drifted past familiar residents until he reached the point he figured he had lost the cop car, pulling up in someone's driveway.

Then, to his dismay, another car pulled up behind him in the driveway he had just pulled into for temporary purposes. He'd just been about to pull out when the unfamiliar car blocked his way out.

"Damn it!" Robert cursed in instant frustration, wondering how he was going to get out of this situation. He checked his Rolex and frowned, seeing that he was going to be late for his important meeting.

Behind him, a female got out of her Mitsubishi Galant with a toddler in her arms.

Through his rearview mirror, he observed the woman and child, quickly thinking of a strategic plan. Strategy was his specialty, and before the woman shut her car door, he was exiting his.

"Excuse me, ma'am?"

"Yes." She regarded him with curiosity. "Do I know you?"

Robert said, "I'm not sure. But is this the Hayes residence?" The man looked every bit the district attorney he was, attired in his three-piece Hugo Boss suit.

The question gave her pause. "No." She seemed a bit unsure of the situation. She was a soft, walnut-brown-skinned sister who appeared to be in her mid-twenties, looking damned good in her high-waist McGuire denim jeans and open-toe sandals to show off her pretty, pedicured feet. Ma was sexy as hell—no makeup, no nothing! "I don't know anyone by that name."

A second later, the front door of the house opened. Another older female stood there in the doorway.

"Then I guess I got the wrong address," he said, glancing over toward the house.

"What address are you looking for?"

Hesitantly, Robert realized he'd placed himself in a bind. He couldn't just come up with any address, or else she would know he was telling a goddamn lie.

The older woman came marching toward them from the house. Robert's sense of alarm kicked in when a group of niggas exited a house from across the street.

"Is there a problem?" asked the older woman.

"This man said he's looking for somebody named Hayes. He thought he lived here, Ms. Viv," said the younger female.

"I apologize for the inconvenience, ladies," said Robert. "I'll just be on my way."

"There ain't no Hayes live nowhere around here," said Ms. Viv, a slightly overweight woman with a large bosom and lovely face with sparkling, brown eyes.

"Thank you," Robert replied anxiously.

"Hey!" Mx. Viv called out to him, stepping up to his car door with that suspicious look in her eyes. "Ain't you that lawyer guy?"

"Please, Miss, I must get going."

"Mama, he got a gun in there on the seat!"

"Yeah, you're him." Ms. Viv peered inside the car, and sure enough, there was a gun lying on the passenger seat inside. "What you need a gun for, lawyer man?"

The other female shielded the child and hurried along to the house.

"I don't want no trouble, ma'am."

"Then you better get the hell outta my damn driveway before there will be some trouble," she threatened, her voice hard now with a hint of fear.

Sliding inside the shiny black Mercedes-Benz, Robert shut the door and cranked the car up.

Ms. Viv stood right there with her heavy-looking arms folded across her large breasts.

Avoiding the opportunity of running her fat ass over, Robert steered the Benz to the right and made a sharp U-turn through the neighbor's yard. He bumped over the curb and onto the street and shot a glare in the big woman's direction. He then sped off and away from there with his heart pounding violently in his chest. All because of a punk ass cop car following him and causing him to panic a little, he ended up where he could have easily found more trouble than he needed. He had enough of it on his hands as it was. He'd escaped it this time, but would he escape it when trouble popped its ugly head up next time?

A few blocks away, Robert allowed himself to breathe easier. That was a close call. Still, he had a meeting to attend that he couldn't miss. He never saw the car following him.

***

General woke up to the arousing sensation of his dick being engulfed in a warm, slippery mouth. When he cracked his eyelids open, he watched as Olivia, his gorgeous and most loyal Cuban-integrated marketing coordinator, worked his piece slowly and magically. General felt himself grow to full length inside her talented mouth. Now that was how a nigga should wake up every morning—to some serious head game from a bad bitch, and that same bad bitch had connections.

He reached up to place a hand at the back of her head to goad her on, and Olivia lifted her gray eyes at him and smiled around his dick. He smiled back.

At that moment, General didn't think about Roe, who was down the hallway in the empty guestroom of the unfinished structured house. The interior of the house had a cool, faintly damp smell of plaster and fresh paint. All the walls in range were a dazzling, pale hue, the unadorned windows of drapes and curtains stark and tall.

The living room in which Olivia tended to Roe's wound in a professional manner, some six and a half hours before, consisted of a few matching armchairs, chunky and oversized, upholstered in a neutral-toned material that merged imperceptibly with the gray cement floor. The quilted comforter General lived on, including a couple of throw pillows to complete his makeshift bedding, also set upon a large area rug that showed a densely woven grid of black and gray patterns. It was enough for General, considering his dire situation.

For the while, that muthafucka felt like a king-sized bed as he lay, getting some mean head from his Cuban princess. After treating the dick with class for a few more minutes, Olivia got nasty on it, spitting and all that good shit, as she lost herself in her own pleasure. Already naked as a newborn, she reached her hand between her legs to stroke her clit, moaning with pure ecstasy at the feeling of her wetness.

"I need this big, black dick in me," she said after plopping his dick from her sloppy mouth like a fat candy cane.

"Then whatcha waitin' on, ma?" he replied.

She tugged his boxers down and off before straddling his lap, reaching behind her to stroke his manhood for a moment. She stared down at him with eyes glazed with lust, her beautiful, full lips wet with saliva.

"Stop playing with it."

She didn't have to be told twice.

There was a change of plans. Olivia spun around on him, reverse-cowgirl style, and impaled herself on his rigid dick. "My god!" She moaned with pleasure as she eased down to take every inch of him in.

General couldn't help it. He had to grab ahold of her round, creamy ass and drive the rest of it inside her to the hilt, and Olivia howled like the animal she was. She rode him like a true stallion; the bitch had porn star potential.

When she slapped his hands away and leaned all the way forward on her elbows, Olivia bounced and ground on top of him like her life depended on it. General threw his arms behind his head and shut his eyes while enjoying the ride. This was something new to him because Olivia had never fucked him like she was now, and the pussy was tighter than a glove.

It wasn't that he had been neglecting the pussy; the streets had him so damned busy he couldn't get around to her. Plus, he had other bitches in his stable that desired his attention too. As it turned out, Olivia had been keeping it tight for him, though, or at least that was what he assumed.

Although bitches weren't worth shit nowadays, there was something he saw in Olivia that he didn't compare with the others. The girl had come from a hard life, but shit, that was majority of the women he had on his team. It wasn't the fact that she was the niece of Anthony Kerr, the right-hand man of his Miami cocaine connect he met through her, but it was that Olivia was the real deal, having been raised from loyalty and burned from it as well. Olivia was his most desirable one.

Suddenly, General sensed a presence other than Olivia's near him, and when he opened his eyes, he damn near went into cardiac arrest. Standing over him with his pistol aimed at General's shocked face was Roe, staring in his eyes with a murderous glare. How the hell did he get loose?

General couldn't believe his luck.

He'd slipped.

Or was it Olivia that slipped?

"This the part where shit really gets drastic, son," said Roe with the most wicked sneer General had ever seen.

Chapter 9

In passing, Thad detached some curious and disturbing stares from his neighbors as he trudged along the sidewalk. He was en route to Vega's house, which was just around the corner. What he might've found when he got there—he didn't know—but one thing for sure was he wanted to check up on his homie.

Of course, Thad figured Vega had just been mad about the situation when he called him the night before. Part of him didn't take Vega seriously because Thad knew how his nigga got at times when he was heated. But there was another part of him that remained cautious, which was why Thad brought his gun with him; Vega could be very unpredictable.

Upon reaching Vega's house, he climbed the porch steps and knocked on the front door. A minute later, the door opened to reveal eight-year-old Tiera, whose hazel-brown eyes gleamed up at him with glee. She was a beautiful little girl with curly, brown hair, and she was mischievous as hell, but Thad loved her all the same, as if she were his very own sibling.

The girl hugged him happily as Sue, the grimy coke head who was Vega's mama, stepped up behind Tiera with a mean look on her used-to-be-pretty face.

"Girl, get your ass back in the house. What I told you 'bout opening the damn door without asking who it is first?" snapped Sue.

"But I saw who it was first, Mama," Tiera said.

71

Sue gave her that *I'ma tear your ass up* look, and Tiera dropped her head, dragging her feet back inside the house.

"What do you want, boy?" Sue finally acknowledged Thad, clutching a cigarette that was already sizzling at the butt between her fingers. She hit it one last time and flicked it away.

Thad loved that mean-ass woman to death, but sometimes, she could be an absolute bitch.

"Is my man's home, Mama?"

She frowned and looked Thad up and down. Then she yelled, "Troy!" before turning away from the door.

With a nonchalant shrug, Thad waited where he stood. He was used to her fucked-up attitude. Over the years, Sue never actually welcomed him into her home. It was Vega who had always done so. She would leave him standing out on the doorstep, just like she did moments ago, but there were several times when Thad would come over for Vega, and only she would be home, high as she wanted to be, giving him that freaky look that said she wanted to fuck. All those times, Thad would leave her stink ass standing there in the doorway, hoping one day she'd seduce him.

Thad would never fuck his boy's mama, no matter how juicy and big her Nicki Minaj ass was. He just couldn't stoop that low, but he knew of some young niggas who had. Though Vega didn't really give a fuck about his mama, it was Tiera he was crazy over. That nigga would've died a million deaths for his baby sister, and Thad would, too.

When Vega finally came to the door, he halted in his tracks, snarling at Thad like a vicious hyena. The look in his eyes was dark and empty of life.

"Look, brah, I don't know—"

"You think this shit is a game, nigga?" Vega cut in and stepped into Thad's face.

"You trippin', Vega. This me, son! I'm not trying to go through it with you over no bullshit you may assume."

"You a bitch!" Vega shoved him.

Thad regarded him coldly. "Nigga—"

Vega upped his gun and placed it at Thad's left temple, his finger curled around the trigger. That made Thad pause.

From nearby, people watched the confrontation at a safer distance, just as stunned by the situation as Thad. They were aware of the brotherly bond the two shared, but to see it go down like that was troubling indeed.

Sue watched from just beyond her son's shoulder, standing in her kitchen doorway. From the first moment she laid eyes on her son that morning, she knew he wasn't the same.

"The only reason I won't blow your muthafuckin' brains out right now is my love for Mama Dee. But nigga, don't push me, dawg," Vega said. "It's no love now, nigga."

If Thad attempted to reach for his gun, he was a dead man.

"Now get the fuck outta my face, chump."

"You got that, brah." It stung Thad to be handled in such a fashion by the only true brother he knew, but to avoid further trouble, he stepped back and walked away from Vega, quietly descending the porch steps in the direction he'd come.

Tears of anger welled up in Thad's eyes, but he willed them to stay, holding his chin up proudly. Vega didn't take his pride whatsoever; he took what love Thad did have for him. Now the feeling was mutual.

***

That morning, Melvin woke up in St. Mary's Hospital, where he had to have Rosie rushed after she'd fractured her hip bone in a fall the night before. When he found her, she was at the bottom of the stairs on the floor that led to the exit behind the pool house. She had mistakenly slipped on one of the rungs, falling back down to the concrete floor of the tunnel, seconds before she was about to make a successful exit.

In the process, she had banged her head pretty badly and injured her left shoulder. Rosie was in a bad mood and refused to look at him for any reason. Sometime around ten o'clock that morning, they received their first visitor of the day—two visitors actually, but only one of them counted.

The other was Rita Brown.

The guy who followed Rita through the door had an oval-shaped, freckled face and short, brownish hair with multiple strands of gray that rolled back from his forehead in tight waves. Melvin knew the face but couldn't put a name on it. The guy's tweed jacket covered a broad chest across, and he gave Melvin an unsettling glance, to which Melvin returned a darker one of his own.

While Rita shut the door behind them, the guy approached the foot of the bed and said, "My name is Charles Bennett, and I'm a homicide lieutenant with the NYPD."

Melvin didn't respond. Luckily, Rosie was still asleep after being heavily sedated for the pain she was experiencing. Knowing her, she would have sent them both running out of there if she'd been awake.

"We have a lot to talk about, Mr. Whitaker," Bennett said, pulling up a chair and parking it before Melvin.

"I'm quite sure you do, sir." Melvin shot a glance up at Rita, who looked about as worried as ever.

Bennett's dark-brown eyes, set close to his wide nose, were utterly flat and dead, far past the boundary where they could have been called expressionless. They didn't even possess enough life in them to be lifeless.

"You gonna sit there and fucking stare at me, or are you gonna get with the program?" Melvin asked firmly but impatiently as well, with the meanest glare.

"I'ma get with the program, sir."

Rita smirked over the detective's shoulder and found herself a seat close by.

"How is the missus, may I ask? "Bennett started.

"She's a champion—no serious damage."

"Yeah, I talked to the doctor myself." That took care of the social portion of their encounter. "And yourself?"

"About bored with your questions!" Melvin snapped and looked back over at Rita. "Brown, where did you get this guy from?"

She just shrugged in response. Now Bennett was a bit offended.

"Mr. Whitaker, last night, around three-thirty in the morning, a call came through the dispatch, reporting a shooting at your residence. When patrol units arrived at the location, we found your front door forced open by what was assumed to be a firearm before being kicked in. Upon entry, a body was found just outside your home office with a shot to the face." Bennett paused for a long second. "You mind telling me if you know anything about that, sir?"

"I have no problem with that, detective."

Bennett nodded. "You got the floor."

Melvin told him what happened from the moment he heard the first gunshot to shooting two men and his escape through the hidden passage when shit got too real.

"And it took you up until now to give your account on the situation?" Bennett's pen was posed above his notepad.

"My wife's well-being and safety is more important. However, I was gonna get around to it."

"Any idea why you were targeted by those gunmen?"

"Clueless."

"I take it you're not being totally honest with me. Sir, I'm only here to help you, not hinder your situation any more than it already has been," said Bennett.

"Good," retorted Melvin as he sat back in his seat. "The only help you can give me is by helping yourself up out of that chair and out of my face. I gave you my statement, detective, and we have nothing else to talk about. Bye."

Silence followed.

The detective exchanged glances with Rita Brown and shrugged his massive shoulders. Then he grudgingly stood and made his way over to the door, stopping with a last glance over his shoulder.

"Just so that you know, sir, there are quite a few people who don't take too kindly—"

That's when Melvin rose out of the chair and said, "I don't give a fuck about you or what or how anyone may take my position, as I'm a man of honor, and I will remain to be that. Now, detective, please, see yourself out before I am forced to become physical, man." His eyes were as cold as a pack of hot dogs.

With a wicked smirk, Bennett took his leave.

Then Melvin turned to Rita. "Who is that man, Rita?"

"He's new to the division."

"Fuckin' with me, I'll tear him a new asshole!" Melvin fumed.

**

Ceasing her gyrating motion on top of General's hard dick, Olivia looked over her shoulder in total bewilderment, freaking the fuck out at the sight of Roe with a gun.

To General's surprise, Roe turned the gun on her and put a bullet through her muthafuckin' head.

"Oh shit!" General gasped.

Olivia died with dick all up in her guts, lying atop General with her last thoughts splattered all over the place.

"You always underestimate a nigga, son," Roe said before kicking General several times in the head with his bare foot. Despite the throbbing pain in his shoulder, he felt damned good about the leverage he had over General. "Now look at your ass, lookin' all scared and shit."

"Fuck you!" spat General, shoving Olivia's dead body away from him with disgust. He was more shocked than scared.

"The tables have turned now, General."

"Then do what you gotta do, nigga. This the shit I signed up for anyway. My heart don't pump no fear for no nigga!"

"I'm not gonna kill you, though."

"You better!" Without so much as a flicker of dreaded caution, General stood up as naked as a jaybird. He snarled over at his enemy like the true gangster he was.

A bemused expression masked Roe's face. "You ready to die?"

"Been ready!" General clenched his fists tightly, his heart pounding with excitement in his inked-up chest.

"I can't kill you, Jarrod," said Roe. "But I could, though. If I didn't have no love for you, nigga, you'll be laying next t that dumb-ass bitch. She knew how serious this shit was and still left them muthafuckin' scissors in the room with me." He shook his head in absolute disappointment.

General looked over at the dead Cuban with malice.

"I spent damn near four hours fightin' wit' them shits with my hands tied behind my back."

There wasn't a word from General, but he remained guarded. What a critical situation it was.

"Like I told you off top, I had nothing to do with what went down with your old man. That's what I came to tell you before your boy Vega got trigger-happy. But of course,"— Roe said with earnest—"under different circumstances, if it had happened to my old man, I woulda got at you too. I respect the game for what it is, nigga, but can you say the same thing?"

All General did was look up at him as his words threatened to penetrate. He was ready for whatever.

Roe held his gaze long and hard. "We been acting like straight-up shorties all these years over some shorties courtroom beef our old men got. You brought that shit to me first."

General interjected in that low, deadly tone. "You the one threw that brick, Roe."

"Yeah. You made me throw it when you stabbed my old man's car tires that night. I saw you!"

"I ain't do shit!"

"So, your old man did it?" Roe questioned, and when General did not answer, he knew the truth. So, it wasn't General who had punctured Robert's tires on his old '69 Camaro, but Melvin. Roe remembered that night as though it were last night, but he did see General and his daddy dash off back to their car just down the street after the mission. Roe had been sneaking and smoking weed behind the house when he heard the mission in progress.

Robert had adored that damned Camaro! Now the truth was out.

"Yeah, I did it! So what!" General said, but his words were nonsense to Roe now.

"Yeah, whatever," Roe said. "Still, we was on some bullshit then and still on it. Now look what all that unnecessary bullshit done got us. I heard the news this morning, man. They think I'm the one who killed that cop."

That was as true as told. Due to Roe's gun being found, which was the same caliber weapon that had been used to kill Yolanda Dovolani, it made it easier to pin it on Roe. Now Roe was wanted for a murder he didn't commit, and there was nothing he could do about it.

"This is the stupidity Ms. Lynn told me about the other day." General wasn't feeling this shit at all, standing there naked before another man—his enemy, to be exact. He reached down to retrieve his boxer shorts as if he weren't standing under the gun that could very much be the death of him. Then he suddenly went still after what Roe said finally registered.

"What did you say about my mama, muthafucka?"

"She stopped me last week at the gas station," said Roe.

That really fucked General up. "What?"

"She told me she loved me no matter what we go through, son. But fuck all that. You wanna know how I really feel about your ass, nigga?" Roe stepped forward with the gun clutched tightly in his grasp.

General stood his ground unwearyingly.

When Roe stopped before him, looking deep into General's eyes, holding his gaze, he then pushed the gun into his childhood friend's chest. "I can't kill a nigga I love, brah. Fuck what we been through. It's what we gotta go through now." Then he released the gun and turned his back on General, the gun now fumbling in General's hands as he attempted to catch it before it fell onto the floor.

He looked at Roe's retreating figure slouching over to have a seat in one of the chairs. General didn't know what to make of the situation. This was the most important decision he'd ever have to make in his life.

"I knew that cop, brah," said Roe with a dazed expression as he looked at General attentively.

General looked from the gun back up at him.

"I know where she came from, too, son," added Roe. "But what's coming to us behind her murder is a whole other story. All I gotta say is I'm down for whatever."

"Me too."

"Then let's make it do what it do, son."

"We got no other choice."

"Except die," Roe replied with a wince.

General shook his head. "Not on my watch, brah." he said.

"Okay," was all Roe said before he blacked out.

Chapter 10

After leaving the car dealership in his new Chevy Impala rental in his old neighborhood of Harlem, Melvin realized he wanted to go somewhere else first. He turned the car toward Hudson Street, the accumulating cloud cover overhead generating an official twilight, and the whiff of approaching rain gathering infused the air.

Melvin was on a mission. He needed some new wheels to throw off anyone wise enough to look for him in any of his vehicles. Of course, the one he'd chosen could be anyone out of the hundreds alike driving around the surrounding cities at that moment. Now, the only thing Melvin needed was another cell phone and more firepower.

The two guns he had the night before were still at Fred's place, one of his good old friends he'd run to for safety through the night, several houses down. Melvin phoned Fred in advance and explained the situation, asking him to meet him at a nearby location to retrieve them. From there, Melvin could make more things happen.

"Say no more, buddy." Fred was down with it.

Twenty minutes later, Melvin was in possession of several guns, including his own, with extra ammunition.

His next step was on to the next phase.

Melvin made a quick stop by his office building and grabbed a few things, brushing off any and everybody who dared to say anything to him. Back safely in his rental,

Melvin searched through his directory and found the number he was looking for after disposing of his own cell phone.

He needed someone who was thorough, ruthless, and could be trusted, and there was no better person to help him accomplish his task than K'wan.

K'wan was Harlem, through and through—the son of one of the most admirable women Melvin knew. Her name was Brenda, whom God had called home before her time and would always be missed. Because of the love and respect he had for Brenda, he promised her loving soul if K'wan ever needed his assistance in any way, he wouldn't hesitate to prove it. Now he needed K'wan's assistance more than ever.

"Hello?" a voice answered on the third ring.

"K'wan, this is Melvin." There was no need to say his last name. "I need your help, man."

There was a pause.

"Where are you?" K'wan asked.

"Wherever you need me to be."

That was all it took to get things done. Now it was to the bank. Money talked.

***

When Thad lifted the cigarette to his lips for a drag, he was prevented from doing so when a raindrop extinguished its flame. He looked at the dead cigarette and up into the cloudy sky, then frowned with discontent, for which the sky seemed to mock his current mood. Or maybe he needed a little rain to wash away his pain. And his anger. He allowed the rain to shower upon him.

As he trudged down the sidewalk with his head down, in deep thought, Thad's attention was snatched away by the sound of his name being called. When he lifted his head and looked in the direction from which he was being called, he saw Old Man Crow waving him over from his porch.

"C'mon, youngin'!" Crow shouted after him.

Thad didn't even think twice about it. He hustled over beneath the shelter of the old man's porch.

Gesturing toward one of the two chairs present, Crow welcomed him to have a seat. "Sit on down and rest your nerves. Tell me what's on your mind, Thad."

Reluctant to speak, Thad sat down and let out an exasperated breath before reaching for his pack of Newports. Crow watched him carefully.

The rain was pouring down hard while knocking against the porch roof like miniature fists falling from the sky. The low grumbling of thunder was heard over the heavy rain. It was definitely about to go down, and Thad knew he'd be stuck there for a while until the storm passed.

"I gather you just came from seeing your brotha?" Crow finally broke their silence. "I take it it didn't go well."

Thad looked over at the old man as he sat in his wheelchair in the doorway of the front door. "That nigga done made himself a new enemy,' he said and told Crow what happened.

Hearing the burn in Thad's voice made him feel some type of way.

"I'm the last nigga he should ever want to make an enemy. Vega ain't the same, Crow. Something happened to him last night that I don't know."

"But I do," said Crow.

Now Thad was looking at him crazily.

"Whatcha mean, you do?"

Crow told him about the discovery of Trel three hours prior, behind the old Baptist church. He described what he knew of the situation, and Thad found himself staring at Crow in open disbelief.

"So, yeah, youngin', I think your brotha went through one of the most disturbing moments he'd ever experienced in his life. For someone to savagely rip your throat out with his mouth…" Crow shook his head sadly. "That's enough to turn a person into a monster. That youngin' saw his life flash before his eyes last night, and he had to do what he had to do to survive," he professed with a sour expression.

To imagine Vega doing something so barbaric was so very unnerving that Thad shuddered in response.

"He was left with no choice, youngin', and that same choice has changed his life forever. "

"How did you find out what happened?" asked Thad.

The old man shot him a mischievous grin. "I'm not only old and paralyzed, Thad. I have resources too. In my former line of work, before my accident, those same resources were the ones that kept me relevant in the game."

"The game?" Thad gave the man a curious glance. "What game you talkin' 'bout, Crow?"

"The same game you call yourself playing."

"I don't play games."

"Oh, but you're a part of it!"

Thad said, "Man, what the hell you talkin' 'bout?"

"I can show you better than I can tell you." Crow reached for the wheels of his chair and put it in reverse. "Come, youngin'. Lemme show you something." When the old man disappeared from the doorway, Thad hesitantly stood up and entered the house behind him.

***

The passenger door of the Impala opened, and in slid K'wan, dressed in his dope boy gear and fitted cap turned backward, with an unopened Black & Mild cigar in hand. Before he could even shut the door behind himself, the car was already lurching forward toward the exit of the 7-Eleven parking lot.

By this time, the driving rain had calmed to a light sprinkle. It wouldn't be long before it started up again, drenching the city with its presence.

For a minute, neither of them spoke, as they waited for the other to speak up first.

"How you been, man?" Melvin broke first.

"I'm good, yo, but save the social shit for later. What's up with this help you say you need?" K'wan retorted, getting straight to the point.

It was another reason Melvin liked the young cat. K'wan was honest and straightforward. After representing two of K'wan's former cases and beating them both, Melvin had developed a bond with the Harlem hustler. They had mutual respect, and that respect was about to be exercised now.

"I need you to help me find General before them swines get hold of him. You know how those crooked bastards play." Melvin referred to his son by his hood name, having committed himself to taking matters into his own hands—to the streets!

K'wan nodded while unwrapping his cigar. Then Melvin gave him the full rundown of what he needed done, giving some familiar names, updating him on the whole situation.

"I know how to handle it, yo," said K'wan.

"They'll be watching me closely now, hoping General will contact me. I'll only reach you by phone from here on out unless—"

"Mel!"

Melvin glanced at him.

"I got this, son. Don't worry. You wouldn't have called me if you didn't know I wouldn't come through," K'wan reassured him and put flame to his cigar. "Finding bro is top priority."

That was what Melvin wanted to hear.

A brief silence ensued.

"So how's your writing going?" Melvin asked, bringing the car to a halt two cars back from a stoplight.

"I'm in the process of gettin' one of my books reviewed now," said K'wan. Because his mother hadn't gotten the opportunity to further her pursuit as a novelist, K'wan took it upon himself to sustain her legacy by becoming a writer. So far, he'd had quite a few novels published in the urban genre and planned to start his own publishing company one day. Besides, it brought in some honest income, and he was a beast with his pen.

"That's great," Melvin complimented. "Maybe, one day, you'll write about the bullshit that's going on now."

"Maybe." K'wan also admired Melvin's wife's penmanship, too.

"And one more thing before I forget." Melvin opened the middle console between them and extracted a white envelope from it. He handed the envelope to K'wan. "That's for you."

After peering inside the envelope and seeing the multiple c-notes it contained, K'wan sucked his teeth and tossed the envelope on the dashboard before shooting him a dark glare.

"Why you tryna play me, yo!"

"Play you how? That's ten G's right there!"

"Fuck that muthafuckin' ten G's, nigga! You don't ever have to pay me for shit. What I do for you, I do outta respect, homie." K'wan was heated, and it showed in his eyes.

Reluctantly, Melvin said, "I was just trying to help out.

"I don't need your money!"

"Good." Melvin shrugged. "More for me, then."

***

Vega plunged across 134th Street and walked east on a block lined with two-story frames and red-brimmed houses, separated by thick, low shrubbery. Some of the small front lawns were littered with children's toys and such, and many were definitely in need of proper landscaping. In passing, Vega heard Kendrick Lamar blasting from an upstairs window.

After bumping into Worm and his crew earlier at the neighborhood corner store, he was enlightened on the matter regarding Twin and Forty. He had a plan. Now he was on the hunt again. Twin was about to wish he hadn't crossed that line.

Eventually, Felicia Carter's house was in his sight, just up ahead. She was Twin's seven-month-pregnant aunt. She was the closest thing to a true mother he would've ever had than the biological alcoholic who'd pushed him out of her womb.

As he made his way up the stone-block path that led to the front door, Vega already knew what he was gonna do to have Twin served to him on a platter. Things were about to get ugly. He was about to make someone feel how he felt the night before, but they would also die instead.

Vega could taste revenge at the tip of his tongue—sweet revenge. Besides, he'd already wanted to murk Twin anyway.

At the doorsteps, Vega rang the doorbell with a knuckle and observed his immediate surroundings—perfect. Nothing appeared to be alarming enough about his presence. He tried the doorbell again and waited patiently.

After several more tries, to no avail, Vega was about to say fuck it and leave, but then something else came to mind. Sneaky as could be, Vega snuck around the back of the house and, with minor difficulty, let himself in. From there, he would wait some more, a task he was determined to do in order to capitalize on the cruelty he was itching to administer.

***

When Roe came to, he was riding on the passenger side of Olivia's Q30 Infiniti, vision hazy and stomach growling like a muthafucka. He looked over and saw General mumbling to himself as he flipped through the radio station trying to find something to ride to.

The last thing Roe slightly remembered, though, was being half-carried and half-dragged down a hallway toward the back door of the house. He was back out cold before

General shoved his heavy ass into the car. The large amount of blood loss had him weak as fuck. Roe needed serious medical treatment.

"The fuck you doing?" Roe managed to ask.

General glanced over at him. "I need some motivation to ride to, and it ain't shit on the radio."

"The situation is motivation enough."

"Yeah, but I need to hear some gangsta shit," General said. "I wish I had some of Thad's shit to ride to. My nigga keep a nigga riding good."

"Brah."

"Yeah?"

"We gotta call Doc. I'm fucked up, B," Roe complained.

Without a word, General retrieved the cell phone and tossed it over to Roe. "Call him up."

That was exactly what Roe did, stressing the matter to the point that Doc was begging him to stop by. Roe was lightheaded and could barely raise his voice above a murmur. Despite the bullshit they'd taken each other through throughout the years, to see his brother in such a condition bothered General.

"We gotta go to his place, over in Queens, brah," Roe said and struggled to recline his seat back.

"Nah, bro, get in the back!"

"I'm good."

General knew he was to blame for his brother's condition, but shit, he wasn't in his right state of mind when the shit went down. Also, General knew who Doc was. Doc had his own private practice where all the street niggas could afford his service without any paper trail. He was good, trustworthy and just as felonious as those he treated medically.

"Hold on, Roe," General told him. "I gotcha, son." He did indeed.

They needed all the strength they could get to conquer the street war that was headed their way, and that plane would be landing in the next hour, and then trouble would come.

Chapter 11

Shutting the unhinged door as best he could, Thad followed the old man through the spacious house toward what appeared to be the bathroom.

'Why he bringing me here?' thought Thad.

Crow beckoned him inside the bathroom while he steered the chair out of the way. When Thad hesitated, he assured him all was well, for him to trust him, and there shouldn't be any doubt when he had Thad's best interest at heart.

Slowly but surely, Thad entered the bathroom before him.

"Now, grab hold of that tub there, youngin', and pull it back against the wall there," Crow instructed him with a gesture of the hand.

Thad looked at him strangely but did as he was told.

The large tub didn't budge at first, but when Thad applied more pressure at the front of the tub, it moved. Then he pulled the tub away from the wall and pushed it against the far wall just beneath the bathroom sink.

"Take that jackhammer there," said Crow.

Thad could see a jackhammer resting against the edge of the wall where the foot of the tub had been. No telling how long that bitch been there, but Thad took it, looking down at it oddly in his hand.

With that same jackhammer, Crow instructed him to pry the floorboard up and push it back against the wall. Before he could, Thad was already getting a whiff of what lay beneath it.

Beneath the floorboard were pounds and pounds of shrink-wrapped grade-A marijuana, grown from fresh Colombian soil, in a two-foot shallow grave dug for its hidden purpose. Thad's sense of smell was assaulted by the full blast now from the potent herb before his own two eyes.

He looked over at Crow with open wonder, and then he saw the .38 Caliber Smith & Wesson revolver Crow had managed to slip from beneath the bathroom sink. It was lying on the old man's lap with his finger wrapped around the trigger. There was no mistaking the grave look Thad saw in his eyes.

"I'ma tell you this one time and one time only." Crow finally spoke up in that dead serious tone. "I can kill you now rather than kill you later if you decide to cross me."

Thad didn't respond.

"I will die before I let you or anybody take what I won— what I risked my life for! And best believe, youngin', no matter how it goes down, I will murder someone about that. So, make your choice now, Thad. You wanna keep my trust or break it by crossing me?" Crow didn't stray away from his eyes as he searched deep within them. One slightest hint of distrust in them, and Crow would not hesitate to pull that trigger.

This was a life-or-death situation, and the tension was thick.

Swallowing hard, Thad said, "I'll always have your trust me, old man. You can trust me wholeheartedly."

Crow studied him carefully.

Turning back to the stash and picking up one of the packages to examine it closely, Thad knew without a doubt that what he had in his hands was pure fire. Just the smell of it alone was effective.

"I've been watching you hustle out there on that corner for a long time, youngin'." Crow let his voice be heard. "You handle your customers well, and you're always on point. You're a lot different from those others out there, and I'd like for you to utilize what you have there and make yourself some money."

"You want me to sell this for you?"

"No," Crow said. "I want you to lock the city down with it, youngin'."

Then he gave Thad the game.

***

By one o'clock, having gotten the majority of his legalities out of the way, Robert found himself driving once more along the Upper East Side in search of one particular person because he couldn't reach them by cell phone. The sky was steel gray, the earlier patches of blue blanketing it with thick clouds again.

Robert was in a fucked-up mood, having been given more cases to take, but he was gonna throw them off on his assistant to handle for the time being. There were more grave matters at stake, and he needed to tend to them personally, without the extra shit. He loved his work, true enough, but his life and the well-being of his son were more important.

He needed to find Rolando as soon as possible. The heat was on now—pressure.

He knew the authorities were also watching him closely, hoping he'd lead them to his son. They would do whatever it took to get his son, even if it meant ruining his life in the process. Another worry was that damned Melvin, who he had ordered some goons to take care of, and the muthafuckas missed! That had him boiling mad.

Old Melvin was swifter than Robert gave him credit for, but how in the hell did he up and disappear like that? That was the million-dollar question. He knew his old crony was smart, but damn! He pulled some smooth shit then.

The phone lying on the passenger seat rang.

"Hunt?" he answered.

"You won't believe who just landed on a flight from Chicago," said the gruffy voice on the other end.

Robert had a bad feeling he already knew. "Was there an entourage with them?"

"Thirteen of them total, sir," the unidentified caller replied. "And I think it's time for you to make that call."

"Precisely." Robert sighed.

"I'll keep in touch."

"You do that." Robert ended the call and had to pull over on the side of the road to gather his bearings. What he had just been told was what he feared the most. It was just what he needed—a bunch of grieving and ruthless Italians to come and destroy some shit that would definitely hinder his mission. Mario Napoli, capo of the Napoli Family, had finally arrived, and what he brought along with him was enough to make the devil shiver and cringe.

"Shit," was all Robert could say. Then he turned the car around and hauled ass in the opposite direction. He needed to get home first. The shit was surely about to hit the fan, and no one was safe.

***

That was the same thing Mango was thinking at that very moment. Nobody was safe now. Standing in the doorway of Lisa's house, clutching his big 44 Bulldog, he looked out among his immediate surroundings with the evilest expression. While several of his goons went about the house, with more on the way, Mango feared the worst.

He knew his brother was dead; he felt it in his heart. With all the blood he saw all over the place, he did not doubt in his mind that General was the cause of his sudden sorrow. Refusing to cry yet, Mango turned to Cuda, who had just exited the house. "Burn this muthafucka down," he ordered.

With a nod, Cuda retreated inside.

Ten minutes later, they were riding two cars deep through Harlem, everybody strapped and ready to murder something. The tension in the first car was suffocating. Mango wanted blood for what he felt happened to Dred. He felt untouchable now, invincible, and no one was gonna stop him from turning Harlem upside down and inside out with a bloody vengeance. Now he had a personal vendetta with General. He wanted to hit him where it hurt most.

Up ahead, Mango saw a lone, young hoodlum walking down the sidewalk, leaving the candy lady's house. He was biting into a pickled egg while clutching a bag of chips, oblivious to the threat lurking behind him. He was fucking up his pickled egg too much to care about anything else.

That would be his first victim.

"Snatch him up and bring his ass to me!" Mango ordered the two armed goons in the back of the Chevy Caprice Classic—the box kind.

The second Cuda pulled the car alongside the young nigga, both goons jumped out and rushed him with guns drawn. One of them pushed him into the back of the car. Within a matter of eight seconds, the young nigga was sitting between both goons in the back seat, about to be taken on that gangsta ride.

"Show him who he's fuckin with, yo," said Mango

On command, both goons pistol whipped the little nigga, leaving him bloody in the back seat, breaking his nose and savagely breaking two of his fingers and all. Mango relished in the agonizing cry of the young nigga.

Taye knew for sure he was about to die right there in that back seat. He was in so much pain. He felt as though he was about to black out. He knew he shouldn't have let Lil' Beezo's fat ass talk him into going to the candy lady's house to buy some goddamn Fritos and a cigar to roll a sack up. Now look where it had gotten him!

Turning back to look at Taye with bloodshot eyes of rage, Mango said, "You know General, little nigga?"

Taye didn't answer. Then one of the goons shot him in the thigh, and Taye howled in excruciating pain.

"Where the fuck is General?" Mango demanded.

Still, Taye refused to talk.

"Oh, you think you bad, huh?" Mango frowned darkly,

Taye cried, and Mango cocked his pistol back, turned back around, and blew his muthafuckin' brains out the back of his head.

"Dump that fool, and let's go!" said Mango, hating and respecting Taye's loyalty all at the same time. "We got some more bodies to bury."

Chapter 12

Washing his hands in a nearby sink, Doc confirmed the vital description of Roe's condition, which was good. He would live. "But he'll need plenty of rest and special needs to build his strength back up," Doc said and glanced in Roe's direction. "He's lost a considerable amount of blood."

General nodded as he chewed on the six-inch Subway sandwich Doc had just bought before Roe's call. He was famished.

Lying on a padded table several feet away in the operating room was Roe, with tubes and IVs protruding from his muscular frame that had taken a serious beating, but he was a fighter, even at this stage, refusing to bow down for any reason. Also, General knew he would hate to swim with the sharks by himself now because Roe needed serious time to heal and get proper rest. He had to step up to the plate now and make it do what it did.

There was no way he could reach his old man, for fear of him being watched, so that meant he had to go for what he knew—beast mode. After finishing his meal, General stood and tossed the trash in a red hazard can to his right. "I need a car, Doc," he said. "The one I got out there, I gotta dispose of fast. I need something—"

"I understand, General. Maybe I can hook you up."

"I need that right now."

Doc, who was of average height, Spanish, and about the size of a mop handle, was a jack-of-all-trades. He had his hands in all kinds of shit, having gotten very busy in the underworld. He went off to make some calls, and while he did that, General snatched up his car keys.

Outside, General eased into Doc's 2014 Porsche Boxster S and brought it to life. Doc was gonna be hot about him taking his car, but General didn't give a damn. He said he needed a car right now.

Minutes later, he was riding down Park Avenue. He'd gotten word about how Harlem was under siege with the authorities from the multiple bodies that were discovered. So much shit had been going on with his situation, and he had no clue how serious it was back in the hood. The news of Quint's death stunned him, for that was one of his little homies, and how much it might affect Baby Thad. He knew how much Baby Thad liked the young cat.

A chain reaction of events about his and Roe's situation had escalated majorly. The city was in complete mayhem.

"I knew that shit was gonna happen!" General banged the steering wheel when he made it back to Harlem. Even from a distance, he knew the body lying on the side of the road was Taye. The young nigga was the only one in the hood who had those bright-orange Chuck Taylor converse sneakers.

General couldn't believe his eyes as he drove right by Taye's dead body alongside the street. He was unaware that seconds before he turned onto the street, Taye was dumped into it. That meant the killer himself was still in the area and had just driven by him in the dark-blue Chevy Caprice. If only either one of them had known the other was just in passing range in two different vehicles.

Little did General know, Taye died because of his loyalty to him. It was hard to find those of Taye's caliber in the game nowadays, and he was fresh off the porch. The young nigga respected the G-code.

Knowing Taye's body was gonna attract a lot of attention, General got as far away as possible. He needed to get to his safehouse to pick up some things. The safehouse was that of

Rhonda's, who was General's Godmother and a drug addict herself. Despite her addiction, General trusted her and had for years, since hiding his stash at her house. She refused to bite the hand that fed her but would no doubt feast from other niggas' tables with her deviousness.

Something in the distance made him bring the car to a sudden halt. Leaning forward to peer through the windshield up ahead, General had a bad feeling. A dark, black cloud of smoke was lifting into the sky somewhere nearby, around the corner. Then there was a strange feeling in his heart that he knew exactly where it was coming from.

Two minutes later, General was yet again stunned by the sight before him. Lisa's house was a giant ball of fire as it burned from the inside out. The roof had already caved in, and the fire was licking flames from every direction, leaving no room untouched by its existence. That's when he thought the worst.

'Could Lisa be in there, too?' he questioned himself. A dull ache somewhere near his heart made him flinch as he allowed his fear for Lisa's safety to affect him. The first person who came to mind was Mango because no one else would have done such a thing but him. There was no coincidence that he murdered Dred in that same house just the night before, and all of a sudden, it was burning down to the ground. Mango did it, and he was probably the one who killed Taye, too.

"I'ma kill that muthafucka," muttered General the same instant the passenger's door opened, and a body slid in beside him. Startled, General looked to his right and saw Little Rabbit there, a twelve-year-old cat who would do anything to prove his worth. The young, black sheep had his heart set on being a street legend one day and was determined to see that it became his reality.

"I saw who did it," said Rabbit, a little, thin muthafucka with mischievous eyes, as audacious as they came. "He just left here a second ago."

"Who?" General asked.

"Mango."

General figured as much.

"And they killed Taye, too," said Rabbit excitedly.

"Yeah." General stared at the burning house four houses down from Lisa's. "I know." And no sooner than the words left his mouth did something shoot past on his left. General looked up and saw Lisa running from her burning house and shooting across the front yard from the porch.

General panicked, forcing the door open and bolting from the car in her direction. "No, sis! Stop!" he shouted but felt it was already too late. Lisa ran into the burning house. Now, General was scared.

***

Standing before the toilet, taking a piss, Twin paused when he felt the cell phone buzz in his right pocket. He finished his business and shook himself off, taking his precious damn time. A moment later, he retrieved the phone from his pocket and read the text message he'd just received. Then he spun on his heels and went to the bathroom door immediately. He didn't even get the opportunity to flush the toilet or wash his dirty ass hands. His Aunt Felicia needed him quickly.

The message he assumed came from his aunt explained that she was in pain and needed him to get there ASAP. That was all he needed to see to put him on the move, racing through Burger King for the exit door.

No more than an hour ago, Twin hijacked some pesky white guy for his car, the same one he was now pointing in the direction of his aunt's house. Luckily, he wasn't that far away and hoped he'd make it there in time, but it was what awaited him that would change everything.

"Shit!" He cursed when a red light caught him two trucks up ahead. There was no time to wait. Twin pulled around both vehicles and dodged others to get to where he was going, hoping his violating traffic laws didn't alarm any patrol unit, or else he'd be forced to buck on them. Nothing would stop him from getting to his aunt.

Eventually, Twin made it to her house in fourteen minutes and dashed from the car to her front door. The fact that it was ajar didn't stop him as he barged inside the house into a real-life horror.

"Oh, God, No!" Twin cried from the instant dread, the moment he turned into the living room doorway.

Sprawled upon the sofa was no doubt his aunt Felicia—well, what was left of her, to say the least. Her throat had been slit from ear to ear, but what disturbed him most was what lay on the floor just at her left, the large hole which was her belly, and the mess it caused in the process of her butchered body. It made him drop to his knees.

Felicia's seven-month fetus was lying on the floor, having been savagely ripped from her stomach in the worst way. Twin had never seen any shit like that in his life, and all of a sudden, he was now scared for his life. Just when the thought crossed his mind, he felt the tip of a pistol kiss the back of his head.

"You shoulda killed me when you had the chance, son," Vega hissed just behind Twin's right shoulder.

Twin went rigid with fear.

Blocka!

One shot was all it took to paint the rest of the room with his brains.

Bringing the Payday candy bar to his mouth for another bite, Vega frowned down at Twin's skinny body twitching repeatedly before he went still in death. Chewing, he said, "Now the nigga Forty is next."

He took his leave—a muthafuckin' real life monster on the loose.

***

Back in the hood, General was sprinting toward Lisa's burning house. He was mentally cursing her ass out for putting her life in jeopardy like that. To his relief, Lisa dashed back outside through the smothering door, waving thick, black smoke away from her face. It was obvious she couldn't handle the fire.

While Losa stood on the porch, looking disoriented through the open front door of her house, the porch's roof from beneath was looking as if it was about to cave in. General had seen enough and grabbed hold of Lisa, wrapping her in a bear hug, and carried her away in just the nick of time.

The roof of the porch caved in, shooting hot coals of fire in all directions.

"Lemme go!" Lisa screamed. "Let—"

"Calm your ass down, ma," said General in that aggressive tone. He carried her over to the curb and dropped her to her feet, taking her arm in a vice grip. "Don't ever do no stupid shit like that again, sis. You coulda got burned to death in that house!"

"Mango did this to my fucking house!"

"I know."

"I want him dead for that, Jarrod." Lisa was badly shaken by the prospect of what could have just happened.

"I'ma make sure of that, sis."

When she turned to face him, General saw something in her eyes he'd never seen. "I want you to bring that nigga to me so I can do it myself."

The rest of the porch crumbled at that moment, leaving no way to enter through the front anymore.

Sirens blared nearby.

"I gotta get off the scene, sis," General said.

"Promise me, bro." Lisa held his gaze. "Promise me you gonna bring that muthafucka to me for destroying my mama shit." She had nothing other than murder in her eyes.

"I gotcha," he promised her with a kiss on the cheek.

"Go!" She avoided his eyes now.

As if on cue, the white Porsche pulled up behind them with Little Rabbit at the wheel, calling out to General for him to come. General looked back at the young cat. Down the street to his left, a fire truck came roaring toward the scene. Just behind it was a police cruiser, and that had General moving.

"Jarrod!" Lisa called to him.

He looked back at her.

"I love you, nigga," she told him. "Now, gone!"

With a brief nod, General ran for the car and got in on the passenger side. The Porsche screeched away from the smoky scene and around the corner, out of sight.

For a twelve-year-old, Rabbit was pushing the whip as though it was something he did on a regular.

"Where we going, B?"

General shot the little nigga a glance as if seeing him for the first time. Reluctantly, he said, "Get me outta the hood for a minute, lil' one. It's too hot 'round her for me right now."

Rabbit couldn't have been happier to do so. The little nigga had his big homies life in his hands, and he couldn't wait to tell the hood this shit!

After a while, General directed him to a convenience store just outside the hood. They pulled up in the parking lot, and Rabbit brought the car to a halt next to one of the gas pumps. Despite his sour mood, General admired how the young cat was handling himself behind the wheel. When he was that age, General was still riding bicycles and learning the game, barely could see over the damn dashboard.

"Check this out, little one," General pulled a lot of bills out from his pocket and peeled off a twenty. "Go in there and grab me something to drink. It don't matter what it is."

"Alright." Rabbit took the money and was gone. The young cat was eager to please.

The cell phone General fished from his pocket next was Olivia's, though where she was, she wouldn't need it. He put in a call to Rhonda and hoped she was home because what he needed her to do was very important. Those three kilos he stashed would make a major difference in what he needed done, and the guns too because shit was about to get a little more drastic in a minute.

"Hello?" replied Rhonda's ghetto tongue on the fifth ring.

"Am I happy to hear you, ma," he stated with a devilish smirk on his face, but in actuality, he was burning with rage.

K'wan had just gotten dropped off by Melvin on the other side of the parking lot. General had missed him by seconds before he hopped in his car and drove away.

Chapter 13

When Mario found her, she was out back in her greenhouse, busily tending to her flowers. Upon entering the greenhouse, a variety of sensuous smells caressed his nostrils. He was surrounded by multiple colors and textures of the many plants of various flowers that had long won his sister's true affection.

Patricia didn't even look his way but spoke in a tone that Mario knew, hidden just beneath its surface, was an indescribable pain. His poor, beautiful sister was grieving hard.

"Yolanda adored the yellow roses and Jasmine flowers. She would spend many afternoons here, studying and just enjoying the peace and quiet, nurturing these same flowers with her warm and lovely presence." Patricia placed a light fingertip on a petal of a yellow rose. It was in full bloom. "Now my child will never find comfort here again."

Quietly, Mario watched his sister intently.

"I shouldn't have to tell you what needs to be done, Mario." She finally turned to face him.

Mario, at fifty-four years old and very lean with dark, wavy hair cut short on his head, was dressed in casual Italian linen worth a mortgage payment. At that point, he looked every bit of his fifty-four years, having not slept since receiving that call the evening before. As he stared in his sister's weary eyes, he knew exactly what needed to be done to give her the closure she now desired, in regards to her daughter's death.

"Isn't that why I was called?" he asked. "To see that it's done accordingly?"

"I called because I needed your support. Can't you see I'm dying, Mario? I've lost the only thing that truly matters to me." Tears streamed from her lovely, light-brown eyes.

This fucked Mario up, and he finally went to her, enveloping his sister into his arms and kissing her head softly, and she let it go. Patricia cried like a baby, her slender body shaking badly with heart-wrenching sobs. It was tearing him to pieces inside at that moment, sharing with her a sorrow that was about to result in dark calamity.

Mario decided to hold her for however long it would take to assure her that she had him—that he wouldn't let her down.

"We will talk later, okay? I gotta go see some people." Mario stroked her silky, black hair affectionately.

She nodded.

"You're gonna be alright 'til I get back?"

Without answering him directly, Patricia got a hold of herself and shook off her weariness. When she looked back up at him, there was no more sadness in her eyes. What Mario saw in them was pure fire, and then she turned away from him and disappeared somewhere behind a shelf of daisies.

There wasn't anything else to talk about, so Mario took his leave.

Once back inside the mansion, Mario was directed to the large parlor by the old, black housemaid, saying that a visitor was waiting for him there.

To Mario's surprise, that visitor was Detective Vincent Pratt, someone Mario knew not only by reputation but personally. He frowned at the sight of the detective and made his way over to him, and Pratt stood, extending his hand in greeting.

"Mr. Napoli."

"Detective Pratt." Mario shook his hand.

Several of Mario's henchmen stood about the room with grave expressions, nothing light about their presence. They were ready to destroy some shit on command—five of some of the most dangerous men to ever run across.

After the brief pleasantries, both men took their seats.

"Let's cut straight to the chase, Mr. Napoli. I understand why you're here, and my great condolences for your loss. I also know that you're planning to conduct your own investigation of the matter at hand," said the detective, a black guy who resembled the actor Wesley Snipes but not as dark.

Mario sighed as he lit up a Cuban cigar for a smoke.

"I'm asking that you please not hinder my investigation by taking matters into your own hands," said Pratt. "It's bad enough—"

"Detective Pratt, you're wasting my time here."

"This is a dire situation, Mr. Napoli, and I'm only asking that you let the authorities handle this one."

Mario raised his hand and snapped his fingers once.

Before the detective even knew what was happening, a thick arm snaked around his neck from behind, adding considerable pressure against his throat. Another one of the henchmen relieved the detective of his weapon.

"Like I said, detective, you're wasting my time. The investigation is no longer yours but mine now," said Mario with a puff of his expensive cigar. "I do what I damn well please, and as for you…" Mario gave his man one look.

Just like that, the detective's neck was snapped like a muthafuckin' twig.

"You're a dead man," Mario added, blowing out a cloud of smoke from his lungs.

There was no time to bullshit around. Murder was the mission.

"Call my girls in here, please," said the Napoli capo.

***

In the meantime, Thad was hard at work, replacing the broken lock on the front door. He and Crow worked as a team, the old man dropping jewels of wisdom on him in the process.

After their discussion about the game and what it might consist of, now that the old man was investing in Thad's hustle, Crow thought it was best to fix the door while they had the time. Luckily, the old man already had everything needed to see the job properly done. He may as well teach the youngin' a thing or two about carpentry and tools.

All Thad knew was street life.

The job completed, Thad and the old man enjoyed a nice smoke session and some oldie goldies from the old jukebox Crow had collected from way back when.

"This some fiyah!" Thad coughed, feeling his chest burn from the effects of the weed. Crow had the nigga smoking from a pipe the first time. The weed was so good it had his eyes brimming with tears.

Crow just nodded in acknowledgment, chillin' and rocking to some old Teddy P. The old man was in his groove.

Suddenly, there was a knock at the front door, causing Thad to sit upright in his seat. He looked over to Crow, and Crow gave him the okay to see who was at the door.

Handing the pipe over to its rightful owner, Thad got up and approached the door.

"Who is it?" Thad called out, standing next to the door with a hand near the pistol tucked at his waist.

"Angelica," a feminine voice answered.

That definitely perked the old man up instantly. "Open the door, youngin'!"

When the door opened, Thad was taken aback by the sight before him. The beautiful, young lady that stood on the doorstep before him was enough to make a nigga's dick stand up instantly. Not only was she classy, but she had an air of confidence in her appearance, regarding him with just as much curiosity as he did.

"Hey," she said.

"Hey." Thad stepped aside. "Come in, beautiful."

She stepped over the threshold and into the house, and the second her eyes landed on Crow, she hurried over to where he sat in his favorite recliner. "Uncle Willie!"

"My girl!" Crow beamed. It was the first time Thad had actually seen the old man smile. The permanent scowl had another side to it after all.

"You changed the lock on the door. My key wouldn't work!" said Angelica, in a City Chic polyester, sleeveless-style dress and Sam Edelman Snake-embossed sandals.

"That's because I just had to put another one on."

"Why?"

Both Crow and Thad exchanged glances.

"It's not a big deal. I'll have you a key made." Crow gave her a tone that said, in so many words, the subject was dropped. "How have you been? How is school? Sit down, honey."

Reclaiming his seat across from the old man, Thad watched as Angelica perched her fine ass on the arm of the recliner. 'Damn,' he thought. 'Ma is a bad bitch.'

"I saw the news and heard about what's been going on over here," she said and shot a sly glance in Thad's direction. "I came to check up on you and see how you were doing."

"I'm doing fine."

"And I see that," she smartly retorted.

Finally, Crow remembered his manners and introduced her to Thad, who had been patiently waiting for him to do so.

"This is my niece, youngin', my brotha Joe's daughter," said a happy Crow, eyes sparkling with excitement. Again, both Thad and Crow's niece spoke, and Thad stood back up, taking her hand in his.

"Alright now, youngin'. Don't make me break your hand, here!" Crow said to Thad when he held her soft hand longer than he should've. Angelica chuckled and pulled her hand out of his grasp.

"Uncle Willie is very protective of me," she said.

"Damn right, I am!"

Thad said, "Who wouldn't be? As beautiful and jazzy as you are, it's worth the energy."

She just smiled in response. "Thank you." She blushed.

"That's it, baby! Hand me my gun!" Crow said, and they all laughed simultaneously. "Youngin', that one is surely off limits."

Thad couldn't take his eyes off her. If Ciera had been present, she would've slapped those same eyes to the back of his muthafuckin' head. Angelica seemed to have that effect on many men.

***

Brooklyn's Crown Heights was buzzing with activity that late afternoon as the hustlers hustled, and the players played. Children were running to and from throughout the place, while dopeheads and tricks went about the premise doing their usual.

It was your typical day in the projects, but not for Worm, Lil' Beezo, and Marc, who were on the prowl, searching for Forty. It was told he frequented Crown Heights a lot because he hooked up this chick that had the nigga sprung on her. That was exactly where they hoped to find him.

From behind the wheel of the old '66 GTO Pontiac that was Worm's, Lil' Beezo cruised along in a slow creep toward their intended destination. "He don't know we're lookin' for him, so he should have driven his car here," he said.

"That's if he's here," Marc retorted from the back seat, rolling an unopened Black & Mild cigar between his palms.

Worm was silent; he was in his zone. Everybody was out for blood. The trio was grieving Taye's sudden death, especially Lil' Beezo, who had been the one to send him out on the mission. Two of their homies died within a matter of twenty-four hours, but it was Taye's death that hit them hard. Shit, it was Taye who had brought them all together as a team.

Who Worm really wanted to get at was Mango, but first things first—Forty needed to be dealt with. Eventually, Mango would show his face, and Worm was gonna put so many holes in him that they were gonna think he was a piñata.

"Niggas walkin' around here like it's a muthafuckin' game, son. Then you got this fool Mango thinking he's untouchable!" Marc was saying in the back. "They just don't know we 'bout to set this bitch off!"

"Like Queen Latifah," said Lil' Beezo.

A minute later, the Pontiac pulled into a parking space next to the apartment building they were about to invade. Then, they all checked their guns and prepared themselves for what was about to go down.

"Beezo,"—Marc said—"don't be with that scary shit, or you can stay in the car."

Little did he know, Lil' Beezo was just as ready as he was. After what happened to Quint last night and then Taye a few hours ago, he had a lot of tension built up that was ready to explode. The pain and hate brewing inside of him as a result of those two losses were all the motivation he needed to prove he could be ruthless, too.

"I'm ready when y'all ready," said Lil' Beezo.

"I don't see his car" Marc spoke up again.

Worm tucked his pistol and downed the rest of the gin he had been sipping on, then he opened the door and got out.

Both Lil' Beezo and Marc exchanged a glance. They got out next.

Minutes later, Worm kicked in the front door of Stacy's apartment, the chick Forty was fuckin', and when they rushed inside, no one was there. The crib was laid out, but not one soul was present.

"Trash this bitch!" Worm said, and trash that bitch, they did, but where in the fuck was Forty?

Chapter 14

By nightfall, K'wan was becoming a little frustrated with his mission, and the fact that Harlem was so hot was making it hard on what else he needed to get done. The hood was a circus, and he wasn't comfortable with all the bullshit.

K'wan sat behind the wheel of his X5 BMW, brewing over the situation he was faced with. He'd checked all of General's spots and still came up short. Well, the location was where Melvin provided, but there were still quite a few others that K'wan had in mind to check out, but something else was irking him—something that he was missing. He knew it had to be something valuable, or else the primitive sense of it wouldn't bother him so.

What the hell was it?

It finally hit him. One of them had been shot, which meant they needed medical treatment. They couldn't get it from just any hospital, because the authorities would've been searching for them there. That could've been anywhere in the state of New York, so any general hospital or anything close to one was questionable.

Who could they have gone to under such duress?

Reaching for his phone, K'wan knew just who to call that could shed some light on the situation. Meanwhile, four young girls passed by his window along the sidewalk. Two of them were walking arm-in-arm, while the other two trekked a few steps behind them. K'wan wondered why those young girls were out at that time of night with the way shit was going down.

"What's up, bro?" a voice answered on the first ring.

"Animal, I need your help real quick, son."

"Talk to me."

"Remember that spot Trigger went to go see that night he got hit up over in Grant Projects to get worked on?"

"Doc," said Animal, one of K'wan's closest homies. Animal remembered that night vividly because he was the one who rushed Trigger off to see Doc. That night, Trigger had been shot five times, and Doc worked his magic, saving his life by determination not to allow a soul to die on his table.

'Bingo!' K'wan thought. "That's who I need to see."

"What?"

K'wan briefly explained the situation.

"Yeah. Doc should be the one you're lookin' for, bro. Other than that, you're okay, right?" Animal asked with concern.

"You'll be the first person to know if I'm not."

"Keep me posted," Animal said. "I got some new toys I've been dying to try out." Beyond that calm tone was yet another beast that didn't take much to release. Vega thought he was in a dark place right now, but Animal was the darkness itself.

"I'ma need his contact info and location like right now," K'wan told him.

Minutes later, K'wan was back on the road, en route to the hood doctor's location, as a strong feeling overwhelmed him to the point it made him smile, despite his mood. He knew that was exactly where he would find General once and for all.

***

Lisa was still tripping over the fact that she let Peaches talk her into borrowing General's car to make a quick stop at the grocery store before it got too late. That quick stop ended up being nearly two hours, and the bitch still hadn't come back yet. Lisa had some words for her ass when she did.

Picking over the salad she'd made for herself, Lisa wondered what General was up to.

She'd been forcing herself to focus on anything but her mama's house. She'd passed a year ago after serving eighteen years on a life sentence. She had killed a man for passing on the H.I.V. virus to her during their brief fling before the truth finally came out. Having grown tired of life and its never-ending bullshit, Linda Marie Clark provoked another inmate to stab her to death in her prison cell since she was too much of a coward to do it herself.

The multiple letters, photos, and all the valuable items Lisa cherished that once belonged to her mama were gone. Mango burned it all to the ground. That was what hurt Lisa the most about the situation. She couldn't save the sentimental values of her life, one that had once been of her dead mama.

That nigga had to pay for that! Somebody had to.

Tired of sitting around and doing nothing, Lisa dumped the half-eaten salad in the trash can and went into the living room. Both NuNu and SonnyBoy were transfixed on the TV, watching a Disney movie on DVD, which was *Monsters' University*. It was a movie even Lisa herself had watched before in that same living room, and she could've sworn her cousin's kids watched that damn movie every day.

"I'm hungry, Lisa," five-year-old NuNu looked over her shoulder and said with those big-ass eyes.

"Your mama gonna cook y'all something to eat when she gets back, boo. Alright?" 'Whenever she brought her tired ass back home and fed her children,' thought Lisa.

"Okay." NuNu turned back to her movie.

On cue, the sound of a car pulling up outside made Lisa sigh with relief as she got up from the sofa to see if the bitch needed some help.

Seconds before Lisa reached the door, she heard a terrifying, blood-curdling scream pierce through the door from outside. When Lisa finally snatched the door open and looked outside, she froze in sudden fear.

Several yards away, in the driveway, four little girls were huddled around Peaches, who was sprawled out on the ground with the trunk of the car open. The four little black girls were all clutching sharp objects of some kind that Lisa couldn't detect, but at the sound of the front door opening and slamming against the inner wall of the foyer, four pairs of glassy, empty eyes looked up at Lisa at once. Before Lisa could even utter one word, the four girls moved in unison, vanishing into the night like a thick fog lifting into nothing, and Lisa ran over to her cousin.

"Oh my god!" Lisa's hands shot up to her mouth in instant horror, and she looked away from the gruesome sight before her.

Lying next to General's car was Peaches, with both of her eyes gouged out and multiple puncture wounds to her face and torso. The most disturbing thing was Peaches' mouth, which appeared to have been savagely forced open wide to the point her jaws split to accommodate a hand that ripped her tongue out.

"Mama?" NuNu called out from the doorway, her mouth quivering, as she was on the verge of crying.

Standing behind the girl was seven-year-old SonnyBoy, and he, too, appeared to be about to go hysterical any second now. Fighting back her tears of fear and agony, Lisa ran to her little cousins to shield them from the gruesome sight of their dead mama, but it was too late for that. They'd already seen enough.

Mario's girls were now in action, and it was gonna take more than Harlem to stop them before they turned that muthafucka into a real life horror show.

***

With the blender now stuffed with buds of weed, Thad sealed the top with its cap, pressing the button to let the machine do its job. Thad was in the kitchen, making it do what it did with the package of weed Crow had put in his hands.

What he thought was a pound was actually twenty-three ounces stuffed in a large, shrink-wrapped package. The weed compressed good, but not anymore, as Thad broke everything down and decided to move only ten-dollar bags, nothing more. He was gonna get everything he could out of the package because with Dred dead, there weren't many other suppliers who had anything else worth smoking.

Thad definitely was about to lock it down with the quality of weed he had in his possession at the moment, and since Mama Doll agreed to work an extra shift of overtime, he had all the time and space he needed to bag up and hopefully put his product in the streets tomorrow. That thought was cut short when there was a knock at his front door.

Thad shut off the blender and exited the kitchen to see who was at the door. Pulling out his 9mm on the way there, he came to a halt next to the front door. Peeping through the peephole for a few seconds, Thad sucked his teeth and opened the door to let Ciera in.

"Just in time," he said and shut the door behind her.

"Just in time for what?" she asked

"To put your ass to work!"

Ciera was a thick, redbone chick with a body that would put K. Michelle to shame. She wasn't ugly nor pretty, but a damned good, loyal bitch, with two college degrees to brag about. Tonight, she had on a $150 crepe-woven jumpsuit and pumps that complemented her frame.

"Boy, puh-leeze! The only work I came to do is work on that big ol' dick!" she replied with sass. "I've been dick deprived by your ass for a week."

"That's 'cause you the one took your ass to Atlanta."

She slapped him on the back of the shoulder. "And I told you that you could come with me."

Thad didn't respond as he dumped the blender full of weed into a large purple bowl, then reached over to put the remainder of the package into the blender to break down. That would be the last of it, which filled damn near four more bowls.

"Damn, bae." Ciera picked up a bud of weed and sniffed it, crinkling up her nose as a result. "I don't even have to smoke any to know it's some good shit."

"Just wait 'til you smoke some, though."

"Speaking of smoking..." She licked her big-ass, shiny, red lips and dropped to her knees, reaching for his zipper, and pulled out his manhood. "Hey, boo! I miss you!" she sang to his dick before taking it into her warm mouth.

Thad had to grab hold of the kitchen counter. "You better make him spit just like that, too."

"Don't I always?" She licked the base of his lil' nigga.

"No."

"Whatever." She swallowed him whole.

Before long, she had that nigga's toes curled in his Air Forces. Ciera was bobbing on that dick as if she were listening to a Young Jeezy song.

"Suck that dick, bitch!" he encouraged.

With no hands, just neck and mouth, Ciera clutched the counter on each side of him and worked his dick like a true headhunter. After several minutes, Thad took hold of her head and began fucking her face, driving dick all down her throat. Although she gagged every now and then, Ciera took that dick like a pro., and homie pounded that shit like it was straight pussy!

"S-shit!" Thad cussed when he felt his piece swell up then explode in her mouth. "Swallow that shit. Shit! That's right. Take all that shit." Thad tossed his head back as he slowly plunged in and out of her slippery mouth.

Moments later, Ciera stood up, wiping her mouth with the back of her hand.

"Damn, bae, you tried to kill a bitch!"

He chuckled. "You beautiful as fuck. You know that?"

"Whatever, boy. I'm not done with your ass," she said and headed down the hallway to his room. "Bring that dick here, nigga!" Ciera shouted at him.

"Later. We got all night for that shit."

Little did he know…

***

As the BMW pulled up around the back of Doc's clinic, which was actually being operated out of a large, three-story house with six bedrooms, K'wan only saw one car occupying a space. That car was Olivia's Infiniti that hadn't yet been disposed of. Parking his car next to the Infiniti, K'wan took a deep breath and got out.

This was where it would all come to light.

Beyond the drapes, K'wan could see the lights were on inside, so he knew someone was in there. As he made his way to the back door, which was the main entrance of the clinic, the doors suddenly opened the moment K'wan stepped foot on the welcome mat.

There was Doc, dressed in casual attire, with a stainless white lab coat and penny loafers.

"How may I help you, sir?" Doc replied.

"By lettin' me in, and we can discuss the matter inside."

Doc stepped aside and beckoned him in. "Be my guest," he said, and K'wan stepped inside to pass him. He followed

Doc down a short hallway, and they turned left into what was supposed to be the den area but was Doc's main office. The room was decked out like a real office but supersized, as plaques and such hung along the back wall behind the large desk. K'wan had to admit it; the man had his shit tight, but he was about to see how tight Doc really was.

"Now." Doc, perched on the edge of his desk, removed his eyeglasses to wipe the lenses with the hem of his coat. "What is it that you want to discuss?"

K'wan pulled out his gun and aimed it at the doctor's face. "Where the fuck is my homeboys?" he asked with menace. "That's the discussion, son."

To K'wan's dismay, Doc didn't even look fazed by the gun. He just put his glasses back on and looked him dead in the eyes.

"What homeboys do you speak of, sir?"

Before K'wan could answer, he heard a voice behind him. "K'wan? That's you, son?"

K'wan whirled around and saw Roe standing in the doorway, nearly slumped over with an IV pole and shirtless, his shoulder bandaged. The nigga looked like he was about to tumble over any moment now.

"Damn," was all K'wan could say.

"Where bro at?" Roe asked. "Where's General?"

Chapter 15

General was about to show muthafuckas his name wasn't for decoration but by reputation, and Mango's time was just about up. For a nigga who considered himself untouchable, he was surely making himself a sitting duck as he and his team dominated three table booths in a local fast food joint. McDonald's was pretty crowded tonight, but not crowded enough to create a fucking massacre.

"Niggas make this shit easy," General mumbled to himself.

Lying across his lap was a Mac-11 submachine gun, cocked and loaded, ready to tear some shit up. He was wondering if he should wait 'til they came outside to chop their asses down like a brick of coke or run up in that bitch like Rambo and serve every last one of them what he had hiding in the clip. Either way, they were gonna get it tonight.

'You muthafuckaz did your thing today,' thought General from behind the wheel of Doc's Porsche. 'Now it's my turn.'

Just when he was about to get out of the car, the phone shrilled. Snatching it up to check the number, General was astounded when he recognized K'wan's number. 'Why in the hell would he be calling Olivia's phone?' he wondered.

"Yeah?" General answered the phone with suspicion.

"What's cracking, homie?"

"You tell me, yo."

"Making sure old Doc taking care of big homie like he should," K'wan replied, knowing General would catch on.

He did indeed. "What's really good, Kay?"

There was a pause.

"You know who put me up to it, homie. Your old man wants to see about you, but—"

General interjected. "I'm on a mission right now, son."

"But you're good, though, right?"

"No," said General. "Not 'til I'm done making these muthafuckaz bleed out here."

"That's part of the game, homeboy."

"Then I'm never gonna be good." General hung up the phone. He didn't have time for conversation; he needed to be on point at all times, so he decided to lay on them niggas. It wouldn't be long.

***

"Rosie, don't do me like that," Melvin pleaded. "Don't shut me out. You can do anything but shut me out like that." He held her warm hand in his own, squeezing it reassuringly, but Rosie just turned her gaze away from him.

For the past three hours since Melvin had returned to her bedside, she hadn't said three words to him. The first had been, "Leave," before falling back asleep on him for an hour or so. Then, when she woke up and saw him there, she whispered, "No." Melvin remained where he was, occasionally stepping out to use the phone. He refused to let her run him away.

His first thought was not to show up for fear of placing her in danger again and, of course, to avoid being detected by the authorities. His love and concern for Rosie brought him right back to her bedside, and Rosie was being hard on him.

"I won't give up on you, honey," Melvin told her when she pulled her hand away from his. "You're my wife, and I love you dearly, and I made a vow to always honor and protect you. You're my queen, the sparkle in my eyes. I can't—I won't give up on all of that for nothing in the world."

"You already have, Melvin," a voice replied.

Melvin whirled his head around in the direction of the speaker and saw Pam there, the wife of Robert, and Roe's very own mother. She approached the foot of the bed and gave him a long, hard gaze.

"What are you doing here?" he asked coldly.

That same instant the door opened, in came Lynn, followed by Thad's mama, Doll, both women carrying grim faces and heavy hearts in their wake. For some reason, Melvin felt trapped.

"We are here for closure, Melvin," Pam spoke up again. "And for us to do that, you need to leave."

"You can't make me leave!" Melvin bolted to his feet. He shot Lynn a questioning glance. That was where his heart truly stood and had since day one, but life was a nasty bitch that had no understanding whatsoever.

"But we all can, Melvin," Mama Doll said.

"Just go," Rosie told him, her voice stronger now for some particular reason.

Were they coming together against him?

"We came here for Rosie—nothing else, Mellie." Lynn stepped up to face him toe-to-toe. "Don't make it anything else. You got a job to do, and you need to be out there doing it. We will take care of Rosie for now."

"This is some bullshit!" Melvin raved on.

"Call it what you want. You still gotta leave."

One more glance at his wife, then Lynn and Mama Doll, he knew he had been left no other choice. He left the room grudgingly, slamming the door behind him, but at least Rosie wasn't being left alone.

"Now," Lynn said while finding her seat next to the bed. "Let's get down to business."

***

Robert had no clue his wife wasn't on her way to New Jersey like she was supposed to be. He didn't know she had found safety and comfort elsewhere, other than back in her hometown in South Orange. He was soon gonna be one mad muthafucka.

As he sat in his unmarked car just down the street from Patricia Napoli's house with wicked intentions in mind, he figured this was the right move. Next to him in the passenger seat was Forty, and he was gripping an AK-47 with two Glocks tucked in his waist. Behind them in the back was Ugly, a young goon Robert had sent along with Forty to kill Melvin the night before. It was Forty who had taken three slugs to the chest of his double-breasted bulletproof vest.

The nigga was still wincing from that shit. Luckily for him, he had decided to double up on the vests, or else he might've been in worse condition than he was now.

A blunt was being rotated between the two young goons while Robert waited to give them the call. Both were trained to go and feared nothing.

Robert thought it would be best to murder Mario Napoli and his people first because, as long as they were alive, it could very well be over for him. Those Italians were out to play for keeps, and he didn't want to play around with them. Kill the head, and the body would die; that was his motto.

They'd already been to both of Robert's homes to give him a taste of their Italian medicine. How they knew about his second house over in Mount Vernon, he didn't know, for he hadn't purchased the Georgian-style two-story not even six months ago, and he hadn't been there but twice.

To underestimate Mario Napoli could be mean death, so Robert's plan was to bring the Italian straight pressure, no bullshitting around! If the big capo wanted it, then he surely was gonna get it. But what Mario might not have known was that Robert was also connected with both the Crip Nation and one of the head chiefs of the Mexican Cartel based in New York.

It first started off with them trying to extort him but figured a close bond would be best, then his having spared some very well-respected Crips from an indictment put him good with them too. In order to survive in this crazy world, one had to play dirty and still keep his face clean.

One call could bring both sides together and crush those punk ass Italians, but Robert decided to hold off on that call until he was left with no other choice.

Being an army veteran himself, he was a warrior, too, but most of all, he was Harlem-bred to the fullest. The man had heart.

"What the fuck is we waitin' on, son!" Ugly asked from the backseat. For someone who had such a name as that, one would be assumed to be ugly indeed, but the young, crazy nigga was quite handsome. He had more girls than a little bit, but it was what he did to niggas in the streets that earned him that name.

Ugly definitely played ugly.

"I rather wait on them to show up outside," said Ugly.

"Me, too," Forty chimed in.

"Then if that's what you wanna do, do it! Just don't fuck this one up this time. The stakes are high now, fellas. This ain't no petty criminal lawyer we're dealing with here," Robert explained and reached for his gun, a .25 Caliber Beretta palm gun, the Colt Python .357 magnum, and his .45 Caliber also resting on his person.

Forty was the first to exit the car, which was well hidden in the shadows.

"Keep an eye on him, Ugly," Robert said. "That situation with Twin is messing with his mind."

"I got 'em, man," Ugly promised. "Say no more."

***

Two young girls entered the McDonald's fast-food joint one after the other and made their way to the front counter. They were twin Gambian girls, about thirteen years old, and dark as ebony but beautiful little creatures sold from an African tribe for their talents. That was five years ago, when they were just eight years old, forced to kill and hunt potential foes, which made them who they were.

Buuwa and Tu looked like two ordinary girls, but just as deadly as a poisonous snake. The other two were worse than them, but no one in the restaurant knew for a fact, not even when they looked into those girls' eyes and saw nothing there. Their beauty alone was the ultimate deception.

These were ruthless killers. With a five-dollar bill in her hand, Buuwa, the oldest by six minutes, placed the bill on the counter before the cashier. She held up her index finger for one, then pointed just over the freckle-faced female cashier's shoulder at the menu overhead.

"Bi'Mac!" said Buuwa.

"You want the Big Mac combo, you mean?" the cashier asked.

The girl nodded eagerly.

While the order was being rang up, Tu observed her surroundings, looking toward Mango's section curiously. She went off to claim the empty booth just across from theirs to wait for her sister.

From outside, General noticed all this but didn't think anything of it. His mind was on murder, oblivious to the murder that was about to happen before his eyes. It was about to be a disaster.

"Here you go, sweetie," said the kind cashier, handing over the bag of food to Buuwa. In response, Buuwa sniffed the bag and offered the cashier a bright, dazzling smile. The cashier thought she was just so adorable.

With her bag in hand, Buuwa approached her sister's booth and bypassed it for the restroom. She wasn't inside even ten seconds before retreating with the bag and sitting across from her sister. They both exchanged glances and reached inside the bag for the food.

After about two minutes of eating a little of the food, both girls got up and headed for the exit. Time was of the essence, and they couldn't waste any.

Then, to General's surprise, as he looked through the large glass window at Mango and his crew, the bag the girls left on the table across from them exploded. The explosion was so great that it shattered the windows of the parked vehicles just outside the establishment.

"God damn!" General was stunned as the impact-explosion rocked the Porsche from nearly fifteen yards away. That muthafucka shook the earth in its wake but only destroyed that section of the restaurant the most.

There was no doubt that Mango and his crew were dead. Out of the corner of General's eye, he watched as a dark sedan turned onto the main highway from the parking lot and disappeared. It was the same car those two pretty girls he'd seen get out of just several minutes ago.

"What the fuck is going on out here?" he murmured with sudden discomfort toward the matter.

Then his phone rang. It was Melvin. Daddy was on some other shit too.

***

"What time is it?" Ugly asked.

Forty looked over at him and said, "I don't fuckin' know! What I do know is these muthafuckaz need to hurry up. You smoked all the weed, bro?" He was squatting low with the AK-47 across his knees.

Ugly shrugged his shoulders. "That shit gone, man."

"Shit."

"The same shit going on down there!"

"Not like this," said Ugly. "Plus, I met this chick from Florida who wants me to move down there with her. She say her stepdad has this new club he just opened up—"

"Ugly?"

"Yeah."

"Miss me with that righteous shit! You know damn well your ass ain't leaving New York, son."

"Shh!" Ugly went still for a second. "You heard that?"

"Heard what?" Forty stood up.

There was silence.

A faint sound of giggling at Forty's left, just beyond a row of dark hedges, made him pause. He and Ugly were not standing next to one another near the entrance gate that led up the gravel driveway to the mansion. They were in perfect cover, hidden within the darkness between two thick hedges.

Out of that same darkness stumbled a young girl who would have been invisible if not for her short, white miniskirt. This was Ava, the oldest out of her pack. She was a fifteen-year-old Gambian girl herself, the worst one of them all.

To both Forty and Ugly, she appeared to be in a drunken state, heading their way along the row of thick hedges. She giggled to herself, her left hand beneath her dark blouse, seeming to be cradling her sour stomach.

"This shorty is drunk as fuck, son," Ugly muttered, not really all that alarmed about the situation. However, he was kind of taken aback by her unexpected, drunken presence.

Leaning the assault rifle against his left side so as not to alarm the young girl of trouble, Forty watched as she suddenly came to a halt before him.

"What's up, ma? You alright?" asked Forty.

A blur of movement caught Forty by surprise as he was suddenly struck by something sharp that pierced his belly. Ava reached behind her and spun like a ballerina, bringing up the dagger that slipped through Forty's right temple, into his brain, killing him where he stood.

Sensing the movement behind him, Ugly turned with fear and saw another young girl in a blue dress. Before he could do anything, a quick, powerful force from an unseen object nearly caved his face in. He was dead before he hit the ground.

That was Zoe, a twelve-year-old pit bull in a dress, but from where he sat behind the wheel of the car, Robert suspected enough. After hearing the short, deathly cry in the night, he knew something evil was about. He saw Ava in her white miniskirt, moving toward him with haste, not really seeing Zoey, but he knew she was a threat as well.

Starting the car, Robert threw it in reverse and pushed the pedal to the floor. Although he had seen them, there was no telling who or what else was out there. Robert would rather live now to fight another day. He wasn't stupid. He was getting the hell away from there!

Chapter 16

For the next two days, Roe and General watched the city fall apart on local television. They were now hiding out at the Melbrook Projects in K'wan's baby mama, Denise's, old apartment that they used as a lay-low spot. This was where K'wan wanted to get away from Harlem and the streets, to put in some quality time with his writing. Now it was harboring two of the state's most wanted men.

Having had a couple of days to rest and build up some strength, Roe was feeling up to going to war now. The shoulder wound wasn't anything a few painkillers couldn't fix, and some Paul Masson on top of that would get the blood flowing right, and some fire ass weed would rest his mind. Roe was bored with just lying around and waiting.

Waiting for what?

Tossing the Xbox 360 Afterglow controller aside and standing up from the posh sofa, General stretched his limbs and let out a loud yawn.

"That's the same shit I'm talkin' about, bro," Roe complained some more.

"A nigga tired of sittin' 'round, collecting dust and shit! We need to be out there where the action is."

"Tonight, Roe."

"Tonight!" Roe was feeling that shit.

General glanced at him. "We can't make no moves during the day, bro. You know the game; stop acting like you just jumped off the porch, nigga." He left for the small kitchen.

Several seconds later, the front door opened.

"'Bout time, son!" Roe said as K'wan entered the crib with carry-out bags of food loaded in his arms. "Thought them bitch ass Italians ran down on you."

Ignoring Roe's attempt to get on his fucking nerves, K'wan dropped the bags of food on the low coffee table in front of him. Roe wasted no time reaching for the bag with the Golden Krust logo on the side. He was a fool for Caribbean food, Golden Krust especially.

Exiting from the kitchen, General sipped his fresh cup of brown liquor. Roe made him do it, tired of his bitching.

"What's going on out there?" General wanted to know.

"Other than that bullshit they showing on TV, the streets are quiet right now. The hood is so hot, that bitch look like a ghost town. But I did see Baby Thad, though. Lil' homie was one of the few niggas still out there grindin'."

"Oh yeah?" This astonished General.

"Yeah, lil' homie pushin' some fire bud out there," K'wan said. "As a matter of fact, I copped some for you niggas too. And lil' homie sent his love and respect to you too, bro."

General nodded. Damn, he missed his little nigga immensely.

"And your boy Bega, G." K'wan spoke up again.

"What about him?"

Now K'wan was shaking his head wearily. "Bro ain't the same no more." They all heard about the incident with Trel and put the pieces together. It was a disturbing reality, but what could they do about it? "Vega walk around that muthafucka like the walkin' dead, son."

No one said a word for a long moment. The issue with Vega was bothersome. The three of them sat down and conducted small talk for a while before the conversation changed over to a more dire subject—the Italians.

"How the hell are we gonna handle these people?"

"There's only one way, bro." General sat back in his seat. "We gotta bring it to them just as hard as they—"

"It won't be that easy." Roe doubted that.

"Who said war was easy, Roe? Yeah, we done been through some shit, coming up in the streets, but this shit here?" General said and looked his childhood friend in the eyes. "This shit is a whole different ball game with them Italians. They're sophisticated when it comes to war, so we gotta exercise our own intelligence to beat them at their own game."

At that moment, Roe thought about those two little girls General had spoken of. That was all the proof he needed to know they were up against some bad muthafuckas.

"We going to war with the same people we should have on our team," said K'wan as he finished up his meal, and that gave General an idea.

"Roe, in all, how many muthafuckas you can say will ride for you on command?"

"How many?" Roe looked at him like he was crazy.

"I'm talkin' about niggas who'll die for you, bro," General said.

A question like that made Roe think hard because he wasn't sure himself. "I got a squad, General. You know that!"

"I got a hundred killas who'll ride for me right now." General didn't mean to exaggerate, but he did have a large number of niggas who'd line up for him. A thought came to mind that made General pause pensively.

"What?" K'wan questioned the weird look on General's face.

Roe regarded him attentively.

'Would it be worth the call?' wondered General.

Retrieving the cell phone from the table before him, General punched in the seven-digit number he knew by heart. He waited anxiously, exchanging glances with both of his homies.

"Hello?" a familiar voice answered.

"Yo, Anthony. We need to have a serious talk."

"You're okay, G-man? What seems to be the problem?"

"It's about your niece, man." General thought about Olivia and avoided the stern expression on Roe's face.

"What about Olivia, G-man?" There was venom in his tone now.

General shut his eyes and told Anthony Kerr what he knew. The Cuban would no doubt grieve in a major way, blaming it all on the Italians, and from Miami, Florida, they would come, bringing with them a mob of crazy Cuban gangsters New York definitely wouldn't be ready for.

***

The next day...

It was a very sad moment for both the Napoli and the Dovolani family, including the colleagues and friends who attended Yolanda's funeral ceremony. People had been coming into the room in threes and twos, filling the chapel almost to capacity.

As the service progressed, there was a lot of tension in the air. In honor of Yolanda's death, the Napoli and the Dovolani set their differences aside. They came together as a whole, but the fact that Mario had ordered the death of Joey Dovolani, Yolanda's father, would never be forgotten. The two families would always be at odds because of that. The Napoli Family's presence dominated the Dovolani's by nearly fifty, and with NYPD law enforcement officials crawling about the place, who were also aware of the many killers present, there was no telling how things might go. There was bound to be some trouble. You could feel it in the air.

At the front of the room, a young man entered the room in tow of the chief of police. He turned away from Yolanda's coffin and made a wide circle around Mario, who turned his back on him, either by chance or intentionally. Luckily, the bullet that entered Yolanda's head from the side made it possible for an open casket.

Suddenly, heads turned around in the room as the large doors at the back of the chapel admitted three senior men. One of them, a bald man about as broad as a bull, wore a row of medals on the chest of his uniform, like a German general. The second guy appeared to wear the same uniform with fewer medals, but it was Mayor William Lofton who attracted so much attention as a dozen or so reporters pushed themselves into the room behind him. The big, silver-haired man marched into the place like he owned it, looking dashing in his $3,000 three-piece suit and Gators.

Mario moved in his direction.

"Mario!" Patricia reached out to her brother, recognizing the look in his eyes, but Mario was beyond reasoning at that point. He had something to get off his chest.

Reporters lined up along the sides of the room, already scribbling in notebooks and talking into their tape recorders, snapping off photos. It was a circus in there!

The mayor stopped and chatted for a few moments, waving at others like he was in a fucking parade, and then he kept it moving in that same fashion. All that came to a sudden halt when he found himself staring into the cold, hard eyes of Mario Napoli.

"M-Mr. Napoli," said the mayor with a hint of uneasiness.

Mario gripped the man's lapels aggressively and jacked him up. Suddenly, the guns came out from every direction you could name. Police and Italian gangsters drew their weapons, freaking the hell out of everybody in the room. For a moment, everything was at a standstill.

"What the hell you think you are doing, Lofton? Does this look like the fuckin' red carpet to you?"

"No, sir."

"Is this a fuckin' social hour for you, man?"

"No, sir."

"Mario, please!" Patricia was at her brother's side with a hand on his shoulder. "This isn't the time or place for that."

Mario glared into the mayor's eyes and released him, smoothing the old man's lapels. "This is a time for mourning, Mr. Mayor. You will conduct yourself like one or deal with the consequences accordingly." Then he patted the man's cheek and returned to his seat, gesturing toward his people with a hand to order them to stand down.

The capo wasn't up for the bullshit. He was in mourning, and one had to respect that, or else.

"You need to behave yourself, Mario," said Patricia as she sat next to her little brother, laying her head on his shoulder, but Mario was already in that zone. Someone had to die today.

***

While sitting on a red milk crate on the corner, Baby Thad had his pen and pad in hand while in the process of maintaining his grind. He had a studio session today, and he was kind of fucked up about it that neither of his main two niggas would be there like always. General was caught up in a war with the Italians and was hiding out somewhere. Vega was also at war, but with his inner demons. The nigga didn't know if he was coming or going at times. Thad would have to go into the studio as a one-man army and put on like he'd been doing since day one.

Within the next fifteen minutes, traffic was nonstop, as customers came and left with their purchases. For the past two days, his product had been selling like hotcakes. It was too bad for those who wanted to purchase in weight and couldn't get it yet.

Maybe after he moved the first package by dining everybody to death, he would discuss the matter with Crow about moving more of his product in weight. For now, Thad would feed them piece by piece of his new fortune—the product that was nearly gone by now. Yeah, he needed to get at Crow immediately, as soon as his shift was over.

Thad looked up when an all-black Acura Legend came to a halt in the street in front of him. He reached for his gun when the car just sat there, standing up, with the intent to let his gun blast. Then the dark-tinted driver's side window wound down.

To Thad's astonishment, it was Angelica. She regarded him suspiciously and frowned up at him.

"Well, hey to you too, Thad!" she said with an attitude.

Thad tucked his gun and picked up his fallen pen and pad from the ground. "Don't be doing shit like that, ma. That's how people get killed around here."

"Boy, you ain't gonna kill nobody!"

"That's what your mouth say," he retorted.

"You'll kill me?"

"In a physical sense, no."

Her brows rose with curiosity. "But you would in what perception?"

Moving over to her car door and leaning into the window, Thad reached inside and stroked her smooth, sharp jaw. "With kindness and admiration. Damn, ma, you're so beautiful," he whispered tenderly.

She took his hand, rubbed it, and moved it away from her face.

"Get in," said Angelica.

Without hesitation, Thad rounded the car and got in.

Putting the car in reverse, Angelica backed the Acura into a driveway and aimed it in the direction it came from. Thad wondered where she was going but didn't ask, though she took it upon herself to tell him anyway.

"Uncle Willie's birthday is today, and I was gonna take him shopping and out for lunch."

"For real?"

"Why would I lie?"

He shrugged. "I guess because he didn't tell me," said Thad. "But if that's what you came to do, where are you taking me?"

"Instead of lunch, I'll just take him out to dinner and go shoppin' later." Then Angelica looked over at him with a straight face. "And I'm taking you somewhere private."

"For what?"

She reached over and squeezed his dick through his Pelle Pelle denims. "Need I say more?"

"Say no more." Thad lounged back in his seat more comfortably.

Yeah, Ciera was really going to kill his ass.

***

"Troy!"

Instantly, Vega stopped and turned toward the familiar voice of the dearest Mama Doll. He had just stepped out of the store when she pulled up.

Mama Doll got out of the car and approached him, watching as Vega ripped open a Zebra cake and bit into it.

"Go get in the car and wait on me," she said.

"Something wrong, Mama Dee?"

She lifted up her chin. "Everything is wrong, and I'm here to make it right. Now, do as I say, and wait in the car, Tory." Mama Doll's eyes were hard on his, empty of life. She recognized it as much but did not say anything, just stepped around him and went inside the store.

Taking another bite of his Debbie cake, he scanned his surroundings, chewing eagerly. He had no idea a threat was lurking in his proximity. Finishing his snack and tossing the empty wrapper, Vega went to do as he was told. There was no way he could deny her anything.

Moments later, Buuwa and Zoey exited the store, carrying two brown paper bags, and slipped into a black G-Class Benz. If only Vega really knew how serious a threat they were. Three monsters were in one another's vicinity and didn't know it, but would they ever meet?

Minutes later, Mama Doll was sliding back behind the wheel of her Dodge Intrepid. She set the bag in the back seat and backed out of the parking space. She didn't speak up until she was on the highway, heading in the opposite direction from the neighborhood. They were about to have a long, serious talk.

"I know you're the one that killed that boy behind that church the other night," she started and frowned when she didn't get any reaction from Vega. That confirmed what she said was true. With a sigh, she continued. "And you did that bullshit to Ranny in the neighborhood park that same night. That's my godbrother, whether you know it or not, Troy! What the hell's wrong with you?"

Vega shot her a glance but said not a damned thing.

"If you don't answer me, boy—"

"Ask your muthafuckin' son what the hell's wrong with me!" Vega snapped and punched the dashboard.

"So you blaming Thad?"

"He left me!" Vega said before he realized he had said it. Then, in a small whisper, he said again, "He left me for dead, Mama."

Hearing the pain in his voice disturbed her greatly. She knew he had been through some serious things these past few days, but blaming Thad for it made her worry. What could her son have possibly done to cause his best friend—his childhood brother from another mother—to become the demonic soul that he was?

"Troy," she said with emotion. "Please tell me what really happened to you."

He told her everything in full detail, not holding shit back. Vega told her what it felt like to really be scared.

Chapter 17

By the time Vega was done talking, Mama Doll was crying softly as she drove, her tears racing those that also fell from his cyes. Vega's tears were from madness and anger, whereas she cried from the shattered heart Vega had just caused her. For a long moment, there was silence between them. Both were overwhelmed with emotion.

Mama Doll was so messed up at that moment, she no longer had the desire to drive anymore. After searching the immediate area, she steered the car toward the parking lot of Kiddie Land Daycare Center off of East 19th of Brooklyn. From where she parked, she had a wide view of about twenty-something children at play beyond the gate several yards away.

By this time, Vega's tears were gone.

"Mama," he replied without giving her any eye contact as she stared ahead, watching the kids play. "Remember when we used to come here too?" he asked, nodding toward the building.

"Yes, baby. I think it was named Little Big World back then."

"Yep."

She didn't realize it until he mentioned it. That was so many years ago, years that were still logged in her memory. Her house had also burned up pretty badly and needed a lot of reconstruction.

Thanks to her sister, Joyce, she'd let her and Thad stay with her during that period, and Thad was only three at the time. Joyce lived just down the street, and it was at Little Big World where his and Vega's bond first started. His mama, Sue, was employed there before quitting two years later. That was when her life as an alcoholic and coke head started. Those were rough years for Vega, giving him a difficult childhood.

It was Mama Doll who had taken it upon herself to see that he was well taken care of, despite the objection from Sue. She took him in as her own, fought with Sue over him for years, and still, to this day, he was her boy.

"Sue used to hate when you'd stop by on your lunch break to come play with us."

"Those were the days." Mama Doll sighed.

Something else came to mind, and Vega found himself looking at her in an odd way.

"What?"

Vega turned away. "Two cats tried to kill Thad that night, and I had to get at one of them," he said. "I couldn't find the other one, so I took it all out on him." There was something else in his tone that Mama Doll detected.

"What else did you do, Vega?"

Shocked by her using his street name, Vega stared out over the gate and into the playground where children fought, played, cried, and screamed in absolute glee. "I killed a child a couple days ago."

"You what!"

"I couldn't stop myself, even if I tried. I was just that gone in the head. I wanted somebody to suffer like I did. And the bad thing about it"—Vega looked at her—"I'm still suffering."

"Please tell me that wasn't you who did that to that pregnant woman over." Mama Doll's heart thudded. "Troy, you didn't?"

"I did," he said.

That was when Mama Doll finally realized she'd been sitting next to a monster all along.

***

When the call came that Anthony Kerr had finally arrived in the Big Apple, General felt a surge of adrenaline kick in. The time had finally come when a story of the violent hail of Cuban fury was about to rain down on New York.

K'wan was sent to retrieve the Cuban gangster and bring him straight to General.

It was a good thing General had destroyed all evidence and cleaned up the place before taking his leave. He didn't want anything to come back to him, relating to Olivia's murder. He had a lot on his plate to begin with, and now he had to deal with Anthony and his wrath.

Roe was anxious to meet the Cuban.

"Just let me handle this, Roe," said General as he paced the living room floor. "No tellin' what that fool is capable of doing."

That brought Roe's head up with a start. "You think that Cuban might pull some grimy shit on us, bro? Because I'm tellin' you now, I'll put one in his head the second he walks through that door like I did that bitch—"

"Roe!" General glared at him.

"Oh. This nigga still salty about his Cuban princess."

"Fuck you, nigga!"

Now Roe was heated. "It comes with the game, bro. It is what it is. Be salty all you want, but what's done is done."

Stepping over to Roe and snatching the freshly rolled blunt from his hand, General looked for a lighter and put fire to it. The nigga didn't even smoke, yet there he was, puffing on greenery. A moment later, his chest was burning, and he was coughing like hell, already buzzing from the effects of the weed.

"Nigga, let a first class chiefer hit that shit, show you how we do it on the other side," Roe boasted, reaching for the blunt.

"Fuck the other side!"

"It didn't stop you from sliding through to see old Rhonda."

"There ain't nowhere in Harlem I can't go, son. Be it your side or whoever side, Harlem is my shit!"

"You got a lot of people who feel the same way."

"Like I said, Roe—" General was cut short by the sound of gunshots ringing outside somewhere. At once, they both moved to the window and the door to look outside to see what was up. More gunshots exploded in the vicinity of the building.

"The fuck's going on out there?"

"I can't see shit from here, bro."

At the door, General cracked it open a little bit more. Then he said 'fuck it' and stepped outside, gripping his steel tightly.

"Oh, shit. General?" a voice asked in surprise.

General looked to his left and saw his homeboy Block and some other nigga posted up. The cat standing next to Block was a very familiar face, but General couldn't seem to put a name to it.

"What it do, son!" General acknowledged Block.

The same instant, Block peered to Geneal's right, and his eyes widened with confusion and astonishment.

"Damn, kid! Yo, Roe, the streets said you was dead, B."

Roe shrugged. "You know how the streets talk."

A baffled Block just shook his head. "Damn. The whole while, everybody thought you'd killed Roe and got missing. You two niggas been chillin' together all along. Ain't that some shit!"

"What's going on out here?"

"Just some domestic violence shit. A nigga got caught up, and his chick wanna body him over it," Block explained as he nursed a red plastic cup, sipping on whatever it was he was drinking. "But check it. I'm about to bounce before somebody calls them pigs."

"When you got out, yo?" Roe asked.

"Two days ago." Block had just done a five-year bid in the joint for domestic violence shit himself. It was said that one of his bitches had been hitting his stash, and he pounded the bitch something badly. He, too, was from Harlem but resided in Brooklyn before his incarceration.

Roe nodded. "When all this shit is over, get at me. "

"Word, son." Block wasn't sure about that.

Back in the apartment, General was wondering if it was still cool to bring Anthony there. Now that he'd shown his face, within the hour, the whole projects would probably have known he and Roe were lying low there. Plus, there might've been cops on the way, and that definitely would not look good to Anthony when he arrived.

"What's up, bro?"

"I'm hittin' K'wan up. I think we should relocate now. We'll have to meet up with Anthony somewhere else instead." General dialed K'wan's number to put him up on game.

As he thought about it, Roe had to agree with him.

"Yeah," he said. "Don't want them showing up with the police all over the place, and we definitely need to get up outta here."

***

Meanwhile, peering through his rearview mirror at the unmarked car that had been discreetly tailing him for the past two hours since visiting Rosie at the hospital, Melvin was scheming on a getaway plan. He had to lose them as fast as he could, but he didn't want to warn them as of yet that he'd made them. He knew just the action to take.

141

Melvin knew the car contained one or more with an official badge because, if anyone else, maybe he wouldn't have lasted as long. He knew the feds were in town too, probably preparing for a bigger street war than the one that had been going on recently. With two mob families in town and the results of what brought them together, extra law enforcement officials were on standby. The city was under siege, and Melvin was tired of the shit.

Turning into the parking lot of a shopping plaza off Broadway and bringing the Impala to a halt before a record store, he went over his plan briefly. In his rearview mirror, the unmarked car drove by the entrance of the shopping plaza. Melvin wasn't dumb, not for a long shot. He knew they would circle back around or park somewhere nearby so they could watch his every move.

Yeah, until he mysteriously vanished!

Sure enough, Melvin noticed the unmarked car had indeed circled back and decided to stake out across the street. That way, they had a larger view of the whole front area of the Plaza.

Snatching up the few things he needed, including the backpack loaded with ammunition and guns, along with ten thousand cash he'd yet to spend, Melvin abandoned the rental. From there, he entered the record store, and to his surprise, there was someone he wouldn't have expected to bump into. Melvin damn near busted a nut with gladness. Boy, was he definitely in luck today.

"Mr. Whitaker!" Lushena looked up in surprise from behind the counter, setting her Hip Hop Weekly magazine down and lowering her IPOD headphones. Then she smirked. "Lemme find out!"

"I need your help, Lushena."

Lushena Murray, who was a twenty-nine-year-old Far Rockaway, Queens, raised redbone honey with the resemblance of Kerry Washington, had once been a client of Melvin's. Two years or so ago, she was apprehended during a sting operation, facing fifteen years of fed time. Melvin got her down to eighteen months and a serious warning. Now, there she was, working behind the counter in a local record store, trying to go the honest route of living.

Well, not exactly, but she wasn't allowing her former trap-star brother to influence her to work for him anymore. That nigga was doing a fifty-year bid right now, wishing he would have stayed in church and listened to his mama.

Lushena regarded Melvin intently now. "You need my help? What's up?" she asked, ready to do anything for the man who legally and faithfully saved her life.

"You have a car outside?"

"Yeah, why?"

"I need to use it. I'll pay a thousand dollars and promise to get it back to you later."

"What's going on, Mr. Whitaker? You in some kinda trouble? Is this about what's going on with General?"

"Yes, all the above," he responded anxiously.

"Rakim!" Lushena called out over her shoulder. Moments later, a young, dark-skinned cat stepped through the door of a backroom behind the counter. Lushena looked at him sourly and said, "Hold the post down 'til I get back."

"Where in the hell you going?"

While Lushena spoke to Rakim with an attitude dripping from her tongue, Melvin was counting out a thousand dollars from his pocket stash. The second she reached the other side of the counter with her car keys in hand., Melvin was pushing the money toward her.

"I'ma need you to show me the back door and meet me around back with the car," Melvin explained.

"Don't fuck my car up, Mr. Whitaker!" She took the money.

"Honey, I'll buy you five cars; just help me get away from here!" he demanded.

She was down with it. "Follow me," said Lushena.

"Lead the way."

Rakim was left looking stupid in the face.

***

In the back seat of the Acura, Thad had Angelica bent all kinds of ways, pounding that pussy something viciously.

"Mmm, yes! Beat it, Thad! Beat this… Oooh!" Angelica was talking all type of nasty shit as the walls of her slick pussy gripped his dick like a pit bull lock. The nigga had pure stamina, having busted a nut already, still as hard as a light pole. Thad was giving her the business.

Laid out on her back in the backseat with her legs thrown over his shoulder, Angelica was cumming for the second damn time. Ma was flooding the backseat with her juices.

"Ahhh… Oh, shit, I'm cumming!" She moaned.

Going twenty minutes strong now, Thad was working up a sweat, but when Angelica suddenly placed a hand against his chest and reached for his dick, Thad looked at her like she was crazy as hell.

"Whatcha doin, ma?" he asked.

Stroking his slippery manhood in her hand, she gazed up into his eyes. She whispered, "Tell me you want it, baby."

His eyes were glazed with lust. "I need it," replied Thad.

She placed the head of his lil' nigga at her asshole, pulling him back into her with remarkable ease, hissing like a snake as he drove deep into her ass.

"God damn!" Thad damn near passed out!

"Slow and steady, baby."

"Damn, baby." Thad grunted, slowly pulling out of her and plunging into her juicy ass with pleasure.

"Just like that," she encouraged.

Thad wasn't trying to hear that shit and gave her ass the real deal, giving her straight pound game. Angelica screamed with ecstasy, bucking against him and talking nastily, but for Thad, it didn't take long for him to blast off in that shit like a bottle rocket.

"Fuck!" He was dizzy with pleasure.

Minutes after they untangled from one another in the back, Thad got behind the wheel and fixed up his cigar. Then he looked back at her with a straight face. "You good, ma?"

"Am I good?" She gave him a devilish glance. "Boo, I'm fantastic!" Angelica climbed up front and eased down into the passenger seat. "You tried to kill me, boy!" That was what they all said.

"Shit, that's what you wanted."

She sighed and slouched down in the seat, twirling a lock of her shoulder-length, crinkled hair, smiling beautifully to herself.

Releasing a cloud of smoke into the air, Thad felt like getting high instead. Then he started the car and cracked the windows a little with Silk's 'Loving You' pouring from the sound system at a gentle volume. Putting the car in gear, Thad proceeded to back out of the garage of Angelica's Upper West Side townhouse. They never made it to the bedroom.

'Maybe next time,' thought Thad.

"We're going back already?" asked Angelica, shrugging her shoulders after checking the time. "It's still early."

"I know."

"Then where are we going?"

Thad looked over at her. "To get some blunts to roll up."

"Boy, stop the car, boo."

"Why?"

Angelica straightened up in her seat and reached for the door. "I got those in the house," she said.

"What?"

"What? I'm too beautiful to burn trees, too?" She smirked over her shoulder and jumped out of the car.

A stupid looked was plastered on his face as he watched her fine ass walk back into her garage. She walked over to the far-right corner of the garage, where an old dresser was, squatting down to reach for the bottom drawer. A second later, she waved a box of Peach White Owls at him, ginning devilishly.

I told you, she mouthed.

Thad nodded. He never would've expected her to smoke weed. She was just so damn beautiful to him.

Chapter 18

Short and stocky built, Anthony Kerr had the appearance and humble manners of an academic, indeed. He read philosophy and could speak eight different languages, but he was also the only man whose essence and strength evolved General's through six years of shared exile.

Roe thought the Cuban looked like a straight mark, but he could see the evil in his eyes. The second he and General walked through the door that evening, Roe looked at the man and saw the pain in them, too.

Upon them seeing one another, Anthony rose from the couch and took General's hand, pulling him into a brief embrace.

"You look like shit, G-man."

"But I feel like a gladiator right now." General's hard expression didn't move. "I'm ready for war."

"My soldiers are on their way up here now, son. What they're coming with, customs won't allow on a plane. Now,"—Anthony turned to Roe and offered him a brief nod—"this is the Rolando you've told me about?"

Both Roe and General exchanged silent glances.

"Yeah." General shrugged.

"Your friend speaks highly of you, Rolando. You have a loyal man here on your side, so see that you keep him." Again, Roe looked at General, but this time, General didn't meet his gaze. He wondered what General had told the Cuban, which he would find out later.

Also present were two of Anthony's men and K'wan, whose house they were occupying at that moment. Having sent Denise and the girls off to a movie and treat for a couple of hours, he used the meeting location at his own crib in Harlem, back in the hood where it all started, but only several blocks away.

After the introductions, both General and Anthony moved over into the kitchen. Of course, Roe didn't like being left out to babysit Anthony's two silent, ever-so-glaring-ass goons in their expensive linens and guns. They were the only two permitted to carry from the troops Anthony had on the road.

Inside the kitchen, General checked the fridge for something to drink. That bitch was loaded with stuff, and the moment General laid eyes on a bottle of sparkling Hypnotic, he grabbed it.

"Tell me everything." Anthony finally spoke up after lowering himself into one of the cushioned kitchen barstools at the counter. "I mean everything, G-man."

"It's crazy," General said and told him about the situation that led to his and Roe's war, to the discovery of Olivia's death. That part, he made up, fabricating a story about the Italian's finding out about his and her relationship and killing her while hunting for him.

"And what made you seek after Olivia when all this mayhem—" Anthony was cut short.

"There was no one else I trusted at the moment."

The Cuban nodded quietly.

General finally poured them both a glass of the drink and sat next to him on the other stool. "I still can't believe she's gone," he said and stared down into the glass for a moment.

"And how much have you progressed so far with what's needed to avenge her death?" asked Anthony, tasting his drink and raising a brow in thought, liking its unique flavor.

General then told him what he knew about Mario Napoli and what he had accomplished since arriving in New York.

Thanks to Rita, who had filled him in on more valuable information on the Napoli family, General gave his connect's right-hand man all he had to give. By the time they were done talking in private, after going over the extent of the matter a few times, Anthony consulted with his two goons. Seeing that they were done, Roe got up to see about his homie in the kitchen.

Still sitting down at the counter was where Roe found General. "What's on your mind, bro?"

"I'm ready to get this shit over with."

"And get back to the money, huh?" Roe looked at the bottle of Hypnotic and turned his nose up in disgust.

"Yep." General lifted his glass for another sip. "Back to the money, as always."

"You still want that million, huh?"

General finally looked at him, knowing exactly what his old friend was getting at. When they were just seventeen and sixteen, before becoming enemies, General had sworn he'd make a million dollars before Roe. They'd made a bet, and the first one to make it would get five thousand dollars from the other.

Grinning, General said, "Hell yeah!"

"Me too."

"Ghetto millionaires." General remembered their future title.

Roe repeated, "Ghetto millionaires!" They both reminisced for a minute until Roe suddenly switched lanes on him.

"And you just might beat me, too."

"I know I am, son! You just watch and see." General paused at the dejected expression Roe now had etched on his face, staring down into the empty glass Anthony left behind. "What's up, bro?"

"Even if we do take care of this street shit, I still gotta deal with them pigs. That's if I even make it that far. It's over with for me, Jarrod. My mission is to help you win now while I'm still here. You feel me?" Roe spun the empty glass before him.

"Hell no, nigga! General snapped. "You talkin' reckless, son. We're in this shit together! You ride, I ride. We die together. Now feel that!" He glared over at him, sliding off the stool to face Roe like a man.

Roe remained seated.

"Get up," he demanded of him.

Reaching for the Hypnotic bottle, Roe turned it up to his mouth for a swallow. General slapped the bottle away, and it crashed into the side of the fridge, shattering on the tiled floor.

That really got Roe's blood boiling, and he stood up, turning to face General head-on. "This whatcha want, son?" His eyes were harder than a Lil' Boosie album.

K'wan then banged into the kitchen next.

"You gotta be a coward because the Roe I know don't back down from nothing, son!"

Roe said, "I never been no coward, bro."

"Then stop acting like one! Pick your fuckin' head up and poke your chest out, son. We living in a muthafuckin' jungle, and the only way to survive is to be beasts of our own."

"And that's exactly what we aim to be," Anthony interjected just behind K'wan's right shoulder.

Meeting the Cuban's eyes with his own, Roe replied in the most earnest tone. "Then let's bomb on them fools."

"That's what I wanna hear, yo!" General smirked and slapped Roe across the shoulder, and he grunted in intense pain, shooting his brother a wicked glare. "My bad, son. My bad!"

***

It was sometime around nine-thirty that evening when Thad finally stepped out of the studio booth. He was perspiring lightly, having just done three hits back-to-back without ever stepping out of the booth. There was nothing he desired more at that moment than losing himself. Inside the booth, his headphones on, with a mic before him, and expressing himself was the best way he knew how. Not even Angelica's presence was as special as this, though he really did enjoy her company.

"That was so amazing, Thad," said Angelica.

With a nonchalant shrug, Thad accepted the bottle of water she held out to him.

"You were so vocalized with that last one. What was it named?" she asked with blatant curiosity.

Thad thought about it for a moment. "Armageddon."

Taken aback just a little by the title, Angelica took his arm and stepped closer to him. She knew exactly why he had named it such. Thad had expressed its essence to her just hours before arriving there. She listened to him tell his story on top of what her uncle Willie had provided her during their earlier time together. Angelica saw the emotion in his actions while observing Thad in the booth from where she sat next to the music engineer's sound table. Thad had spoken of love, war, and pain in that last session, making her all the more willing to offer him her sympathy for the recent losses of those he truly cared about.

"Well," she said softly. "They were all wonderful, Thad."

Turning to Black Boi at the soundboard, Thad acknowledged the beat master directly. "I'll hit you up tomorrow, Black, and check out the master copies," he said.

Black Boi, who was originally from Atlanta, Georgia, and so black that he looked purple at times, nodded in response. "By the time I get done with it, it's gonna be a masterpiece."

"It's a masterpiece already," Angelica cut in confidently.

"Word, ma!" Black Boi nodded again.

After kicking it in the studio for a few more minutes, both Thad and Angelica took their leave.

On their way toward the car outside, the two walked alongside one another, enjoying the gentle night breeze.

While they talked and laughed in the process, they were unaware of what awaited them just around the corner.

Once there, Thad halted instantly when he saw Ciera and the other females waiting patiently for them. Ciera rose from the hood of Angelica's car, and both of her girls did the same, all carrying salty and grim expressions. Angelica knew drama when she saw it.

"If one of those are your peoples, then I suggest you—"

"I got this," Thad assured her.

The three females waited until they were in each other's proximity before Ciera finally spoke up.

"Who the hell is this bitch, Thaddaeus?" she asked icily.

Now, Angelica was offended. "You can chill with the disrespect."

"Bitch, shut the fuck up while I'm talkin' to my man!" Ciera snapped instinctively. "Nobody's talking to your ass."

"You left your bitch at home, bitch!" Angelica sneered, refusing to back down. "That's a bitch that had yo' bitch ass."

"What?" Ciera then drew her blade.

Thad stepped in at that moment. "Chill out, Cee!" he said, knowing how dangerous Ciera could get under circumstances where her heart was involved. "It ain't even that serious."

"Too late for that shit now, bae."

Both of Ciera's girls had their blades out now. Thad made a move toward his girl before he came to a sudden halt when he felt Angelica reach beneath his shirt and take his gun. When he turned around to look at her, she was sliding a bullet in the chamber, ready to get it on and poppin' on those hoes.

"Get away from my damn car," Angelica ordered.

Ciera turned to her man. "For real, bae?"

Blocka!

The bullet kicked up dirt inches away from Ciera's feet. "Don't make me say it again," warned Angelica.

At that instant, Thad stood in front of Angelica and reached for the gun. "Lemme hold the gun, ma, before you hurt somebody," he said and frowned when she stepped back and to the side, away from him. Angelica was dead ass serious, and there was no doubt she was about her issue when pushed.

"Let's go, Thad. Fuck that bitch!" Ciera said.

"Go!" he told her.

"Go?" Ciera looked at him with disbelief.

"Just go, ma. I'll see you later. I got this!" Thad told her, the whole while staring at Angelica with the gun.

Moments later, niggas stepped outside the studio to see what was going on. Several of them had their guns out and were shocked at what they found in the parking lot. It was a very intense situation.

"I'll be at the house when you get there," said Ciera before shooting Angelica a dark glare. "You fucked up when you did that shit, ma. We'll see each other again."

Angelica smirked. "I'm so scared," she said.

"You better be!" Ciera said over her shoulder before heading for her car.

***

Turning the nose of the car into the driveway of the old, red, brick four-bedroom house, Robert knew damn well he wasn't supposed to be there, but he had no choice, for Pam had left him none. He was heated with her for not getting out of town like he told her to. Now, there he was, returning to the same home that had, just days ago, been invaded by loco Italians who wanted his hide for something his son had done.

Robert wanted to strangle the damned woman. Where could she have run off to, if not back to Jersey, where she promised? There was no doubt that she would wait for him there, and how wrong he was!

One thing he was sure of was that she hadn't been taken, or else there would have been a random demand of some sort—well, that was what he assumed—nor could she have been taken and murdered either, or she'd have been found. Another assumption? He didn't know what the hell to think. All he wanted was his loving wife and to ensure her absolute safety, wherever the hell she was.

Maybe she'd called home and left a message for him as to where the hell she was? He could only hope so.

Robert got out of the car and scanned his surroundings, then made a hasty move for the door. He wished he had some type of illumination to work with, the porch light or something. No sooner had the thought crossed his mind, he heard a flicking sound to his left. A fraction of a second later, something solid soared through the darkness and hit him just above his right eye. A rushing movement sent him crashing to the ground by a force he wasn't prepared for, and when that force landed on him, Robert immediately knew who the source of the assault was.

"Now I'm about to beat you to death, punk!" came the snarling voice of Melvin before damn near breaking Robert's jaw with a heavy left hook. He had the element of surprise, and Robert was useless beneath Melvin's 265 pounds of pure pressure. It was about to be a slaughter indeed.

"I told you." Melvin talked to him in between blows. "I told you I was gonna punch you!"

The only free hand Robert had was his right, and he used it for a counterattack, punching wildly and desperately from where he lay underneath his assailant. If only he could reach the gun tucked at his waist, but it was difficult to do so in the position he was in. He couldn't let Melvin beat him to death either. He had to do something fast, but what could he do to get this big bear of a man off of him?

"Fight me head up like—" *Whop!* Melvin knocked the taste out of his mouth, but Robert's determination to get through to him was what kept him going. "Fight me like a man!"

Whop! Whop!

"Whatcha say?" Melvin heaved, his large chest rising and falling with every intake of breath. At least he stopped swinging on him.

"I said fight—" Robert's words came to a sudden halt when he noticed movement just beyond Melvin's massive shoulders behind him. Once his vision focused, and he saw Tu's sharp dagger rise into the air over her head with both hands, he panicked. Then Tu came down with a dagger.

"No!" With surprising strength, Robert shoved the big guy aside, but not fast enough.

Melvin cried out suddenly when the blade sliced through his shirt and penetrated flesh like a knife through melting butter. The slash, which was as deep as a trench, went from his left shoulder down, almost diagonally, to his right lower back.

The little girl laughed and lifted the dagger, one-handed this time, and like a blur, Melvin felt the blade piercing through the back of his arm. His triceps were punctured.

He fumbled for his gun when his eyes landed on Ava coming up behind Tu. Robert knew he had to act quickly. Melvin suddenly keeled over.

With two daggers in her hands, Ava glared down at Robert from two feet away, the mulling reflecting from her lifeless eyes. She struck the instant his finger squeezed the trigger. The deadly impact of the bullet snapped her head back, and Ava was lifted off her feet and into the air.

Spinning around instinctively as a result of the violent blast from Robert's Colt Python .357 Magnum, Tu looked over at Ava's fallen, dead body at her right. A wicked smile turned toward Robert, and he could've sworn he saw her eyes glow in the dark. With the amazing speed of a rattlesnake striking, Tu went after him.

Boom!

The bullet seared just past Tu's ear by a mere inch, for Melvin had managed to clip her feet from beneath her. Still, to Robert's horror, she drove the dagger into his thigh, laughing devilishly before her little girly chest exploded, spraying blood everywhere. This freaked Robert the fuck out. The girl fell on him, still breathing, but struggling for breath. Seconds later, she became as still as a piece of plywood.

"Robert, you alright?" Melvin called out with a groan.

Pushing the dead girl away and feeling nauseated with her blood all over his face, Robert howled when he realized her hand was still clutching the dagger. That had Melvin crawling over quickly but in agonizing pain to inspect his wound.

"That little bitch stabbed me!"

"There's two more of them," Melvin warned him, and that notion seemed to give Robert pause. That was all the time Melvin needed to snatch the dagger out of his leg.

Robert clenched his teeth and let out a loud, guttural gurgle.

"Son of a bitch!" he said and looked down at his wounded leg in disbelief. "Fuck."

There was silence.

When he looked back over at Melvin, he was no longer moving. With a shaky hand, Robert reached to check his pulse and found him still breathing. He muttered some very expletive, choice words once he realized what he was faced with now.

Suddenly, a shadowed figure appeared, and Robert lifted the gun and shot it down, seeing that it was one of those Italian henchmen. That was when he knew it was time to get the fuck away from there immediately, especially when there were two more of those killing little girls out there somewhere.

"Oh, hell no!"

Chapter 19

For the past thirteen years, Tony Bardem had been working for Mario Napoli faithfully. He would deny the Italian capo nothing. Shit, if it weren't for Mario, he wouldn't have been alive, nor would he be able to provide for his blended family like his father hadn't.

To be given the job to babysit a couple of demonic little girls was nothing to him, especially when he was being paid handsomely for his services. The less he was out on the battlefield, the better for him. Besides, he'd put in enough work and endured more pain than a little bit over the past thirteen years, working for Mario, so he deserved to kick back now and watch the action go down from a safer distance.

Little did he know, he wasn't safe at all. No one was safe.

Having been around the girls for the last five years since Mario had bought them, Tony had grown to care for them in a strange little way, and they protected him, shared fruit with him. The little ones were crazy about fruit. The bond they shared with him was like no other. Tony had been almost like their guardian since the beginning, when they first arrived in the United States, and he liked Tu the most.

She was the one he pretty understood the most. Zoey, the youngest out of the bunch, was the bossy one, while Ava was the quiet before the storm, and Buuwa was the most audacious one, the one whom Tony felt they all feared. She had the most kills, but Ava was the skilled one, always coming up with new tricks to show her sisters. Tony had been there through it all.

As the G-Class Benz pulled to a stop at the red light near the Union Square Green Market, which was a block away, Tony was startled by a piercing shriek. He turned and looked in the back, where Zoey and Buuwa were, and saw Buuwa covering her face with her hands.

"Tu!" Buuwa cried out suddenly. "Tu! No!" She began shaking violently in the back seat as if having the holy ghost, the whole while with her face covered.

Tony looked at Zoey, who stared at Buuwa unblinkingly, with an expression on her face he couldn't describe.

'Tu?' thought Tony. 'What's wrong with Tu?' he wondered. Suddenly, Buuwa went quietly still, then she dropped her hands from her face.

"What's wrong, Buuwa?" Tony asked with concern.

Without a verbal response, Buuwa reached for her seven-inch SOG fighting knife next to her. Buuwa stared down at it as if to admire it for the first time, then she reached for the door and bolted from the car.

"No!" Tony protested to a useless effect. Putting the car in park, he got out next, hoping to catch a glimpse of Buuwa, but it was too late, the girl was gone. Buuwa was on the loose.

Back in the car, Tony cursed in great anger and fear for what may become of this situation. Mario was gonna be pissed, and there was nothing he could do about it. He turned around to look in the back seat and saw Zoey still sitting there, looking out into the open passenger door with that same expression.

"I can't believe this shit!" Tony said angrily and banged a fist against the steering wheel.

Believe it or not, there would be hell to pay, and Buuwa was hell on earth.

***

The Acura came to a halt behind Ciera's car at Thad's house. Sure enough, Ciera had kept her promise, but there was no doubt in Thad's mind she'd be waiting for him to get home.

Angelica suspected as much but didn't say anything. She knew her place in matters like this.

On the drive there, Thad had smoothed her ruffled feathers with the assurance that nothing had changed between them. They both came to a mutual understanding that there wouldn't be any more fucking, though Angelica had to damn near wrestle him into honoring it, and he had. Because their first encounter had been great indeed, she thought it would be enough to call it a done deal for now.

Thad had to smoke a cigarette after that one.

"So, when's the next time I'ma see you again, ma?"

She said, "The next time you see me."

"Whatever, yo!" Thad reached for the door.

"Hey!"

Thad turned to look at her, and that was when she kissed him at the corner of his mouth, stroking his jaw affectionately.

"You want me to break that promise?"

"Go, Thad!"

"Then keep them crusty lips off me," he retorted with a grin, and she punched him in the arm.

"Bye, boy, before your girl kill your ass."

As he stepped out of the car, something down the street up ahead caught his attention. Thad squinted his eyes to focus on the lone figure walking along the side of the road. Closing the door, he made his way toward the child, fear gripping his heart at the sight of Tiera passing beneath the streetlight. Then he shot past Ciera's car, running and scooping the girl up in his arms.

"Tee Tee, whatcha doing out here?!" he asked, sensing how scared the girl was. She was shaking in his arms like a starving, mangy dog in a winter storm. Looking down at the girl, Thad noticed that she was barefoot and dressed in her pajama bottoms and a T-shirt.

"Mama hurt brotha." She cried softly. "She won't wake up!"

Dread gripped his heart instantly. By this time, both Ciera and Angelica were getting out of their cars and making their way toward Thad and the child.

"Where is Troy?" Thad questioned her.

"He not there," said Tiera. She buried her face into his shoulder as if to black out some image that frightened her. She was sobbing, holding on to him for dear life.

Ciera was the first to reach them. "What's wrong, bae?"

Quickly, Thad put the girl in Ciera's arms and gave her the house keys. "Take her in the house! I'll be back in a minute!"

"But wait!"

Thad jumped in Ciera's car and peeled out.

Cradling the girl in her arms, Ciera turned to Angelica with a worried expression.

"C'mon. Let's get her in the house." Angelica took the keys out of her hand and made her way to Thad's house. Hesitantly, Ciera cast another glance in the direction her bae had gone and shrugged. Then she followed Angelica into that house with more than just the child's well-being on her mind.

What would happen now?

***

Before Thad even realized what he had done, he'd jumped from the car without putting it in gear. Thinking fast on his feet, he rushed back behind the wheel to do so. Then he got out and ran to the front door of Vega's house.

Tiera had to leave from the back door or the patio door because she wouldn't have left the front door open.

160

Then, to Thad's surprise, he heard a familiar voice on the phone from next door, talking to the 911 operator. When she looked up and saw him standing there, she beckoned him over to where she stood. Ms. Faye covered the phone's mouthpiece and gazed those dark, watery, brown eyes into his.

"You know where Troy is?"

"No," he said.

"Well, Tiera is missing, and Sue is dead in the kitchen. I'm on the phone with the police now," she replied emotionally, badly shaken herself. "We gotta find that child, baby."

"She's at my house with my girl."

"Praise God!" Ms. Faye laid a hand over her heart and turned back to the phone. "Yes, ma'am? I heard shooting and came over as soon as I thought it was safe to," she said as Thad left the room for the kitchen.

His heart rate quickened with every step.

Lying on the kitchen floor, with a bullet hole in her forehead, was Sue, still dressed in a pair of cutoff shorts and a wife-beater. Upon closer inspection, Thad could tell she was physically battered from the fresh bruises on her fucked-up face. Someone had swollen her nose two times its normal size, blackened her eye, and split her bottom lip wide open.

"Damn," was all he could say.

He couldn't stand the sight of her anymore. Thad backed out of the kitchen, into the unexpected path of Vega. The sound of the gun click made Thad pause immediately as he stared into the wicked expression of Vega's face.

"You just won't learn, huh, nigga!" Vega sneered.

"Troy!" came Ms. Faye's voice.

When Vega turned his head, Thad knocked his gun away and hit Vega with a vicious right jab that sent him backpedaling. Thad went after him, rushing Vega with another mean jab that sent him crashing into the hallway floor. Now that he had Vega disoriented, Thad immediately disarmed him.

"You better use it," Vega threatened.

"Fuck you, nigga!" Thad dropped the loaded clip into his pocket and pocketed the single round from the chamber. "This shit is real right now, bro."

"The police is on the way," said Ms. Faye.

Still looking up at Thad with a murderous glare, Vega got to his feet slowly.

Thad said, "Mama is dead, bro. Somebody killed her. Tee Tee came 'round to the house and told me. She's 'round there now with Cee. I…" Thad stopped when Vega reached behind him and was instantly alarmed because he knew what he was reaching for.

Blocka!

Thad ducked in the nick of time and dashed back inside the bloody kitchen.

"Troy, Stop! Please! No, baby, stop!"

"Get off me!" Vega shrugged the woman off him and entered the kitchen after Thad.

His heart pounding violently in his chest, Thad watched as Vega rounded the corner to the kitchen, and then Vega stopped in his tracks when he laid eyes on his dead mama. Thad regarded him cautiously as Vega's mouth hung in disbelief. Moving toward his mama, he dropped to his knees. Vega reached for his mama and pulled her into his arms, a bewildered look on his face.

Seeing Vega cry moved Thad deeply.

"Oh, Troy." Ms. Faye's mouth quivered.

With the gun next to him, Vega held his dead mama and cried. Although he'd hated her for years for all the hell she took him through, it was a different story now, seeing her dead. This was the woman who'd brought him into this world.

As he threw caution to the wind, Thad stepped over and laid a hand on his brother's shoulder. "C'mon, bro. We gotta go," he said. "We gotta go check on Tee Tee."

Vega looked over his shoulder at him. "Who did this?"

"That's what we gotta go find out."

Sirens blared from somewhere nearby.

"We gotta go," Thad repeated.

Kissing his mama's bruised and bloody cheek, Vega grabbed his gun and stood up. He faced off with Thad for a second and wiped his tear-stricken face. "A muthafucka gonna burn for this, bro. They done killed my mama," he said and looked back down at her lying at his feet. "I'm already dead now, bro. Now everybody else gotta die."

Chapter 20

Patrica was deep in thought as she made her way along the deserted hallway. She paused to retrieve the bottle of Scotch from the table where she had left it, then proceeded to her bedroom, entering it as if she were moving in a trance. By the time she got settled in, the bedroom door opened, and in ran Zoey, climbing onto the bed and burying herself under her arm.

'This is odd,' a puzzled Patricia thought.

"What's the matter, Zoey?" Patricia was taken aback by the little black girl's behavior.

Zoey mumbled something Patricia didn't comprehend.

A moment later, Mario entered the bedroom and paused, quietly seeing the situation for what it was. He shook his head wearily and made his way over to the bed.

"What is wrong with her, Mario? Where are the others?" Patricia demanded to know, setting her glass aside.

Sighing deeply, Mario reached over to pet the girl's leg. There were no tears from her, nothing. Zoey just lay there beneath his sister's arm, mumbling while staring into space.

"Ava and Tu didn't make it." He told her all he knew of the situation. "And Benny's dead, too."

Patricia found this quite disturbing. "And Buuwa?"

This was the most disturbing part.

"Buuwa is on the loose out there by herself."

"Oh, God."

"This is bad."

"Very bad"

"Bad," Zoey mumbled softly, followed by silence.

"I gotta go find her," said Mario with a worried look in his eyes. "Lock up everything because I'm gonna need all my men. The others won't be here 'til tomorrow. It's over tomorrow, and I'm gonna take you back to Chicago with me."

"Promise." Patricia shook her head.

"Patricia, I will, tomorrow," he swore to her. Then he smiled. "I have to come back to my beautiful big sister. Everything is gonna be okay." Mario kissed her forehead. "Okay?"

Taking his word for it, like always, Patrica gave her head with a brief nod in trust. "Okay."

Mario then pointed a finger at Zoey, a little dragon of a girl, and Zoey nodded. She understood. She knew what to do—protect the princess's queen.

Then Mario was gone, closing the door behind him.

Zoey shot from the bed to lock the door. She stood there for a moment, just looking at the door, until she heard the master's exit. She drew her spiked glove and put it on her left hand. The little black girl with the four-inch shiny piece of pointed metal protruding from her fist, Zoey was the little boxer. It was the same one she punched Peaches' eyeballs out of her head with. She was vicious with her hands, a true warrior fighter.

"Bad." She growled and spun from the door toward Patricia, then shot back to the bed to bury herself back beneath the queen's arm. Zoey watched the door like a little black pit bull, ready to damage something in the worst effect.

Patrica pulled her closer, protectively.

***

Buuwa had always been the night-crawler type, never afraid in the dark. She would hunt in the dark. At eight years old, she would hunt rabbits in a fenced-in backyard at night near the jungle where snakes as long as two car lengths roamed in hunting too. It was just exercise for her to become who she had—a beast that always emerged victoriously in the end.

Buuwa never really went out to play from the battlegrounds during her growth. All she ever knew was darkness, waiting for that ultimate moment where her animalistic skill would be needed.

For the past five years, she'd had the freedom to see the light after Mario purchased her and Tu. They were the first. Then came Ava two years later, and three months after her came Zoey, the little runt of the pack, but Mario never let her out to play either, for her skills were never needed.

In Chicago, Mario just allowed her to stay in the house all the time. He was strict with his most precious one; he had things in order there. Mario had a structure. The master never had serious trouble there. Though this loss of a loved one was warranted vengeance taken for her death, Mario released her, finally letting her out to play in the worst way. His wishes were her every command, and the master wanted destruction.

He wanted the killer himself. He wanted Rolando.

Right now, she wanted her identical twin sister. She wanted her Tu, and nothing was going to stop her. She was gonna find her, their spiritual energy attracting her whole purpose for connecting with her one last time. Buuwa could not live without her sister.

It was almost time for her to die, too, but not without seeing her sister again before it was over. The final showdown. The Champion. The end.

With her knife tucked silently at her side leg, Buuwa ran to that inner connection with Tu as if chasing the same soul. For miles, she would run at a time, every morning, from age seven, then back home from the real true jungle to which she would also train, searching for potential prey.

For the past hour, she had escaped many deaths from being chased by some goon niggas in Brooklyn, damn near getting hit by a truck, and even spraining her ankle in the process. Now, she was climbing over the gate into someone's backyard, adrenaline surging through her with the determination to win. That battle was about to be tested.

Buuwa didn't make it four yards before the first one hit her, biting into her left arm with brutal force. She growled through clenched teeth in sudden pain. Not even three seconds later, Buuwa felt another set of teeth and fangs sink into her.

Meet Bison and Yellow Eyez—two full-blooded German Shepherds. Yellow Eyez, the most dominant one, was giving her a really hard time. She needed her legs.

Instinct made her reach for the handle of the knife, then, with no remorse whatsoever, Buuwa drove the blade straight through Yellow Eyez's heart and head-butted Bison with damaging intent. Yellow Eyez was a done deal. She had to get his big ass out the way first.

Withdrawing her knife and raising it high above them both from the ground, Buuwa lost her leverage when Bison locked onto her wrist. That really made her mad because that was the hand she used to grip her knife, her most valuable protector. She had to do something.

That young true warrior instinct kicked in, and Buuwa bit onto Bison's nose and clamped down on it for dear life. Bison held on for a few seconds longer and cried out when she finally locked in, tasting his gushing blood spray into her mouth. The second he let go of her arm, Buuwa stabbed the dog through the brain, the knife buried to the hilt in his skull.

He didn't last long either. Bison was done. He was finally dead.

As she lay back on the battlefield, staring up into the dark, black sky, through the limbs of the tree, beyond her vision, tears spilled from her eyes. She was hurting. The thought of

Tu brought her up, and she reached for the knife with her good hand, still determined to hunt.

"Tu." She groaned in severe pain, cradling her injured arm against her. She sighed and disappeared into the darkness again. Buuwa would fight to the death. She was a champion.

***

"He had hair like a girl," said Tiera, lying in Angelica's lap, her head resting on her smooth, shapely thighs.

"What else do you remember, honey?"

"Cuda."

"What did you say?"

"Cuda," Tiera repeated sadly, eyes tired and raw from crying. "That's what Mama called him—Cuda," she said with a hint of confidence.

There was the sound of the back door opening, then Vega's voice calling out to her. She popped upright instantly, staring in the direction her brother's voice had come from. Ciera hurried out of the kitchen, still kind of salty and worried sick about her bae, but Vega's familiar voice was music to her ears. Surely, he would be a lot of help at that moment.

When Vega finally appeared, Tiera ran into her brother's arms, crying her eyes out once again. Behind him was Thad, whom Ciera clutched onto immediately, her poor heart sighing with hope again.

"Who is Cuda?" Angelica asked, also very familiar with Vega's face, having seen him around on several occasions.

Instinctively, Thad and Vega exchanged glances.

"Cuda?" Thad's brows furrowed.

Angelica told them what they learned from Tiera while in their absence.

Picking his sister up and holding her in his comforting, protective arms, Vega carried her over to the other sofa. He kissed her head and promised everything was going to be okay. It was the same way Mario had just done to Patricia in a promise. To their surprise and relief, Mama Doll entered through the front door. Then Angelica bolted to her feet with a look of confusion on her beautiful face.

"What's up, Ma?" Thad acknowledged her.

"Angie?" Mama Doll regarded Angelica with astonishment.

"Miss Dee?"

Mama Doll looked at her son. "Baby, what's going on?"

That was Ciera's cue, and she let Mama Doll have it—her version of the matter—and everyone listened attentively, the reality of it all coming through her voice. When everything was all said and done, Vega finally rose from the sofa and looked at Thad with that look in his eyes.

Mama Doll knew what that look meant. Vega pulled out his gun, dashing for the front door with only one thing on his mind—murder.

"Troy!" Mama Doll called after him, but Vega was gone. She looked over at Thad. "Go get your brotha, baby," she ordered him tiredly.

He didn't have to be told twice. Thad reached for the Glock 9mm he'd taken from Vega earlier and popped the clip in from his pocket. He chambered a round and ran out the door.

'It's what he'd signed up for,' thought Angelica with a silent but heavy heart.

Ciera dropped her head sadly, but Mama Doll was proud of her son, knowing he would come back to her when he'd accomplished his goal. He always did, so she had confidence in her baby. "They'll make it out there," Mama Doll finally said, pulling the sleeping child in her arms now. Tiera had cried her poor heart to sleep. "I didn't raise no failures. My boys will come back to us soon."

***

Thanks to Mango having sent him on a mission, Cuda knew he would have been clowned to pieces right along with him. He had escaped that fate, but he was still on a mission to kill, seeking vengeance for Mango's death, but most of all, Trell's death. That was his baby brother, the last child of his father, Al, who had been a rolling stone ever since they could remember. Now, Cuda had more purpose to transform into the certified goon that he was.

He heard in the streets that Vega had killed Twin, whom Cuda had under his wing. That was a little nigga who had heart, the proud father of his niece Kendall's two-year-old son, so he got at Vega, hitting him where it hurt. All of them niggas were playing for keeps, but they were far from even.

Cuda was starving for some more gangster shit. He'd already caught Worm behind the house, tricking with Connie, one of Harlem's notorious prostitutes. He clapped that cat with his pants down, getting head, then snapped Connie's neck before she had any bright ideas in that good ass head. He wasn't leaving Harlem 'til Vega was dead.

Yeah, he murdered Man-Man too, so Cuda definitely had to find that nigga. This was for the other side. He was next.

Chapter 21

After rushing Melvin to the hospital and leaving him there at the emergency entrance, Robert went back out to the battlefield, though the deep worry of his old friend's condition disturbed him greatly. Plus, Melvin saved his life tonight. How could someone ignore something like that?

Robert returned the favor, setting aside their differences. The same man's life he'd ordered a hit on, he was probably saving the life of now. The tables had turned in a dramatic way, and he still hadn't found his damned wife.

Fishing for his phone now, Robert retrieved it and made the call he'd been waiting to make. Now was that time.

Wincing from the pain in his leg behind the wheel, he patiently waited for someone to pick up the phone. On the fifth ring, the voice he was hoping to hear answered, and Robert couldn't be happier at that moment.

"What's crackin', cuz?" replied Trigger, a West Side Crip that Robert had it in good with. He was the one who was about to bring everything together, and he also knew Gordo Lopez, as well as the link to the Mexican Cartel.

"Crip luv, homie," Robert responded.

A chuckle was heard over the phone. "I was wondering when you were gonna call. Say no more. I already know what to do. You don't even have to ask," said Trigger.

"Now that's Crip luv, cuz."

That was all it took, and now it was showtime.

***

"We're expecting some of my men sooner than later now," said Anthony.

General nodded.

"The more, the better," said Roe.

"Precisely." Anthony posed a pensive expression.

A call had just come through that twenty-one of his Cuban soldiers had pirated a private jet in Fort Lauderdale and were now in New York. The goons were coming for blood and war.

K"wan and both of Anthony's henchmen were gone at the moment, K'wan taking them to where Patricia's mansion was so they could get the lay of the land. From there, they would return to the boss with a strategic plan and angle to work from.

Like a game of chess, Anthony wanted to study the board before making his ultimate move.

"Fourth quarter," Roe said, checking his timepiece. "This is where that shit is about to turn all the way up."

Pulling K"wan's old, two-door Monte Carlo up behind a silver Lexus truck at the stoplight, General wondered where his daddy was at that moment. Melvin said he was going to call him back later when he got situated. Damn, he hadn't gotten situated yet?

"I need me a Cuban cigar, and I don't have any," said Anthony from the passenger side. This was the first time he'd ever been riding with General behind the wheel.

"How about we make a stop at that store over there, son," Anthony suggested.

That instant, General looked up ahead, noticing the neighborhood corner store at his right, and paused. Then he leaned forward a little and squinted his eyes to tighten his visual point. "Baby Thad," he said.

"Yep," Roe agreed from the back seat.

General felt a boost of energy kick in at the sight of his right-hand man, and that was exactly where General turned off to, as he honked the horn at his nigga to get his attention.

Thad spun around and stared intently at General from behind the wheel of K'wan's precious Monte Carlo. Then a look of surprise masked his face, and Thad ran to the car. He was happy to see his mans.

He couldn't help himself; General had to get out and show his little home some love, but he then became guarded by the serious look in Thad's eyes.

"What it do, bro?" General asked, checking his boy out.

"I'm looking for Vega," he replied.

General held his gaze for a moment. "What happened?"

Thad told him.

***

Vega had just rounded the corner of a house when he finally noticed the sky aglow with flickering light in the distance. He had a strong feeling he knew where it was coming from. Vega dropped his head for a second and proceeded toward his goal.

The hunt was in progress.

Minutes before, he had to stop and take a shit in the woods, wiping his ass with one of his socks. The nigga was so wired up that it gave him a bowel movement, and he turned to nature like it was nothing, just like an animal ass nigga. It wasn't his first time shitting in the woods.

When somebody had to go, they had to go! Now it was back to business as usual.

He also wondered where Thad had run off to now. While fleeing, he'd heard him call out to him several times from a distance. Vega was so caught up in his rage that he just kept running, shooting through the darkness like a bat out of hell.

Cuda had definitely hit him where it hurt, and already, Vega had thought of fifty ways he would like to murder the nigga. When he found Cuda, he was going to make him suffer to the point he'd be begging Vega to kill him, but the nigga was going to die slowly.

Payback was a muthafucka.

Vega came to a sudden stop as he happened upon something just at the mouth of an alley between two houses. The slower he got, the more he heard the soft, agonizing groans. Vega's heart then began thudding hard when he realized it was a little girl he'd happened upon.

"Oh, shit!" Vega froze when the injured girl made a sudden move. Then he noticed the gleam of a large knife clutched in her grasp. She looked up at him cautiously from where she lay upon the cool earth.

It was Buuwa, who could no longer finish her journey. The girl had worked herself into absolute exhaustion.

"Damn, shorty." Vega thought about his baby sister, and before he even realized what he was doing, he was bending down to take her in his arms.

Buuwa hissed at him from her half-fetal position, lifting her head off the ground to give him a warning look. The girl was a bloody mess, but she would remain a fighter for all it was worth.

"It's okay, shorty. I won't hurt you," Vega found himself whispering to her, then reached for her again and stepped a bit closer to her.

Buuwa didn't sense a threat from Vega at all, especially after looking into his eyes. There was something in his eyes she found trusting, a darkness that she knew well. Buuwa didn't fight him away, instead speaking up to him.

"Hurt." She groaned once again. "Hurt…"

This time, Vega didn't stop and carefully lifted the girl in his arms, her good arm swinging limply while still clutching her weapon. "I gotcha," he said. "I'ma take care of you," promised Vega, feeling emotion in his eyes again. Then he carried Buuwa away, unaware of what he was getting himself into, but he had no choice. She needed him more than anything right now.

Into the shadows they went.

From those same shadows, Cuda looked at Vega and sneered. This was his chance, finally. Without further ado, he stepped out of the darkness and stabbed his prey with deadly intentions. The wait was now over.

Chapter 22

Rabbit froze when he noticed movement just outside his bedroom window. He then hurried across the dark room and eased the curtain back just a fraction of an inch. It was all he needed to prove himself right. Someone was lurking outside his bedroom window, and it alarmed him greatly.

He retreated to his bed and reached between the two mattresses, withdrawing the 25 Caliber Beretta pistol he'd stolen recently. The little gun had yet been put to the test. Rabbit's opportunity to do so lay just moments away. The little homie was on the move.

Shutting the back door behind him while clutching the chrome pistol in his hand, Rabbit crept alongside the back of the house toward his target. The second he rounded the corner, the dark figure up ahead was doing the same thing. Then Rabbit proceeded in its direction.

Within the next several moments, Rabbit stepped around the corner of the house to the front. To his surprise, the silent figure before him moved across the front yard, toward the sidewalk. From his viewpoint, Rabbit saw exactly what he assumed the nigga was looking at and creeping through the shadows toward. When Rabbit noticed Vega, his heart quickened.

"Yo! Son!"

Rabbit went still, hearing the familiar voice of Cuda, fearing the worst immediately.

"Vega!" As cold as a glass of Remy was Cuda's tone, calling out to the person he'd been waiting to catch slipping. Now he had Vega where he wanted him.

Vega paused and looked in Cuda's direction, recognizing the voice. He saw Cuda moving fast toward him from across the street, extending his gun before him. A glance down at Buuwa was all it took to send him running as hard as he could. The nigga was running like Ricky did in the movie 'Boyz In Da Hood' before he got shot down. He couldn't let him kill the little girl, too.

Blocka! Blocka! Blocka! Blocka!

"Don't run now, son!" Cuda shouted after him.

Blocka!

Like the little rabbit he was, Rabbit chased after Cuda and knew to kill him before he got Vega. He wouldn't be able to face himself if he let Cuda murder Vega without at least trying to prevent it from happening.

Once in the middle of the street, Cuda halted and aimed the gun at Vega's fleeing direction.

Blocka!

Rabbit was on him in no damn time, lifting the pistol and putting two slugs in Cuda's back. Seeing Cuda fall in front of him, crying out in pain, made Rabbit gasp, but it was far from over, for Cuda was still fighting, struggling to reach his fallen gun a few feet away. Rabbit walked up to him from behind and stepped onto one of the bullet wounds in Cuda's back, causing him to howl in agony.

"Where you going, B?" asked Rabbit and aimed the gun at the back of Cuda's head. "You shoulda stayed over on the other side, yo."

Cuda turned his head up as far as he could to face his killer. When he saw Rabbit, he looked surprised.

Pow!

"This is my side." Rabbit dome checked him.

That was the end of Cuda's world.

Raising his head, Rabbit looked up and saw Vega staring back at him from down the street. Vega lifted his head in a nod, spun back around, and vanished through the night like a muthafuckin' phantom. It was at that moment that it finally hit Rabbit that what Vega carried in his arms was someone else, but who?

Rabbit took off after Vega to see with his own eyes.

***

While they stood there, talking in front of the store, two ambulances shot past on the main highway with their sirens blaring. Both General and Baby Thad watched in silent discontent as a lone police cruiser shot past just seconds behind.

The first thing that came to Thad's mind was Vega, but for some reason, he didn't feel it in his heart.

What had happened now?

"I'm not feelin' this shit, bro," General said to Thad. "Our hood haven't ever been through no shit like this. I gotta put a stop to it some kinda way."

Thad could see in his big homie's expression that General was blaming himself for what had been going down in their hood. "Yeah," he said. "We need to do something."

Harlem was being turned upside down before their eyes. The hood was in total mayhem.

Now, if Anthony would bring his ass from inside the store, maybe they could see what was going on. Roe still sat in the car, watching everything from his viewpoint. Earlier, he phoned his team and put them all on game, pointing out that he and General were joining forces.

Of course, there were a lot of questions, to which Roe only answered by stating, "It is what it is. That's my brother, and I'm riding with him. If y'all down with it, then meet up with us in the next half hour." That was all that needed to be said.

It was time to team up and reclaim what was left of Harlem. It was time for a hood revolution, once and for all. The time had come to finally unite as one—unity.

It put General's mind at ease to hear that his two little homies were back on solid ground.

"Hey!" a voice called out.

Both heads turned at the same time, and Rhonda was coming from around the corner of the store. The woman hurried over toward them, looking high as a blimp, followed by Apryl, a young trick the streets had turned out as spoiled goods. Although she was still quite pretty, at eighteen, Apryl was a mother of two, with AIDS eating her alive from the inside. The girl was too far gone to bring back. She was dying every step of the way, regretting her life, wishing she had listened to her mama.

"What's up, Mama?" General acknowledged his godmother.

Rhonda got straight to it. "Cuda shot little Worm and killed my girl Connie behind JoyceAnn's house. Next thing you know, Cuda's laid out in the street, dead. They say Tangi's boy, Rabbit, killed him."

"What!"

"Yep," Apryl coincided with Rhonda's story.

This really surprised General. He knew the young cat would catch a body sooner rather than later. Rabbit was too eager for a street reputation, bound to do anything to prove his worth.

A second later, Anthony exited the store and made his way toward the car without acknowledging General or his people.

No sooner than Anthony shut the door, Worm's car pulled into the entrance of the store. Just when Thad thought shit couldn't get more exciting at that moment, Marc's big homie Big Man pulled up in his truck behind the Pontiac. Apprehended by immediate hostility, Thad turned to General with that look in his eyes. This was cause for immediate action, and he didn't want General hanging around.

"Bro, take your mans, and get him away from here. I'll hit you up later," said Thad. "I got something to handle real quick."

General wasn't easily persuaded. "What it do, son?"

Rhonda peeped the play and moved on, taking Apryl by the arm and nearly dragging the girl away. There was no questioning something was about to go down. It could be felt in the air, and General didn't like how Thad was brushing him off without putting him on point. He recognized the dark look on Thad's face at the presence of Worm's car and Big Man's truck. Whatever it was about, General wasn't leaving 'til he knew what it was. Several yards toward the east corner of the store, Big Man got out of his truck, followed by two of his homies. At the same time, Marc and Lil' Beezo exited the car next.

"You got a problem with one of them fools, bro?"

Thad glanced at General. "It's some shit with my cousin I got to take care of," he said and told General what the deal was. "I gotta see that the shit don't go any further."

"You sure you don't need me here?"

"I got this, General!"

After glancing in Big Man's direction and meeting his gaze, General gave him a brief nod and turned back to Thad. "I won't be that far if you need me," he replied.

Thad didn't even respond.

"Be easy." General dapped him up and got in his car.

Thad made his way over to where he was about to get some straightening. He knew how it was gonna be done, but it definitely wasn't going to be easy.

***

About fifteen minutes prior, sometime close to eleven o'clock, four dark SUVs drove into the city. Occupying those same vehicles were twenty of Anthony's men who had finally arrived in the Big Apple. Another troop of Cuban goons was still on the road and would arrive by sunrise. The night clerk at the hotel nearly had a heart attack when they suddenly pulled up in front.

Ten men with dark expressions stepped out of the vehicles and made their way to the reception desk. The young clerk, Penny, a college student majoring in graphic design, fell to her knees and began to tremble. She was about to die right there. She just knew they were about to kill her, and no one would know for hours.

"H-h-how m-may I help you?" she asked when four of the men approached the front desk. The other six stood guard with guns and whatever other type of weapons that bulged beneath their shirts and jackets.

"We have a reservation," said one of the men. They were all huge muthafuckas, with dark hair and cold, hard eyes. "Under Barrera."

"Ten rooms for tonight, all close together. Then—"

Penny, as nervous as a sheep in the presence of a pack of wolves, reached over for a registration card. "Please, sir, if you'll just sign the register."

"That's not necessary," said the Cuban gangster. He passed her two hundred-dollar bills across the counter. "That should make it easy for you. I appreciate your understanding."

"Um, okay. Sure. Thanks."

Penny tossed the reservation card aside and quickly programmed ten keys. It was only when she'd given the men directions and they'd left that she dared to retrieve the money and stash it in the pocket of her pants. Later, she was going to take some of that money and get so high that even God would have to look up to find her. It wasn't every day that someone like her faced men like that and lived to talk about it.

***

It was just five months before when Mama Doll first met Angelica, who was an intern, and Mama Doll did everything in her power to see that the girl was trained properly. Angelica, who was also going to school for nursing, was inspired by Thad's mama and had taken the woman in with her confidence.

Ciera couldn't have cared less about how and when they had met. She was worried about Thad and those gunshots they'd heard. They were all worried to death.

From where they occupied the living room of the house, they also heard the faint blare of sirens somewhere in the distance. Mama Doll wanted so badly to go to Sue's aid, but she knew it was too late. Her heart pained for the women, despite all their differences. She was the mother of her second son, Troy. How could she not feel some way about Sue's death?

"I gotta go look for—"

"Ciera, sit your behind down somewhere!" Mama Doll gave her that don't-test-my-patience look.

Ciera sucked teeth and folded her arms.

Angelica said, "We are in the safest place right now, Ciera. Plus, we gotta be here for Tee Tee." Tiera was now in Mama Doll's bed, sound asleep, exhausted with grief.

"When will this mess ever end?"

"Soon, I pray." Mama Doll looked at Ciera with pity.

The sound of footsteps on the porch outside made them all look in that direction.

"Mama, open up! Hurry!"

Troy. Mama Doll hurried over to the front door and opened it. Her heart damn near burst with dread and panic when Vega barged into the house, carrying Buuwa in his arms. He was drenched in blood and had a crazy look in his eyes.

"Oh, lord, Troy."

"I found her like this," Vega said.

"Troy, quick. Take her into the kitchen. Angelica, you know what to do. Lemme go get my supplies." Mama Doll was already rushing down the nearby hallway.

When Angelica reached for Buuwa, the girl hissed at her, and Angelica jumped back at the threat of the bloody knife.

"It's alright, shorty. Don't worry. She's gonna help you. Let her help," Vega said to Buuwa as he carried her off to the kitchen as ordered.

'What the hell is going on?' thought Ciera. She was stunned by this sudden incident and couldn't take her eyes off that big ass knife the girl was weakly clutching in her grasp.

Cautious now, Angelica followed them into the kitchen and turned on the tap water in the sink. She hoped Mama Doll would hurry back and, perhaps, sweet talk Buuwa into surrendering to her like she'd watched the woman do on many occasions at the hospital. There was something about the girl that disturbed Angelica greatly.

This child had been through some serious shit in her life. The evidence lay in the girl's dark eyes, which scared the hell out of Angelica. This was no ordinary child.

By the time Mama Doll returned, Vega was now holding Buuwa's knife and rubbing her curly hair. Angelica scrubbed and sanitized the kitchen counter as good as she could, knowing it was where Mama Doll would operate on the girl.

Minutes later, Buuwa was moaning and groaning in pain as both Mama Doll and Angelica tended to her wounds. She never took her eyes off Vega, and he couldn't help but do the same. They were bonding in a way that neither one of them knew how to explain. Buuwa trusted only him with what was being done to her at that moment. She saw something in him that would later result in something so deep that nothing would come between them.

Then there was a knock at the front door again.

"I got it!" Ciera called out.

Moments later, little Rabbit was standing in the kitchen doorway with the strangest look on his face.

"Boy." Ciera stepped back inside the kitchen and glared at Rabbit. "Your little bad ass shove me again, and I'ma bop you upside your damn head," she stated firmly.

Rabbit wasn't hearing her. His eyes were locked on Buuwa. He, too, was affected by the sight before his eyes.

"Tu," mumbled Buuwa as a lone tear escaped her eyes. Then she shut them, falling into a deep, unconscious state. Once again, the champion was down for the count, but when she woke up again...

Chapter 23

Five of them stood amongst one another, conversing, as Thad approached their small group. Thad had only one thing in mind at that point. If Big Man decided not to honor that, then there would no doubt be some bloodshed.

Big Man was one of those Suge-Knight-sized niggas with a low cut and inked up with more prison tattoos than the rapper Kidd Ink. When he looked up and saw Thad coming, watching him attentively, he knew something was about to go down, and Marc was very aware of what it was.

Everyone present knew by the negative energy it carried in the air.

"What's poppin', homie?" Big Man spoke up.

Stopping before Big Man and looking up into his eyes, Thad was tempted to break his jaw right there. "What's poppin' is you bringing my lil' cousin home to the nation when you knew what went down with his old man. And because of your awareness of the situation, I feel disrespected, son."

All eyes glanced in Marc's direction.

"Your cousin made that decision himself, B," said Big Man, dressed in red from head to toe, and leaned back against his truck. Both of his enforcers, now on guard, sensed trouble amidst. "Besides, those fools who did that wasn't from my crew."

"It don't matter. Y'all all Blood, homie."

"So whatcha sayin', Thad?" Now, Big Man was feeling some type of way.

Thad stepped up. "I want him out. Big Man, I don't want my cousin running with your crew no more."

"I can't walk out on my fam like that, cuz," Marc interjected and glanced at his cousin. "I put in too much work for the fam—"

"And I'm about to put in work now, nigga!" Thad snarled and put his gun to Marc's head.

There was silence.

Two young girls exited the store, looked in their direction, and retreated inside immediately.

Jake and Nard, both of Big Man's closest men, looked over at their big homie, and Big Man shook his head. The O.G. pushed away from the truck and stepped to Thad, towering over him by a foot and some change.

"Back the fuck up off me, son," Thad warned Big Man, still pressing the gun against Marc's head.

"As long as he's under my set, homie, I'm responsible for him. That's my little homie right there, and you threatening my mans, which is my set."

"What!" Thad looked at him, frowning openly.

"Now you're disrespectin' me, B."

Nard budged, and Thad blew his fucking brains out the back of his head. Then Jake made the mistake by reaching and got two slugs pumped into his chest. Thad felt himself being lifted from the ground and landing hard on the hood of a car. Big Man hit him so hard that Thad felt himself black out momentarily. Before Thad even knew what was happening, Big Man lunged forward and cracked him in the jaw with a deadly left hook while still on the hood of the car.

"You gotta die for that, homie." Big Man drew his pistol.

Blocka! Blocka!

Thad watched Big Man's head explode in front of his eyes, startling him with the unexpected. The nigga's brains splattered everywhere, and Big Man dropped to the ground.

There stood Marc, gripping his .380 automatic pistol tightly. He looked over at his big cousin with open concern.

"You okay, cuz?"

Grimacing as he pulled himself up from the car to his feet onto solid ground, Thad scanned the area for his gun. When he found it, he picked it up and then stepped in Marc's face.

"See what you made me do, Marc?" he replied.

"We gotta bounce," Lil' Beezo chimed in.

Marc met his cousin's gaze.

"Let's go!"

"You lucky I love you, nigga," Thad said to Marc as Lil' Beezo wobbled his fat ass over to the car. "Now go."

Marc hesitated.

"Go, nigga!"

Before Marc did as he was told, he reached and retrieved the red bandana from his back pocket. To Thad's surprise, he kissed it and threw it onto Big Man's dead body.

Then Thad got missing—his baby cousin, too—though the situation was far from over.

***

If Mario had known just thirty minutes prior, while at a stoplight, that General and Roe were just behind his SUV, it would have gone down right there. Now, as he rode past the Magic Johnson Theater, he felt tired of searching for Buuwa, but his heart wouldn't let him give up that easily.

"She's just upset right now, man. She'll blow off a little steam and find her way back to the mansion soon," said Tony from behind the wheel of the Lexus truck.

Mario looked over at him. "You think she would go back?"

"Where else would she go, Mario?"

The two henchmen in the back were quiet as kept.

"This is a big place, though, Tony. It would be difficult to find her way back to Patricia's place."

"You're doubting Buuwa?"

He got no response.

"I've driven them all over New York enough times for her to memorize a route. Coming from where she's been, Mario, the girl has remarkable skills in tracking. This is her playground now," said Tony with confidence in the girl. "When she's tired of playing, she will definitely find her way back."

"I sure hope so."

"Or call first."

Now Mario was looking at him questioningly. "What do you mean, call? What are you saying, Tony?"

"What I'm saying is that I've been teaching the girls how to use the phone, and to be honest, they caught on pretty fast. The only numbers they've memorized so far is yours and mine—you know, just in case of an emergency."

"And how long have this been going on?"

Proudly, Tony said, "For the past year or so now."

Imagining Buuwa making a phone call seemed weird to Mario, but if it was true, then he damn sure hoped his girl called before he went slap crazy with worry. Mario loved all of his girls, truly. He was proud of them, as any father would be toward his children. Sadly, it was Ava who was gone, and Tu, too, leaving him with his precious little Zoey and Buuwa, the two he could not afford to lose.

There would be none other like the four he'd chosen. They were the most unique.

Ava, Tu, Zoe, and Buuwa had been a force to be reckoned with. 'No,' Mario thought sadly. He could get twenty more girls, and neither one would compare to those he'd lost. He believed he had picked the best from the whole litter.

After a moment, Mario was pulled from his thoughts by the ring of his cell phone. Everybody in the truck went still with hope.

"Yeah?" Mario prayed it was Buuwa.

"It's me, boss." Paulie.

"What is it?" Mario demanded.

"I think I may have something you'd like to hear."

"I'm listening, Paulie."

Paulie told him about Melvin's emergency arrival at Harlem Hospital. Then he pointed out to Mario that Rosie was no longer committed and had been secretly removed from the hospital where she was. He had no clue as to where she'd been taken, but he knew who had snatched her from under their noses.

Mario didn't like the sound of that.

"Who's with you now, Paulie?"

"Just me, Rollow, Nitty, and the idiot Frank. I swear, boss, if Frank wasn't your guy, I'd have been whacked him."

"What's he done now?" Mario sighed.

"Can't stay focused, flirting with the women here. I'm just about sick of him, boss. One more mishap, and I'm—"

Mario cut in. "Send Nitty in to see about our man, and spare Frankie. The boy's young. He needs more growing up to do in this business."

"I know what can make him grow up now!"

"Paulie?" Mario was grateful to Paulie. The guy was loyal and one of the most skilled killers of the bunch. He was the chosen guy, Mario's right-hand man, the Cuban kingpin who was back in Havana, Cuba, tending to other business. "I'll handle Frankie later myself, okay?"

"Yeah."

Of course, Mario thought he didn't sound too convinced, but Paulie would honor his command, no matter what the matter was. He was the boss, and what he said went.

"I gotcha, boss. I won't slit his throat tonight."

All Mario could do was shake his head. At least he had those who would kill in a heartbeat.

***

Across the street, sitting behind the wheel of a dark sedan, was Rita Brown, accompanied by Agent Mildred Shackles and Detective Clayton Riddle. They all watched both entrances of Harlem Hospital as Frank, a young, slender, long-haired Italian in expensive slacks and a button-down, engaged in conversation with a young redhead nurse.

Then there was the all-black Cadillac Escalade truck just up ahead, near the corner across the street as well. There was no doubt that there were armed Italian gangsters occupying the big SUV, and they were about to receive the element of surprise as soon as the SWAT unit was in place. Something had to give.

To take away Mario's power players would make the game easier. Then they would go in for the kill.

It was believed that Mario was behind the sudden disappearance of Detective Vincent Pratt after it was noted that the detective had visited the residence of the capo's sister several days before. He was yet to be found. Because of this, an investigation was warranted, and Mario couldn't even use his cell phone without it being monitored. They were watching his every move, allowing him no room to breathe without staying on him like fleas on a mangy mutt.

As for the men he had coming from Chicago and would be arriving the next morning in New York, the FBI saw that they were apprehended immediately. Little did they know, they were taking away Mario's advantage, only to give leverage to the deadly force that was about to befall him.

Their main focus was Mario, and that would be the reason they would lose him. He wasn't that powerful of a man to not have muthafuckas see to him, as he had done to many others. Mario was running on borrowed time, and it was almost over.

"Good," said Rita. "I'm tired of sitting around doing nothing, and I got to go check on Melvin."

"Okay, Matt. Make it happen," ordered Agent Shackles, touching a finger to her right earpiece.

For a moment, there was nothing, just silence.

Then Rita watched as what looked like a dozen black, shadowy figures appeared out of the darkness at once up ahead. All of a sudden, the SWAT unit swarmed the big SUV and drew down on everyone in the truck the second the passenger door opened as Nitty stepped out.

Rita was holding her breath. She just knew there were about to be shots fired, and she waited for the first explosion. None came.

In the meantime, Frank was still dazzling the young redhead nurse with his charm inside the lobby. He was oblivious to what was about to become his fate.

"My turn," said Detective Riddle from the back seat.

"Let's make it happen." Rita reached for the door and got out of the car.

After getting out, Riddle rounded the back of the car to Rita's side, getting in position, while Agent Shackles made her way toward the SWAT unit. Riddle placed a hand at the small of Rita's back. She slightly bent forward and wrapped one arm around her middle, and they approached the entrance of the hospital. To many, they appeared to look like a woman in pain being escorted by her worried companion.

Once inside, they moved toward Frank and the redhead who was beaming like a school kid with her first boy crush. Frank looked up at them for a brief second then turned his attention back to the nurse and her naive ass.

As if they were passing, Riddle drew down on Frank, and Rita relieved him of his weapon with a swift motion. Headfirst to the lobby's floor, Frank went, Riddle putting a large knee in his back to hold him there.

"Go check on Whitaker," Riddle looked up at Rita and spoke.

With a nod, Rita spun on her heels and dashed away, pushing the redhead nurse aside, causing her to fall on her ass. Ensuring Melvin's safety was her priority now, and there was nothing more she desired at that moment than that.

The lawyer was not only a good friend, but her bread and butter were, too, and the father of the nigga she was fucking, that same nigga who was behind their city being painted in blood. She was the only one who knew it had been General who had killed Yolanda Dovolani, not Roe. Then again, she wasn't really the only one, but she surely did know the truth.

Chapter 24

Gordo Lopez forked up another potato, rolled it around in melted butter, and ate it. He'd eaten one loin of lamb chop, and four others crowded his plate. Robert swallowed a cube of filet mignon and washed it down with a swallow of white wine. He waited for Gordo to finally speak up.

"So, you need some reinforcers to help you with your situation," said Gordo, a big bear of a man, too, who'd hailed from Mesilla, New Mexico, years ago to New York to organize his very own empire. "You want me to hand over my men to back you up?"

Robert nodded. "If it isn't too much trouble."

"The trouble has already started, amigo."

There was no response from Robert. They were in one of Gordo's bar and lounge night spots, over in Brooklyn. Gordo looked at the remains of his glass of water, which was also drained.

"You know I cannot deny you that request after all you've done for me and my people."

A spark of hope perked Robert up.

Gordo continued. "But only under one condition will I hand over my men, amigo," he spoke again.

"And what's that, Gordo?"

"For every man I lose in this little war you have is the amount of men you will spare in the court of law."

"That's no problem, amigo."

"No exceptions!"

"No exceptions," Robert repeated with sincerity.

Gordo signaled one of his men nearby, and he came with no hesitation. He spoke to the Mexican goon in Spanish, and the Mexican glanced at Robert, nodding briefly, and responded to Gordo with his vow to do what was needed.

"Okay, Robert, my friend," said Gordo as he looked across the table at him. "You got what you asked for, and Flaco here will see that everything is taken care of as you desire."

"Thank you, Gordo." Robert stood up.

"No problem, amigo." Gordo then returned to his feast.

Twenty minutes later, Robert was commanding the troop of dangerous Mexican killers under the influence of Flaco. He and all nineteen men were on their way to meet up with Trigger and his Crip gangsters to combine forces.

It was the first time Robert had smiled in days. He had an army now.

***

Jogging down the sidewalk toward his house, distancing himself from the murder scene, Thad slowed down to walk once he made it near his street. His heart skipped a beat when a police cruiser turned onto the street up ahead, heading in his direction.

Thad did not panic but kept it moving at an unhurried pace. He dared not give them reason to suspect him of anything. Though he had disposed of his shirt along the way and was bare-chested, it still wasn't reason enough to be harassed by them. He wasn't doing a damn thing wrong. In passing, Thad recognized others hanging about and spectating, trying to get into everything but the right thing.

"Damn." Thad almost whined in response to the cop car creeping down the street, taking its precious time. "Haul ass, son!"

Slowly but surely, the car drove by without incident.

A moment later, Thad turned onto this street, and he saw Vega.

Standing out at the curb in front of his house were Vega, little Rabbit, and Ciera, and to his astonishment, Crow sat in his wheelchair among them. Why the old man was out at that time of night, he didn't know, but Thad was surely about to find out.

Upon seeing her man, Ciera ran to him. "Bae, you alright?" she asked, kissing his lips affectionately and taking his hand in hers.

Thad assured her he was good.

"What happened to your shirt?" she wondered.

He just shrugged and stepped away toward Crow, laying a hand on the old man's shoulder while exchanging a glance with Vega.

"How ya hanging, youngin'?"

"I'm surviving."

The old man just nodded in response.

"What's up, bro?" Thad acknowledged Vega.

Passing the blunt to Thad, who had a very suspicious feeling that overwhelmed him, Vega explained. With every following moment, Thad could not shake the very eerie feeling that something was wrong.

"Where is Mama, son?" Thad asked after seeing Mama Doll's car out front in the driveway. He could have sworn her assistance would've been needed at the hospital by now. There was blood all over the streets.

"She's inside," Vega enlightened him, receiving the blunt.

Inside was exactly where he wanted to be to see his mama. Thad turned for the house. After all that had happened since he left the first time, he wanted to make sure his mama was okay.

Just when Ciera was about to go after him, Vega reached out and took her arm. She turned around to look at him, and he shook his head no.

"Let bruh do this alone for right now," said Vega. "Stop hounding my mans, and let him take care of it his way."

"I am his way, Vega," she retorted.

"Not tonight," he responded.

Ciera glanced at him worriedly, folding her arms stubbornly across her chest. She didn't like the thought of Thad standing alone with Angelica. Ciera thought the girl was prettier than her.

Seconds later, Thad entered the house, and Rabbit was right behind him.

***

Zoey raised her head and cocked it to the side, listening. She slithered out of the bed from beneath Patricia's protective embrace. Then the lights shut down.

"What is it, Zoey?" a startled Patricia asked.

The girl stopped and glanced back at her. "Bad. Go." She put a finger to her lips, and Zoey turned back to the door. Zoey looked eerily dangerous with her spiked glove on, opening the door to sneak out and venture beyond the queen's comfort.

Reaching beneath her pillow for her gun, Patricia came up with a chrome .38 revolver. She cocked it back and prepared herself for the worst. She got up and ran for the door, peeking out. She missed Zoey descending the staircase by a split second. She shut the door and locked it. Zoey knew what to do; Patrica placed her confidence in the girl.

Zoey would protect her honor to the death. This was her turn to show her combat skills.

Whoever was lurking outside, Zoey was about to see. Zoey clenched her gloved fist, wondering whether she should slip on the second glove.

The second glove was on in a heartbeat.

They were like Wolverine's from 'X-Men', but hers had four-inch daggers protruding from the knuckles of the gloves. Ava had made the gloves for her after recognizing her ultimate fighting skills. The young girl was deadly with her hands.

Easing through the darkness of the mansion, Zoey noticed several shadows moving beyond the windows. The house was dark, but that was what Zoey wanted, for the darkness, she'd prefer over anything else.

A glass broke somewhere, just behind the staircase down the hall, leaving the corridor. Zoey froze on the last step when the front door suddenly exploded inward. She shot across the hallway and into the massive living room sitting area. She moved fast and silently so her presence could not be easily detected. She was an itty-bitty something. Four shadowy figures entered the front, not knowing that, beyond the staircase, somewhere in the back, she had yet to present herself. The four intruders spread out and went in separate directions, their weapons out and ready to shoot something.

Zoey moved in for the kill.

The second intruder was the one who decided to roam the living room area. He was ski-masked up and carrying an AR-15 submachine gun.

Out of the corner of his eye, he sensed movement on his right, and when he turned, he didn't know what hit him. All he saw before the driving pain of something driven through his forehead from a sudden, wicked blow was a shadow. It bounced from the arm of one chair to another and soared through the air at him before he could react. Zoey landed on her feet, bringing the enemy's head down toward her face. The dagger was sunk into his skull and brain. She snarled at the masked face and snatched her fist away. The rest of his body tumbled to the floor in a heap.

Looking up toward the living room's doorway at her left, Zoey stepped away from her first kill and zipped through the darkness. She was hungry for more blood, and more blood, she desired.

The lone figure slowly making its way up the carpeted staircase caught her attention. Zoey advanced on the intruder from behind, and the next thing he knew, he was crying out in pain. Zoey had punched him in the back of the leg, driving the blade through the back of his right kneecap. The nigga bent at the knee and turned toward his attacker. Zoey gave him a mean uppercut, sending the blade beneath his chin and up through his mouth. The second one let out a throaty cry.

Zoey shut him up when she drew back her right hand and shot him a straight jab to the ribcage. After the blade sank and hit its mark, the second intruder was done for good. She let him roll down the stairs.

Startled by a sudden burst of automatic gunfire as bullets flew over her head and inches from her person, Zoey ducked and became a blur in the night. Being forced to the second floor made Zoey just as determined to protect Patricia, the queen; she couldn't let anyone get through that door. Zoey watched the stairs like a hawk, ready for the chance to destroy whoever came up.

The dark was her preference anyway.

Zoey lived in the dark, too, but not like Buuwa had.

She was hidden just to the left at the top of the staircase, fists ready to strike. Death was her mission. Voices from below were faintly heard before Zoey sensed movement coming from downstairs. Then she eased herself flat against the wall behind a large hallway table, waiting.

"He's dead too," a voice said.

Movement, followed by the low voice and two forms, appeared on the staircase. Both intruders were also heavily armed and moving along the wall and the banister before one another. They moved with caution, fingers on their triggers.

Zoey watched quietly from behind her cover at the shadowy figure in front of her. He had his back turned to her, moving with ease down the hall with his partner covering him, but to be the enemy and turn their back on Zoey was the worst thing someone could do.

Then she struck fast, hard, and ruthlessly.

Zoey shoved the closest intruder forward with all her might, causing him to collide with his partner. A shot rang out at the same instant Zoey drove a firm fist into the back of the intruder, making him scream in excruciating pain when his lung was punctured.

One more shot from the gunman furthest from her damn near blew her foot off. Zoey, from behind her first victim, used him as a shield while attacking the other. She had the furthest one pinned to the wall, but only momentarily because her human shield was weakening and slipping to the floor into his death.

A flash of steel warned Zoey of what damage it could do, and with one hand, she shoved the big gun aside and served the gunman with a straight jab to the face. That did it. The gunman released the weapon and reached for his wounded face.

"Bad," Zoey whispered.

The gunman was letting out a terrified cry of agony and fear after realizing his right eyeball was no longer in his head.

To finish him off, Zoey hit him with four body blows, which caused the gunman to double over, and she killed him with her famous uppercut. The blade broke through the fridge of his nose up and into his brain with one powerful blow. He died before hitting the floor. Zoey turned to the staircase. There was somebody else in the house. She glanced at the queen's bedroom door and shrugged her shoulders, then she silently moved toward the darkened staircase, listening and ready for more combat.

Chapter 25

Over fifty armed men were standing there in that warehouse that night. A mixture of Anthony's men, General's, and Roe's, who had all come together as one, it was a very intense atmosphere, but they all knew where they stood.

After an hour of preparation and strategizing a plan and the focal points of the situation, they went into action. Back to the streets they'd go, but with a higher degree of vengeance to serve.

That was what it all boiled down to.

Back in the car, General looked over at Anthony.

"You sending Oliva back home?"

Anthony appeared to be deep in thought. When he gazed over at General, he saw worry. "Sending her back to Cuba would be my pleasure, but it wouldn't be what she'd want. Olivia had a terrible life, growing up in Cuba," he said.

Roe was nodding off in the back seat. The nigga had popped two roxies to fight off the pain but was too high to recognize it, but he said he was ready for war.

"She told me about those days," General said.

Anthony nodded briefly. "Those days still haunt her. Me and her aunt Vivian are all she has left. Everyone else who had existed in her life is either dead or in prison, and since this is where all her friends are, I'll see that Olivia is buried among them."

"And Vivian?"

"It will take some convincing, but she will come."

"Damn." General dropped his head for a second. "If only I could have been there to protect her."

"Don't go blaming yourself for that, son."

But how could he not? General had been lying right there with Olivia straddling his lap, still fucking him, when Roe blew her brains out. What else could he have done to prevent it? At that point, to reason with Roe in an attempt to spare her life was useless.

If only Anthony knew the truth.

"It's part of who we are in our line of work," Anthony spoke up again. "We will always lose something we love and cherish along the way toward greatness."

"But is it worth it?"

There was silence.

"No one's life is worth losing when it should be lived—" Anthony was cut short by the ring of his phone.

Roe was now laid out in the back seat in a slumber.

Anthony answered the phone and conducted an intense conversation with the caller. General let his thoughts on the situation take their course. Tonight would be the night everything would be put to rest. With nearly seventy armed goons out lurking for Mario and his people, General was sure victory would soon be theirs.

"Oh, man," Anthony muttered after hanging up the phone.

"Oh, man, what?" asked General.

Reluctantly, Anthony answered. "Your boy Thaddeus made himself quite a mess back at the store earlier."

"What?"

Anthony explained the situation, and General couldn't believe what he was hearing.

"Who the fuck told you that shit?"

General's outburst snapped Roe out of his sleep. Roe sat upright in the back seat and looked from one man to the other. "What's going on, bro?" he asked.

"Nothing that my men haven't already cleaned up," said Anthony. "I saw to it, and that's that. Now we got to take care of this little business there and—"

"Man, what the fuck is up, yo!" Roe insisted.

General told him. After they'd left Thad back at the store, there was some shooting, and Big Man and his homies got bodied. What Thad didn't know was that as soon as he went missing after the shooting, several men exited from the back door of the store. They cleared the bodies from the scene while two others cleaned up what little they could of the blood and brains that were left. By the time the police got there, there was nothing they could do.

The scene had been thoroughly situated.

"Just what the fuck we need," Roe muttered with dismay in his voice. "Now we gotta deal with the Bloods and their bullshit."

"It's taken care of," Anthony reassured them, but not with General, it wasn't.

He was worried about Thad, and hearing Anthony say in so many words his men had straightened it all out made him wonder. What connections did the Cuban have with the Arab owner of his hood store? *How was it possible that...* General let the thought go and knew it would be foolish to question Anthony's position. There was no question that the Cuban was tied in with more than what met the eye.

"Don't fret, son." Anthony patted General's arm and lit up his Cuban cigar. "Don't fret at all."

***

When the bedroom door opened, little Rabbit slipped inside the room unnoticed. Quietly, he shut the door behind him while allowing his eyes to adjust to the obscurity of the room. He froze when movement across the room caught his eye.

Buuwa slowly raised herself from the bed.

Cautiously, Rabbit took a step toward the foot of the bed and halted instantly when Buuwa released a hissing sound that ran a chill up his spine.

From the moonlight shining through the window from Buuwa's right, Rabbit could see her glassy eyes staring at him. She didn't move a muscle, just watched him closely.

Swallowing hard, Rabbit chanced another step toward her as she sat up in the middle of the bed. "It's a'ight, ma. I ain't gonna hurt you," he said.

She gave no response.

"What happened to you?" he asked.

Still, he got nothing. Rabbit stepped closer.

Wrapped up in bandages with one of Mama Doll's tank top shirts draped over her wounded form, Buuwa was a sight to behold. Her left leg from her ankle up to just two inches below the knee was bandaged tightly. The dog had taken a chunk out of her leg as well as her left arm, but it wasn't as bad as her leg. The wound to her right wrist wasn't anything serious to worry about. Buuwa was heavily sedated but remained alert, refusing to allow herself to be taken down like her body was fighting to. Buuwa was a true fighter; she was a young warrior.

"You can't talk or something?" Rabbit stepped around the guest room bed.

Buuwa tensed up.

"Who are you, shorty? Where you from?" Rabbit questioned and took one final step toward her when it happened. He saw the gleam of the knife's blade before it slashed across the darkness in front of him. "Whoa!" Rabbit jumped back in the nick of time, inches away from being gutted like a fish from her sudden act of violence

"Back!" Buuwa ordered him in a low, hoarse tone. She groaned in pain, glaring over at him, then Rabbit drew his gun.

"You tryna die, ma?" he replied. "The fuck you go and do that shit for? I told you I wasn't gonna hurt you. You don't have to try—"

"Hurt."

"What?"

Buuwa shook her curly head.

Then, to Rabbit's astonishment, she lay down, staring up at the dark ceiling. From several feet away, Rabbit could hear her moan and groan. Then he froze when he recognized that she was crying softly.

"Tu," whispered Buuwa.

There was something Rabbit wasn't sure of awakened inside of him at that moment. He stared over at the crying girl quietly, wrestling with the decision that seemed to keep him placed there next to the bed.

Something was happening to the little one.

Buuwa said, "Hurt." She was hurting badly.

Glancing back at the door for a long moment, Rabbit turned back to face the girl. After releasing a deep breath, the little nigga took another step closer to her, and Buuwa was ready for him.

***

Robert explained to his men that the process wasn't so much about finding the best option as it was eliminating the ones that were not needed—that was, if someone had the time to go through all the other possibilities. After two hours together, Robert made the decision, and Flaco and Champ, Trigger's man, both agreed. Tonight was the perfect opportunity to make their move, and it would happen at the mansion.

Hell, it had already happened at the mansion.

Sitting in the passenger seat of the dark minivan parked just down the street, Robert lifted his hand for another pull of his cigarette. He'd quit years ago, but this was a time when one was needed.

What the man really needed was a strong drink and for all this to be over.

"They've been in there a while," said Robert the moment one of Flaco's men stepped out of the shadows. The big, tall, lanky Mexican made his way toward the vehicle at a hurried pace.

Due to the house being soundproofed, they didn't hear the earlier gunshots, especially from the distance between the house and the main road. They were about to be informed in just a second. Shit was getting hectic.

Flaco rolled down his window. "What is it?"

"Five went in, but no one came out. There were gunshots inside. We got the place surrounded by heavy guards. I'm sending another team inside to check up on things."

"Then why are we having this conversation, Niko?"

Niko shrugged.

"Go see to the others and make it quick."

"I don't think our guy is in there, Flaco," said Niko. "If so, he would've had the place secured. We have checked all the outside areas, and there's no vehicle but one around back. For someone like the person we're after, there should be a war goin' on if he were there."

"If there were shots fired, then the war has already begun." Robert surprised them both with his perfect Spanish. The man spoke three different languages, and Spanish was one of them.

Both Niko and Flaco looked at him

"Get it done, Niko!" Flaco ordered his man.

"It's done, amigo." Niko vanished back into the shadows from which he'd come.

Finishing up a cigarette and lighting up another one with the butt of the other, Robert released an exaggerated breath along with a cloud of smoke. His leg was hurting like hell.

"He's right, Flaco. If Mario was here, so would his soldiers be, and things wouldn't be so—"

"Why were there gunshots fired then?"

"Maybe he left one or two men back to…" Robert paused when, all of a sudden, a thought came to mind. "To protect something he loves," he muttered.

"Patricia."

Robert nodded. "Exactly."

A vehicle turned onto the street behind them with its headlights beaming. When they peered into the rearview mirror, they were taken aback by the train of other vehicles in tow as they turned onto the street and veered in their direction.

Lifting his AR-15 in his grasp. Flaco looked over at Robert with a serious expression. "Get ready, amigo."

Adrenaline surging through him, Robert flicked his cigarette out of the window. "I'm ready for whatever." He filled both of his hands with fully loaded automatic pistols.

There was about to be a showdown.

***

The front door of the house opened, and Mama Doll stepped out, followed by Thad and Angelica. Mama Doll had her purse slung over a shoulder and was hurriedly making her way down to the porch steps. She had a very worried look on her face.

Vega was the first to ask what the matter was.

"They need me back at the hospital," she said when Lil' Beezo and Marc suddenly appeared. The two homies crossed the street over to where they all stood at the edge of the front lawn and sidewalk.

"But what about…" Vega looked toward the house.

"She's resting, Troy, and we still gotta find her parents to inform them of the situation. I'm still tempted to take her to the hospital where she'll receive more proper care."

"She's alright," said Vega.

Seeing the look in her boy's eyes, Mama Doll reached out to touch his arm. "Why won't you let me take her, Troy?"

Vega knew exactly what and who Buuwa was but could not explain it. He was still at a loss for words about the situation, yet he felt in his heart that taking Buuwa to the hospital would be a serious mistake.

"I'll keep an eye on her," Angelica promised.

"Worm is still alive," Lil' Beezo interjected as he and Marc came to a halt before them.

"What?" Thad glanced at an approaching car.

"He didn't die," said Marc. "They just rushed him to the hospital a minute ago."

That was astonishing news to Thad.

"That must be Cathy's boy," said Mama Doll. "She was the one who called me and asked me to meet her at the hospital because her son was shot, and they were giving her a hard time."

"That's his bad ass," Ciera confirmed.

"I'll be back before the night's out." Mama Doll made a hasty retreat to her car. "Y'all watch over those girls!"

An awkward silence hung in the air.

No sooner than the car door closed behind Mama Doll did the sound of an engine roaring nearby startle them all at once.

"Oh, shit!" Vega acted fast.

Suddenly, the night exploded with machinegun fire.

Old Man Crow bolted from the wheelchair and rushed over to Angelica, tackling her to the ground and shielding her with his bulky frame.

In the process, Thad shoved Ciera's screaming ass to the ground and went for his gun. Lil' Beezo took two slugs to the body and dropped instantly. Marc also dropped low but only to duck the flying bullets and return fire with his own weapon as the car drove by.

Meanwhile, Vega, who was standing firm and letting off rounds in the direction of the car, ran out into the street behind it. Next thing he knew, Old Man Crow was squatting down a few feet from him, dumping rounds from his cannon.

The drive-by car turned the next corner up ahead and disappeared. Niggas were bold as hell to pull a drive by when the hood was crawling with cops.

"Fuck boys!" Marc cursed angrily.

Without a word, Vega spun on his heels and ran for the house to see about his sister.

"Thad!" Mama Doll called out from her car.

At the sound of his mama's voice, Thad felt his heart rate quicken. He looked over with relief to see her rushing over toward him. Thad took his mama in his arms, and she cried like a baby.

"I can't do this, baby." Mama Doll cried in agony. "I can't lose you, too." Ciera stepped over to rub her back soothingly.

"We gotta help Beezo!" Marc called out in a panic.

All eyes fell on Lil' Beezo, who had taken a hit in the leg and stomach area, but he was still alive and fighting through the pain on the bloody sidewalk.

After seeing this, Mama Doll demanded they bring Lil' Beezo to her car.

"I got him," Marc said.

"Lemme help you, youngin'." Crow tucked his gun and assisted Marc with Lil' Beezo.

Both Angelica and Thad stared at the old man in disbelief. To see Crow walking and such was a sight that also left them befuddled. The old man had not only played them both for a fool, but everybody else, but why? What was the reason for his deception?

'Yeah,' Thad thought with anger. 'This old muthafucka got a lot of explaining to do.'

Crow knew damn well he had to. Angelica was furious. She was hurt.

Chapter 26

Patricia sat on the edge of the bed, clutching her gun, tapping her foot. It had been nearly twenty minutes since Zoey had left her, and she was having a hell of a time trying to calm her nerves.

She'd heard the terrifying gunshots and the cries of what she assumed was the enemy. Patricia knew those deathly cries came from Zoey's attack, but it was Zoey she was now worried about. The girl was built for this type of shit, but still, Patrica could not help but worry.

Suddenly, there was more commotion downstairs, and another gunshot rang out, then a man's agonizing screams. That shit made Patricia shiver with dread.

Zoey was hard at work with the second team Niko had sent into the house.

They didn't stand a chance in the dark.

Something attracted Patricia's attention, and she found herself rising from the bed, stepping quietly over to the large window door of the outside balcony. She raised her gun and waited, and when the shadow of a form appeared beyond the glass door, she squeezed the trigger.

All it took was two rounds to drop whoever it was that had climbed up onto her outside balcony. Glass rained down upon her kill, leaving Patrica wondering who else might try their luck. She heard voices below on the ground and backed away. Then she stopped abruptly, easing back over toward the balcony door, and kneeled forward to retrieve the dead man's gun. Tucking her gun away, Patricia hoisted the big assault rifle up and slowly backed away.

What startled her next was the knocks at the bedroom door.

"Me!" Zoey knocked harder.

Instantly, Patricia turned around and ran to the door.

Once the door was open, Zoey took her by the hand and pulled her away. The scent of fresh blood and death was in the air as Patrica noticed two still bodies down the hall near the staircase. That was exactly where Zoey was leading her as she gripped her hand tightly.

The girl's hand was slick and wet with something. Patrica had a bad feeling it was the enemy's blood. The little one had definitely been putting in work.

Together, they descended the stairs and leapt over another dead body at the bottom. As her heart pounded in her chest, Patrica searched the darkness for any sudden movement. She just knew someone would pop up soon, and she was ready, the assault rifle ready. In passing, Patrica caught sight of several more bodies laid out through their journey toward the basement.

Patricia stumbled and fell.

"Up!" Zoey urged.

Pain shot up Patricia's twisted ankle.

"Up!" repeated Zoey in that soft but demanding voice as she reached with both hands to pull her to her feet. It was a mission, but Patrica regained her footing.

At the next turn, they stepped into the path of two gunmen, nearly colliding with them. Zoey acted swiftly, shooting out a fast, five-piece combo to the enemy before her. He howled, and Zoey then kicked the second one hard in the stomach. Patricia backed her up by filling his chest with hot lead.

"Go!" Zoey reclaimed her grip on Patricia's hand and led her to the basement up ahead.

Moments later, they were locked down in the basement, holding each other and breathing hard, but the mission was far from over indeed. From the basement, they would make an attempt to escape through the trap door that led to the guesthouse around back outside. If they could only make it outside safely and without being caught, Patricia was sure that they could find safety elsewhere outside of the house.

"My girl." Patricia rubbed the girl's cheek affectionately, placing a gentle kiss upon her curly and sweaty head, but Zoey didn't have time for the sentimental shit. She stepped away from her and ran over toward the trap door. She wanted to have a peek outside before making her next move.

***

Arrogance could be comforting, the belief that one was a blossom of cleverness springing from a load of foolishness and a cozy bit of emotional insulation. But it was a risky delusion, leading to a sudden lack of balance when reality came tumbling down on a person, and cleverness was no longer enough.

It was that kind of vertigo that caused Mario to sway when the truck suddenly shut down. For a moment, it rolled on and came to a halt right there on the highway.

"You gotta be kidding me!" Mario barked the instant his phone shrilled to life. He looked over at Troy with a glare in his eyes.

"Boss?" Tony lifted his hands in confusion. "It just shut off on us."

"You better do something about it quickly."

Tony suddenly looked lost.

Mario answered the call. "What is it, Rico?" he asked after recognizing the number. Rico was one of his lieutenants and a relative of the Napoli family—Mario's cousin, to be exact. He was heading a squad of Italian gangsters of his own as he and eight others roamed the streets of New York, raining hell upon those who got caught in their wrath.

"Do this sound like Rico, muthafucka?" an icy tone replied.

Mario froze. "Who is this?"

"The same nigga who gonna bust your brains out when I catch you, but 'til then, I got a gift for you, son."

A second later, Mario heard the unstoppable screams of his man Rico before a gunshot silenced him. That really shook Mario to the core, and he closed his eyes as the disturbing image of his fellow comrade moved him undeniably.

"You next, yo!" the caller announced in that same tone. Then there was a click. They'd hung up, and there was silence.

A hand lightly rested on Mario's shoulder from behind. "What is it, boss?"

Mario shook his head.

"What happened to Rico, Mario?" Tony questioned and feared the worst when the capo turned his gaze on him.

"Mikey?" said Mario.

"Yes, boss?"

"Get me away from here, now."

With a nod, Mikey opened the door and stepped outside into the street. He drew his weapon and then moved into the lane of approaching vehicles. Mikey lifted the gun and aimed it directly at the car's windshield. Moments later, the car came to a halt several yards in front of him, and Tony wasted no time snatching the driver out of it.

"That's more like it." Mario sighed.

Soon afterward, Mario and his men were peeling out, leaving a frightened young girl standing on the side of the road. Seconds later, a car pulled up to a stop before the girl, and two men with gold badges stepped out to offer her assistance. Another van shot past in a hurry.

"Don't worry, miss," said the lead special agent. "We're about to get them and your car back."

"Who were they?" asked the frightened girl.

The short FBI agent offered her a comforting smile. "Someone we've been waiting to get for a while now."

***

There was a total of twelve vehicles in all, from what Robert could see. They blocked the entrance of the mansion, and to Robert's surprise, multiple armed men began exiting vehicles along the road.

'Something ain't right,' thought Robert.

"Those can't be our men," Flaco stated with ambivalence.

"They aren't."

Flaco asked, "Then who could they be?"

Then Robert recognized quite a few men in the bunch. Some of them, he recognized from the old neighborhood, and Robert had a feeling why they were there.

"Where are you going, man!" Flaco asked when Robert suddenly opened the door and got out. He wasn't about to go after him, but instead, he reached for his phone to make a call.

Stepping out into the middle of the street and tucking both guns, Robert did not want to give them any reason to shoot him dead. He yelled out several names he knew from a distance. At once, all heads turned to look in his direction.

Robert felt a nervous shiver wash over him. He continued to walk toward them down the dark road, his hands held high. He was no fool. Robert knew what he was up against. Several niggas began meeting him halfway. One of them was K'wan, the third person he recognized.

"Whatcha doing out here?" K'wan asked the man.

Robert stopped before the four killers. "The same reason y'all are here," he admitted.

K'wan exchanged a glance with his homies.

"You seen my boy lately?" Robert found himself asking.

"Roe is chilling. He's good," K'wan told him. "But you need to fall back and let us take care of this right here."

"It's already being taken care of."

"Whatcha mean?"

Shots fired in the distance made them all turn. A rapid succession of machinegun fire rained in the night, a matter that demanded immediate attention.

"That's what I mean," Robert said. "I have my own army taking care of everything right now."

"Yo!" someone called out to them from the group of killers standing readily near the mansion's entrance.

K'wan raised a patient hand, then turned back to Roe's father. "Who you rolling with, Rob?"

Robert told him everything.

Surprised by what he was being told, K'wan did not doubt that the D.A. had more than enough help on his side. The man really had a team of thoroughbred killers riding with him for sure. Little did they know, those same killers were dealing with the situation.

Zoey was eliminating their asses like it was no problem.

"Then we need to find some kinda structure before I send my niggas in there with them crazy ass chicos," said Var, the big, black, Marvin-Sapp-looking nigga at K'wan's right.

"Definitely," K'wan agreed.

With a shrug, Robert looked back over his shoulder at Flaco, who was now exiting the minivan down the street, parked on a vacant lot of another unoccupied house. "We're about to see now," he said and called Flaco over.

Joining forces with Robert was about to be the biggest street team K'wan had ever been in. He called General to let him know what was going on. K'wan could see his big homie's face now. General didn't fuck with Mexicans, period.

Chapter 27

When the shots fired and bullets penetrated the wall of the house, Rabbit's first instinct was to protect the girl. Without so much as a moment of hesitation, Rabbit threw himself onto the bed and covered Buuwa's body with his own. He remained there until no more shots were being fired. He was there even when Angelica burst through the door and turned on the light, flooding the room with illumination.

That was when she panicked. "Oh my God!" Angelica rushed over to the bed.

Beneath, Buuwa stared over Rabbit's right shoulder at Angelica almost pleadingly. Blood was soaking the bedsheet beneath them as Rabbit lay there atop Buuwa, unmoving.

"Rabbit?" Angelica touched his shoulder and heard him whimper at her contact. "Rabbit, you okay?"

Thad appeared at the doorway next. Across the hall, Vega was seeing to Tee Tee, but something was wrong with Rabbit. Carefully, Angelica pulled Rabbit off Buuwa, and he cried out in excruciating pain. Biting her bottom lip in concentration, trying not to hurt either one of them as much as she could, she was immediately attacked by Buuwa once she had pulled him off her.

Angelica shrieked and jumped back from the girl's swinging fist.

"Damn." Thad approached the bed.

Tears spilled from her eyes while she mumbled something softly under her breath, and Buuwa crawled over to Rabbit. A deep, guttural sound came from the pathetic-looking girl at the sight of Rabbit being drenched in blood. She lifted his shirt with her badly injured hand, and there it was, the puncture wound her knife had caused when Rabbit threw himself on top of her. Buuwa's bottom lip quivered, and she looked up at Angelica and Thad pitifully. It was a mistake. Rabbit was groaning in pain while lying on the bed next to the girl.

Seeing this encouraged Angelica to see about Rabbit's wound, and Buuwa stopped her with a threat of the bloody knife.

"Troy!" Angelica called out.

Thad didn't like this shit at all. As he stared at the girl, he couldn't help but gawk in stunned silence. Moments later, Vega appeared with Tee Tee in his arms, both Ciera and Crow in tow. Vega analyzed the situation and handed his sister over to Thad. He knew what needed to be done and moved over to the bed.

Just like that, Buuwa pointed at Rabbit sadly, looking up into Vega's eyes pleadingly. Vega sat on the bed next to her and reached for Rabbit, pulling the little homie over to him.

"She didn't mean to do it," Vega whispered.

"I need to see to him," Angelica spoke up suddenly.

After gathering little Rabbit up into his arms, he carried him over to Angelica. Behind him, Buuwa made a protesting sound, but Vega handed him over anyway.

"Hurt," said Buuwa, her eyes on little Rabbit.

Vega turned back for her as Angelica rushed Rabbit out of the room with Ciera on her heels. Vega sat back down at the edge of the bed, and Buuwa went to him, laying her head in his lap. The girl was dealing with some emotions that were new to her, feelings she did not understand. She shut her eyes as if to black out her pain and agony and the emotion that overwhelmed her so.

"Primakov's camp," said Crow

Both Vega and Thad looked at the old man.

"What?"

"Primakov's camp," Crow repeated and leaned back against the wall next to the door. "It's a training camp over in Gambia, Africa. That's where the young one was bought from. She's trained to hunt and kill anything, and they're as loyal as they come. You got yourself a real killer on your hands, Vega."

"Where the fuck you get that bullshit from?" Thad demanded to know. It was obvious that he was still heated with the old man.

Crow pushed away from the wall. "It's no bullshit, Thad," he said with direct eye contact. "I know this for a fact."

"It's bullshit!"

"Call it what you want, youngin'."

"How the fuck you expect me to believe anything you say, old man? You really need to get out of my face right now, or there's gonna be a serious problem, Crow." Thad felt something in him awaken and didn't like the feeling. He had trusted the old man and had even grown to care for him. Now, Thad was tempted to break his muthafuckin' jaw for playing him.

"We'll talk later."

"Fuck you!"

Crow shook his head and walked out.

***

While Mario and his men were being apprehended by the FBI, General was hanging up with K'wan, General had also spoken to Robert, who had given his account of his and Melvin's situation. Melvin had saved his life, and he owed it to his old partner to see that he was medically treated for his wound. In so many words, Robert told General that he and his old man were no longer at odds, and General could only wonder.

So much shit had happened lately that it was difficult to see how the situation was shaping their destinies. It was hard to digest so much at one time.

After speaking with his father briefly, Roe sat back and pondered over his life. What would become of him when all this was finally over? Shit, how would it all end?

'Will I be able to see my kids again before it all did?" brooded Roe. He could not stand the thought of leaving them behind to have another nigga to call Daddy. Despite what he went through in the streets, the nigga truly loved his kids. Roe would trade his life for theirs any day.

Once the line was clear, General phoned Rita's number and got her on the second ring.

"Tell me something good, ma," he said.

"I swear, boy, if you were in front of me right now, I'd break your nose."

"Yeah, right. What's good, ma?"

"I just left the hospital after seeing your father," she said and filled him in on the latest news. Rita told him almost everything he already knew, except for the shooting at Thad's house and Mario's recent arrest along with his men.

"What?"

"I'm not gonna repeat myself."

"What do you mean, there was a shooting at my lil' brotha's house?" General snapped.

"Don't bite my head off, boy. There was a drive-by shooting, and someone was hit. That's all I know about that situation for now." The sympathy in her voice couldn't be missed. She knew how much General cared for Thad.

General leaned back and shut his eyes for a moment. He hoped whoever it was that got hit wasn't Thad or anyone he would set the world on fire about.

"You there, Jarrod?"

"Yeah." General opened his eyes. "You say the feds got that punk ass Italian?"

"He's on his way to jail at this very moment."

"Shit!" he said. "He gotta die, ma."

"I don't wanna hear any of that business, baby."

General hung up on her and looked out the window toward the hotel where Anthony's men were holing up. They had several of Mario's men inside, giving their asses the business, trying whatever possible to get them to talk. Roe sat outside on the hood of the car, appearing to be in deep thought. The nigga had a lot on his mind, and General wondered where the course of those thoughts was taking him.

"Bro!" General called out to him

Roe glanced over his shoulder back at him. "What?"

Getting out of the car instead, General approached Roe and sat down beside him on the car. The fitted cap he had on was pulled low over his eyes. His identity couldn't be detected anyway, because of the dimly lit parking lot. There was no need for him to believe they'd be easily recognized.

"Lemme hit that," General said.

Roe looked over at him oddly. "Let me find out you an undercover weed head." He smirked and handed over the blunt of Kush. After a few pulls from the blunt, General passed it back and blew out a stream of weed smoke into the air.

"What's on your mind, bro?" Roe asked.

"They took Mario Napoli to jail tonight, son."

"To jail?"

General nodded.

"Then he gotta die in that bitch tonight?"

"That's the same thing I told Rita." Then General briefed him on what Rita shared with him a minute ago, stressing the importance of Thad's well-being. "We gotta get bro outta the hood 'til we take care of everything. I can't lose my man, Roe. Vega, too, son."

"You think it was them Bloods that did it?"

He was briefly silent.

"I don't know, man." General sighed and took the blunt again for another pull to fill his lungs.

"We gotta tell your Cuban man what's up."

General hit the blunt one more time. "We gotta contact everybody we know who's in the county right now. The way I feel, I'll go to jail myself just to body that mutafucka, bro. He gotta die ASAP!"

He got no response from Roe.

"Fuck it!" General stood up and faced his brother. "With him in the county right now, it'll be easier to get him touched. He don't get no win, bro. This where we end this shit right now, son!"

Roe lifted his gaze to him. "I know a few people in there who's down for it."

"Me too."

"So, let's make it happen, then."

"Let's make it happen."

General took out the phone and made the first call.

***

Flaco made his way back toward the minivan to make a few more calls himself. After speaking briefly with Robert and his people, Flaco found himself anxious to get away from them all. Robert could deal with it, but it was his people who made him feel uneasy.

Maybe it was because he was the only Spanish descent present that made him uncomfortable. All the dark gazes stared at him, sizing him up like a lion's feast. Flaco was built for war, but he would have felt more secure if one or more of his men were present.

Flaco kicked himself for being shaken. He felt trapped around them. That wasn't normal for the Mexican goon who had killed his share of people without any remorse whatsoever. Little did he know, he was about to be a casualty himself in just a second.

From several yards away, Flaco noticed the cell phone he left on the dashboard glowing in the distance. He took off in a light jog for the van and snatched open the front door.

"Yeah?" he answered.

"Give me an update, amigo."

It was Gordo calling from a more secure phone.

With a deep breath, Flaco told his boss what little he knew of the situation. His men had been gone a while now, with the exception of Niko, and still, no word as to what the problem was now.

"And Angel?" This was Gordo's cousin, a twenty-three-year-old he'd recruited not long ago.

Before Flaco could respond, something from the corner of his eye stole his attention. When Flaco looked, he saw Zoey standing right there in the doorway of the vehicle. The little girl looked up at him with big, round, glassy eyes that seemed to glow in the dark.

Flaco reached for his weapon—big mistake.

Like a striking cobra, Zoey rushed him, pushing into the van and onto him. All Flaco remembered was a bright flash of light behind his eyes when something sharp entered his forehead. The Mexican goon was out of commission.

"Out," Zoey said over her shoulder before climbing out of the vehicle.

Patricia stood right there, then she handed Zoey the big ass assault rifle. She reached in next and dragged Flaco's lifeless body from the van and urged Zoey to get in next. Climbing in behind the wheel, Patricia looked over at her girl and released a sigh.

"Time to go now, honey," she said.

Zoey stared ahead with a dark expression on her face as she held the gun in her arms. "Go," she replied finally, and they went, peeling away from the battlefield, never to return again. The mansion was no longer home.

Chapter 28

By morning, everyone was exhausted with stress, emotionally and physically. The night before was a long, tiring one that could last a lifetime of pain and agony, and it would indeed. This street war would never be forgotten.

Despite the attempts to go back out into the war zone and get at anybody who dared to get in their way, both Vega and Thad stayed home. Angelica, Ciera, Tee Tee, and even Buuwa wouldn't let them leave their sight, so the two brothers stayed at the house amongst their loved ones. But damn, Vega wanted more bloodshed.

Sometime after eight that morning, Thad was awakened by Ciera with his dick in her mouth. Although he had been asleep during her mouth service, his little man was rock hard, and Ciera was working up a sweat, sucking his dick like the beast that she was. Thad grunted and reached down to stroke her head.

"Now you want to get your tired ass up, bae?" Ciera looked up at him with slobber all over her mouth.

Without a word, he guided her head back down to his dick, and she eagerly complied. Thad closed his eyes and concentrated on busting his nut down her throat. After a couple more minutes, Ciera shook away from him and climbed on top of him.

"I want you to cum in my pussy," she said and pulled her panties aside, guiding him into her fat, juicy pussy. Ciera sighed with pleasure as she wiggled down onto him, taking every inch of his meat up in her goodies. "Mmm, I love this dick, bae. Don't ever give my dick away. Ahhh." She was grinding on top of him, slow and hard.

All Thad could do was lie back and enjoy the ride. He knew what she was doing. Ciera felt threatened by Angelica and was out to prove herself. Ma was proving herself well.

"I'm about to come, bae." She moaned. "Come in me. I wanna feel you cum in me."

Grabbing hold of her thick hips now, Thad drove in her deep.

"Yes!" she goaded him on.

Thad pounded that thang a good three more minutes before he busted a nut in her pussy. That shit was so good it made him dizzy. Then, to his surprise, Ciera climbed off him and took his dick back in her mouth, licking and sucking up both of their juices from his little man.

When she'd sucked him dry, Ciera looked up at him with sparkling eyes. "I gotta go to work now, bae. I'll be back later for some more on my break."

"Word, ma."

"I love you, Thaddeaus."

"You better." He smirked at her, but Ciera had this look on her face that made him wonder what was on her mind. "What?"

"Why won't you ever tell me you love me back, bae? Why I always gotta be the one to say it first all the time?"

"Girl!" Thad sat up in bed. "If I didn't love you, ma, you wouldn't be here right now."

"Then why is she here?" Ciera cocked her head in the direction of the bedroom door.

Thad frowned. "This isn't about her, ma. We been doing this shit before she even existed. My heart only belongs to two women, and that's you and Mama. Get the fuck off that insecure shit, and play your muthafuckin' position," he said and stood up.

Putting on her clothes, Ciera had a few more words for him.

"Just so you know, the bitch got one more time to cross me," she told Thad as she stepped into her flats. "Next time, I'ma carve that pretty face of hers."

"Go to work, Cee."

"Whatever."

He slapped her on the ass, and Ciera was gone, slinging her sexy ass out of the room with purpose. Thad shook his head and prepared himself for the day that awaited him.

***

As Ciera walked out the door, Mama Doll was pulling up in the driveway outside. Vega looked up from where he sat perched on the porch steps. He was smoking a solo blunt while drowning himself in deep thought.

"Boy, do you ever sleep?" Ciera rubbed a hand over his head and eased past him down the steps.

"I can sleep when I'm dead, ma," he said.

"Well, don't sleep no time soon, because my boo need you in his corner every step of the way."

"And I'm there."

"I know," she said. "You always have been, and I love you for that, bruh."

Vega nodded and watched her make her way over to Mama Doll and speak with her for a minute.

The hood was quiet this morning. The sun was shining beautifully, and the atmosphere was warm and calm. It was as if there hadn't been total mayhem just the night before. However, Harlem was scarred beyond repair from all the bloodshed, lives lost, and destruction that had befallen it. Now, everything seemed okay, as if there was not a worry in the world, but Vega knew the battle was far from over. It wasn't that easy. It wasn't over 'til it was over.

Mama Doll approached the porch, and Vega stubbed out the blunt before she reached him. He stood up to help her with the bags she carried, relieving her of them, and kissed her cheek gently.

"Good morning, Troy. How are things? I'm sorry I'm just now getting back home, but they needed me—"

"You don't owe me no explanation, Mama."

She nodded solemnly.

Together, they entered the house to find Rabbit lying out on one of the sofas with Angelica curled up on the other one. Mama Doll looked at a shirtless Rabbit's form with a bandage over his abdominal area. She glanced over at Vega questioningly. She gestured for him to follow her into the kitchen, and he followed obediently.

"What happened to that child, son?" she asked once they were in the kitchen and out of earshot.

As Vega explained everything to her, Mama Doll wanted so badly to go to Rabbit. She knew the boy's story well. The whole damn hood knew Rabbit's way of life.

For the past three months, Rabbit had been surviving on his own while his prostitute, drug-addicted mama was serving a year sentence in jail. Her name was Faye. She had birthed Rabbit in a local crack house and had raised him from the dirt ever since. All the young cat knew was the street life, and there was nothing more he desired than the streets.

Rabbit was bred for that shit.

"I wish y'all had called me."

"You had too much on our hands as it was, Mama." Vega sat down at the kitchen table. He was buzzing good from the effects of the blunt he'd smoked. "What's up with Beezo and Worm?" he finally asked her.

She told him that Lil' Beezo was alright and would have to undergo more surgeries for his leg wound. He'd been hit in the side with a through-and-through shot that missed any important organs. As for Worm, he had been shot just above his top lip and was experiencing a minor coma.

"He's fighting. He will come out of it."

"I hope so."

Mama Doll reached over to lay a hand on top of his and squeezed it in assurance. "God will see us through, son," she said. "He hasn't let me down yet."

Vega wasn't sure if he could say the same.

***

While Vega and Mama Doll talked, Buuwa was silently moving down the hallway toward the voices. Though her leg was giving her a hard time, she managed to fight through the pain, and her process was quite slow.

Buuwa was determined.

Upon entering the living room, where the kitchen doorway was a little further up at her left, she stopped short. At her immediate right lay Angelica on the sofa, sound asleep. Just across the room, to her hazy surprise, was Rabbit on the farther one. Buuwa's face crinkled as she analyzed the situation.

A moment later, Buuwa was standing in front of Angelica's sleeping form, studying her for a minute. The girl was lying on her back with an arm across her eyes, her right leg cocked up against the back of the sofa. Buuwa reached over and touched her long, brown hair, reminding her of Ava's, but there was something about Angelica's beautiful hair that amazed Buuwa as she stroked her hair softly. While doing so, she thought about Ava and wondered if she was alive too.

Angelica sensed a presence near her, pulling her from her sleep immediately. When she looked up and saw Buuwa standing over her, she thought her heart would burst. Angelica remained as still as a dead crackhead left behind a bando. She stared at the girl's beautiful, young face with a crazy, bewildered look.

'Is this a dream, or is this little girl really admiring my hair?' Angelica wondered, but she wasn't dumb enough to make any sudden movements.

Stirring at Buuwa's left made her pause and glance over at Rabbit for a brief moment. She took one last look at Angelica and then quietly moved over toward him. Angelica had been holding her breath and let out a sigh of relief when the girl moved away from her.

"Rabbit," whispered Buuwa softly as she now touched Rabbit's bare shoulder. She reflected on the night before when he first showed up in the house and entered her room later. She tried to understand his intentions, and to her incomprehensible surprise, a feeling of emotion welled up in her chest.

It was at that moment that Buuwa concluded that she wasn't in any danger. Since Vega rescued her, all anyone ever did was try to help her. She felt safe in this strange place, no longer threatened by any of them.

Buuwa felt wanted, despite her emotional and physical pain.

"What's up, ma?" Rabbit muttered softly, peeking one of his eyes up at her.

Something surged through her at the sound of his voice, and Buuwa touched his face next, slowly feeling him in a way no one had ever allowed her to. Rabbit had done something to her last night that she could not explain—Vega, too, but she knew, with him, they were spiritually connected. She would forever be grateful to Vega and show her appreciation for what he did for her.

"Rabbit," she repeated and grinned devilishly down at him for some particular reason he didn't understand. Rabbit knew that she was different, that Buuwa had done something to him too.

A shadow fell over Angelica, and she looked up to find Thad watching Buuwa and Rabbit. She reached up and took his hand and watched them too. It didn't take a rocket scientist to see what was happening between the two young ones. Now, what would happen next?

***

The second Melvin opened his eyes, he found himself looking into the eyes of Rosie. She sat close to his side with a gentle hand resting on his arm and the other clutching a cup of hot chocolate cocoa.

Melvin wanted to say something but feared he would run her off with regret for ever opening his damn mouth. He just lay there, staring at the woman he loved, trying his best not to show how much he hurt. The pain in his back was agonizing, and his arm throbbed with the rhythm of his pulse. Melvin felt like shit, laying there on his stomach in front of his wife at his most vulnerable state.

Rosie tipped the cup to her mouth and pulled her hand away with an audible breath.

"Look at us, Melvin," she finally said. "We look damn pathetic. But we're lucky to still be alive."

He didn't respond.

"I have all the right to leave your ass and never come back, but I'll never do you like that, Melvin. I made a vow to you that I'm prepared to honor with every breath in my body while being your wife." She set her cup aside and winced from the pain in her hip in the wheelchair. "But if you ever put me in a situation like this again, I will kill you myself. You got that, Melvin? You understand what I'm saying?"

He nodded.

"I will kill you," Rosie repeated with cold, hard eyes.

Melvin had no doubt in his mind that Rosie would kill him just like she promised. The big man knew he had nearly pushed her over the edge to the point of no return.

"And I don't blame you for all of it," she continued. "Jarrod put himself in that predicament, and you had all the right as a father to want to protect your son."

'Jarrod,' thought Melvin hazily. "Where is my boy?"

"He's safe."

There was a brief silence.

"Jarrod is a gangster, Melvin. You know that just as well as I do, but you're no gangster, and you had no right to stoop to that level. You played your hand wrong, baby," she said with conviction. "He has a team of many more gangsters who would go to the ends of the earth for him at one phone call, and while you were so busy chasing after him—you're a powerful man, Melvin—you should've been using your political and resourceful influence to ensure his safety in advance. You don't go out and battle with the others. You remain on your throne and call the shots from your post. I shouldn't have to tell you something you already know."

"You're right," he replied reluctantly. "As always.

"I know I am."

"It won't ever happen again, Rosie."

She nodded. "I know it won't. I'm gonna make sure you don't make it happen again."

"Or you gonna kill me," he said.

Rosie smiled sweetly. "I damn sure will."

Chapter 29

General awoke partially rested and went through the motions of his morning routine without coming to grips with what he had, for the most part, already decided. He showered, ate a bowl of Froot Loops, and made a call to check up on Anthony. The Cuban had purchased a suite at the Four Seasons for the night, and that was where General reached him.

"I was just about to call you," Anthony said the second he answered the phone.

General looked up and saw Rita enter the living room through the front door of her Queens residence. She was dressed in a pair of khaki shorts and a white blouse, carrying a McDonald's bag in her hand. She glanced in his direction and made her way into the spacious kitchen.

"What it do, yo?" General replied

"You know anyone by the name of Block?"

At the mention of the name, General couldn't deny that he did. "I know him. What's up?"

"Let's just say that he solved our problem a couple of hours ago. It's believed that he sent that bastard Napoli to meet his maker this morning."

"What?"

"Yep. The guy killed Napoli and two of his men with a shank." General was genuinely stunned by this. Why was Block even in jail? Didn't he just get released from prison a week or so ago?

"That's not all, General."

"What now?"

"Block didn't make it," said Anthony.

"He didn't make it? How?"

"The guy was in for attempted murder on some chick and was facing some serious time. After he murdered Napoli and his men, he tossed the shank to one of Napoli's other men. From there, he went after the guy and made him kill him."

"Damn," was all General could say.

Rita returned and headed down the hallway.

"It appears that Block had nothing to live for anymore," said Anthony. "But I would like to contact his family and compensate them for his services."

"No doubt." General knew that Block did it for Harlem.

"I'll be leaving for Miami after the funeral tomorrow. I got more business of importance to tend to."

"I know." General nodded unconsciously. "I might need to make that trip with you," he kidded.

"I can set it up for you."

"We'll talk."

After speaking with Anthony for a few minutes longer, General ended the call and fell back against the couch. He closed his eyes and let his mind wander.

Mario Napli was dead. What now?

A minute later, Rita reappeared and stopped before him with a questioning look on her face. General regarded her for a long moment, holding her gaze intensely.

"I take it that you've heard, huh?" she asked.

He nodded reluctantly.

"Now what?"

"Gotta play the cards how they're dealt, ma."

She sat down on the arm of the couch and took his hand. "You really wanna run from all this now? Where will you go? There's no place on this earth called safe. You really wanna be a fugitive for the rest of your life?"

General didn't respond.

"It's something to seriously think about, Jarrod. Melvin will do everything in his power to help you. You know that." She kissed his head. "Now, where is that silly brotha of yours?" Rita asked.

General looked up at her oddly. "Whatcha mean, ma?"

"Roe."

"He in the back," said General.

"No, he's not."

Suddenly, General sat upright and stared at her. "Roe isn't back there—"

"Jarrod,"—her tone was firm—"he is nowhere in this house at all. Roe is gone."

That was when General felt worse. Where was Roe?

***

During the same moment, Roe was sitting on the passenger side of an Audi S5, smoking a cigarette. His right knee bounced repeatedly with anxiousness. What he was about to do would change everything.

Max Austin, one of the most powerful criminal attorneys in New York City, sat behind the wheel of the car, deliberating over the matter Roe proposed to him.

This definitely was about to put the state in an uproar. It was also dangerous.

"You sure you want to do this, man?" Max asked for the third time.

"You sure you can get me off?"

Max said, "The way you explained to me, I have no doubt I can get you off. Ballistics will prove everything. Besides, you're the victim, man."

In the backseat was a gym bag containing $150,000 in cash. It was Max's retainer fee to represent Roe's case after he turned himself in. He was doing it to clear General's name and take all the heat. Plus, Roe had three reliable witnesses who would testify that they saw the whole thing, and he did not kill that cop.

Also, Max had called his assistant in advance to get everything started. Max was about to earn that money and bring his A-game to save Roe from a murder case.

Once he got booked, Roe would contact his daddy, and best believe, Robert was gonna work his magic too. Everything would fall in place.

"What're you gonna do when all this is done?" asked Max.

"The same shit I was doing before all this bullshit," Roe replied cooly. "Ain't shit gonna change with me, son."

"Something will."

Roe didn't respond.

Ten minutes later, they pulled up in front of the police station, and Max shut the car off. They sat in silence for a moment while collecting their thoughts, Max giving him a window of opportunity to change his mind.

"What we waiting on, son?" Roe looked over at him.

Max shrugged. "Your call, Rolando."

"Then let's go." Roe was ready to get it over with as he reached for the door.

This was where it'd all come to a head, and they were ready for him.

***

When General got word hours later, all he could do was drop his head. He felt bad inside. Roe had turned himself in to the authorities, and General was scared for his brother. He knew it had been a hard pill for Roe to swallow his pride to commit to some shit like that.

'But he did it for me,' thought General.

That shit affected the whole hood. Roe had done the unexpected. The nigga hated the police with a passion, and here it was that he was going in for something he didn't do.

Four days afterward, Roe finally reached General at his baby mama, Angie's, house by prearrangement. Angie was the one whose house was next to the church where Trel got savagely murdered. Little Jamia and VJ were Roe's two little ones, the loves of his life.

The two homies had a deep conversation, General feeling some type of way about this brother's position. Roe was fucking him up emotionally, General fearing he was losing his true brother, but it wasn't until it was time for them to part when Roe touched that nigga.

"I love you, my nigga," said Roe.

"You know what it is, bro," General assured him. "If it ain't love, it ain't nothing, son."

Later that evening, General was sitting before a plate of country-fried chicken and was grubbing good when there was a knock at the front door. Rhonda called out that she would get it, so he continued to pig out.

Earlier, after leaving Roe's baby mama's crib, General stopped by to see Thad and Vega. For the second time since Roe turned himself in, General had been in the presence of Buuwa. The little girl had amazed him greatly after recognizing her from that night of Mango's death. She had been one of the girls involved, and he loved her for that, despite the fact that she had been working for the enemy. Now she was more like Vega's little sidekick than anything. General couldn't stop thinking about Buuwa and wondered what might become of her. It would take some time to trust her wholeheartedly, but as long as she played her loyal part, then everything would be good.

Familiar voices were heard outside the kitchen, and General lifted his head at their physical presence. There was Lisa.

"Just the person I'm looking for," said Lisa as she entered the kitchen with Rhonda and another female in tow.

Instantly, General dropped his chicken drumstick and stood up, wiping his hands on his jeans.

"Come here, ma," beckoned General.

Lisa didn't hesitate to wrap her arms around him.

"Where the fuck you been?" he wanted to know.

Lisa sniffed. "VA," she said. "I couldn't stay here with all that was going on. Plus, I had to take my cousins to Aunt Bev's house in Richmond because I couldn't keep them," she added.

"I miss you, bro."

"I miss you, too, sis," General replied. "Everything's gonna be alright now. It's over with."

"Not really."

"Generally speaking, no, but I assure you that you will be okay for now," he said with strong emphasis.

"I'm not talking about me, Jarrod."

He regarded her curiously. "What're you saying, ma?"

"I'm talking about Patricia." She lifted her chin high. "Mario Napoli is gone, but she's still out there."

'His sister,' thought General with uneasiness.

"And I know where she's at," said the female whom General nor Rhonda knew a thing about.

All eyes were on her.

"And who are you?" General asked.

The woman smirked mischievously. "I'm Cassandria," she answered proudly. "And Patricia's worst enemy."

"How's that?" Rhonda replied.

Both Cassandria and Lisa exchanged a knowledgeable glance with one another, and Lisa nodded encouragingly.

"Patricia's daughter, Yolanda, was my girlfriend before she ruined my life by putting false reports in my permanent file and falsifying client billings at the insurance agency I used to work for. She didn't want me and Yolando to be together, and she got what she wanted." Cassandria was obviously affected by this matter. "Now I want to pay that bitch back for what she did to me."

"Where is she?" That was all General wanted to know, and Cassandria told him exactly what he wanted to hear.

***

Three days later…

Patricia Napoli dangled in the air from a hook bound tightly to her wrists. Her feet hovered several inches from the floor. Her arms ached like nothing she had ever experienced before. She knew this was her punishment because of who and what she was—Mario's sister and Yolanda's mother.

Now, Patricia wished she had gone back to Chicago, where she was wanted, or anywhere else other than New York. She felt that Westchester County, New York, would be safe for her to mourn alone and start a new life there with Zoey. She had bought a house in Westchester County several years ago that she would visit occasionally when she wanted to get away for a while. It was her secret spot, and only a few people knew about it, but she learned who told. She worried about Zoey the most. Patricia wondered what had become of her little fighter.

The last thing Patricia remembered was stepping out to make a quick trip to the grocery store. She had left Zoey at the house by herself. On her way back to the house, Patrica was cornered at a stop sign by three cars full of goons and snatched up like Mario did Mayor Lofton. She was then forced into the trunk of one of the cars and taken to an unknown place. Now, four hours later, after being beaten up and manhandled by Lisa and Cassandra, left to endure the pain, Patricia was ready to die. The Italian queen was fed up and wanted to get it over with.

Patricia was ready to meet her maker.

There was a noise at the door. Seconds later, it opened, and a little illumination poured in. Patricia blinked a few times before she could see that it was Vega.

"I bought a couple of friends for you to play with," Vega sneered from the doorway.

236

To Patricia's horror, two full-blooded, red-nosed pit bulls entered the room, and the door shut behind them.

"I'll check on you in a week!" Vega's laughter came as she hung there in the darkness.

Patricia hated and was terrified of dogs. She willed herself not to scream but knew it wouldn't be long before she did. A week? Wasn't that what he said? By that time, she would be dead, eaten by both of those beasts that roamed around in the darkness. Then it hit her; that was the whole purpose for not killing her.

They wanted her to suffer. The dogs would do it. She was trapped. Patricia screamed at the top of her lungs.

***

Thad had just sold his last sack and was now completely out of product. For the past two days, all he did was grind. Then a thought came to mind. *Crow.*

He hadn't spoken to the old man since that night he revealed his unexpected deception, nor had Angelica. The girl was truly hurt by it. Though he and she kept in close contact, they tiptoed around the matter concerning the old man.

Now, as he entered his house and made his way to his bedroom, Thad thought about just giving the man his profit from what he'd made with his product. Thad had given Crow his word and decided to honor it.

Ten minutes later, Thad was exiting his house, carrying a Timberland shoe box containing the money. He made it to Crow's place in just a few minutes and knocked on the door, but he got no answer.

Thad knew the old man was home. He knocked again.

"Come in, youngin'!" came Crow's signature raspy voice from years of smoking. The old man had that gas.

Without further ado, Thad opened the door and let himself inside the house. The old jukebox was playing at a modest volume. There sat Crow in his favorite recliner, turning on an old wooden guitar that looked older than Thad himself. Crow didn't take his eyes off the instrument and spoke up while concentrating on his task.

"I'm gonna say this once, youngin', and you can take it how you want to," the old man started.

Thad didn't respond.

"I've been walking for the past year and a half now. After I started getting feeling back in my legs, I trained and worked myself to death to earn my legs back. Those damn doctors never knew what they were talking about, youngin'. Or maybe this was God's miracle blessing to me after all the good I've done in life. Who knows? All I know is that whatever happened to me happened for a reason only God could explain. I got my legs back, and that's all that matters."

"But why you continued to play everybody as if you were still paralyzed?" Thad finally spoke up.

Crow shrugged. "To continue to receive those government checks they pay me every month."

"You can come up with a better excuse than that bullshit!"

"Angelica."

That gave Thad a pause. "Huh?"

"That *bullshit* is what's paying her way through college, youngin'. That, along with what I'm being given monthly from serving in the military—all that money is put toward her having a comfortable life."

"Not anymore."

Crow looked away from him. "I know keeping something like that away from her was stupid. I should've told her from the get-go, Thad," he said with a deep sigh. "Now I'm afraid my mistake done cost me my girl. I done lost Angelica."

To Be Continued…

Lock Down Publications and Ca$h Presents
Assisted Publishing Packages

Due to an increase in the price of services we have increased our prices. The prices below reflect the price increase as of 11/1/24.

BASIC PACKAGE	UPGRADED PACKAGE
$699	**$1000**
Editing	Typing
Cover Design	Editing
Formatting	Cover Design
	Formatting
	Upload eBooks to Amazon
	Upload Paperback to Amazon
ADVANCE PACKAGE	**LDP SUPREME PACKAGE**
$1,400	**$1,700**
Typing	Typing
Editing (line editing/content)	Editing (line editing/content)
Cover Design	Cover Design
Formatting	Formatting
Copyright Registration	Copyright Registration
Proofreading	Proofreading
Upload eBooks to Amazon	Set up Amazon Account
Upload Paperback to Amazon	Upload eBooks to Amazon
	Upload Paperback to Amazon
	Advertise on LDP's Amazon and Facebook Page

***

Other services available upon request.
Additional charges may apply

Lock Down Publications
P.O. Box 944
Stockbridge, GA 30281-9998
Phone: 470 303-9761
Email: lockdownpublications@gmail.com

Submission Guideline

Submit the first three chapters of your completed manuscript to ldpsubmissions@gmail.com. In the subject line add **Your Book's Title**. The manuscript must be in a Word Doc file and sent as an attachment. Document should be in Times New Roman, double spaced, and in size 12 font. Also, provide your synopsis and full contact information. If sending multiple submissions, they must each be in a separate email.

Have a story but no way to send it electronically? You can still submit to LDP/Ca$h Presents. Send in the first three chapters, written or typed, of your completed manuscript to:

LDP: Submissions Dept
P.O. Box 944
Stockbridge, GA 30281-9998

DO NOT send original manuscript. Must be a duplicate. Provide your synopsis and a cover letter containing your full contact information.

Thanks for considering LDP and Ca$h Presents.

NEW RELEASES

BLOODLINE OF A SAVAGE 1-3
THESE VICIOUS STREETS 1-3
RELENTLESS GOON 1-3
BY PRINCE A. TAUHID

THE BUTTERFLY MAFIA 1-3
BY FUMIYA PAYNE

A THUG'S STREET PRINCESS 1&2
BY MEESHA

CITY OF SMOKE 3
BY MOLOTTI

GET IT IN SLUGS 1 &2
BY B. STALL

STANDING ON HER BUSINESS 1&2
BY DG SANTANA

STEPPERS 1,2&3
THE REAL BADDIES OF CHI-RAQ
BY KING RIO

THE LANE 1&2
BY KEN-KEN SPENCE

THUG OF SPADES 1&2
LOVE IN THE TRENCHES 2
CORNER BOYS
BY COREY ROBINSON

TIL DEATH 3
BY ARYANNA

FOR MY ENEMY'S SAKE | IRA B.

THE BIRTH OF A GANGSTER 4
BY DELMONT PLAYER

PRODUCT OF THE STREETS 1-3
BY DEMOND "MONEY" ANDERSON

NO TIME FOR ERROR
BY KEESE

MONEY HUNGRY DEMONS 1-2
BY TRANAY ADAMS

HUB CITY MENACE 1-3
BY J. WHITE

A THUGGISH PASSION 1&2
LAND OF DA HOOLIGANZ 1-4
KILLAZ ON STANDBY 1&2
BY IRA B.

FO'EVA ROLLIN 1&2
BY ASSA RAYMOND BAKER

THE LEVEL UP 1&3
BY LUXURY KING

Coming Soon from Lock Down Publications/Ca$h Presents

IF YOU CROSS ME ONCE 6
ANGEL V
By Anthony Fields

A THUGS STREET PRINCESS 3
By Meesha

CORNER BOYS 2
By Corey Robinson

THA TAKEOVER
By Keith Chandler

BETRAYAL OF A G 2
By Ray Vinci

SAVAGE FAMILY EMPIRE 1&2
SOULLESS GOON 1,2&3
THE DIRTY SIDE OF MONEY 1,2&3
By Prince

FOR MY ENEMY'S SAKE
AMBITIONS OF A SLIDER
FRESH OFF DA PORCH
By IRA B.

THE TRUCKLOAD 1-4
TIPPIN' THE SCALES 1-3
BAD BITCHES WIT GUNZ 3
PROBLEM SOLVED 2
By Christopher "Diesel" Hornezes

Available Now

RESTRAINING ORDER 1 & 2
By **CA$H & Coffee**

LOVE KNOWS NO BOUNDARIES 1-3
By **Coffee**

RAISED AS A GOON I, II, III & IV
BRED BY THE SLUMS I, II, III
BLAST FOR ME I & II
ROTTEN TO THE CORE I II III
A BRONX TALE I, II, III
DUFFLE BAG CARTEL I II III IV V VI
HEARTLESS GOON I II III IV V
A SAVAGE DOPEBOY I II
DRUG LORDS I II III
CUTTHROAT MAFIA I II
KING OF THE TRENCHES
By **Ghost**

LAY IT DOWN I & II
LAST OF A DYING BREED I II
BLOOD STAINS OF A SHOTTA I & II III
By **Jamaica**

LOYAL TO THE GAME I II III
LIFE OF SIN I, II III
By **TJ & Jelissa**

IF LOVING HIM IS WRONG…I & II
LOVE ME EVEN WHEN IT HURTS I II III
By **Jelissa**

PUSH IT TO THE LIMIT
By **Bre' Hayes**

FOR MY ENEMY'S SAKE | IRA B.

BLOODY COMMAS I & II
SKI MASK CARTEL I, II & III
KING OF NEW YORK I II, III IV V
RISE TO POWER I II III
COKE KINGS I II III IV V
BORN HEARTLESS I II III IV
KING OF THE TRAP I II
By **T.J. Edwards**

WHEN THE STREETS CLAP BACK I & II III
THE HEART OF A SAVAGE I II III IV
MONEY MAFIA I II
LOYAL TO THE SOIL I II III
By **Jibril Williams**

A DISTINGUISHED THUG STOLE MY HEART I II & III
LOVE SHOULDN'T HURT I II III IV
RENEGADE BOYS 1-4
PAID IN KARMA 1-3
SAVAGE STORMS 1-3
AN UNFORESEEN LOVE 1-3
BABY, I'M WINTERTIME COLD 1-3
A THUG'S STREET PRINCESS 1&2
By **Meesha**

A GANGSTER'S CODE 1-3
A GANGSTER'S SYN 1-3
THE SAVAGE LIFE 1-3
CHAINED TO THE STREETS 1-3
BLOOD ON THE MONEY 1-3
A GANGSTA'S PAIN 1-3
BEAUTIFUL LIES AND UGLY TRUTHS
CHURCH IN THESE STREETS
By **J-Blunt**

CUM FOR ME 1-8
An LDP Erotica Collaboration

FOR MY ENEMY'S SAKE | IRA B.

BLOOD OF A BOSS 1-5
SHADOWS OF THE GAME
TRAP BASTARD
By **Askari**

THE STREETS BLEED MURDER 1-3
THE HEART OF A GANGSTA 1-3
By **Jerry Jackson**

WHEN A GOOD GIRL GOES BAD
By **Adrienne**

THE COST OF LOYALTY 1-3
By **Kweli**

BRIDE OF A HUSTLA 1-3
THE FETTI GIRLS 1-3
CORRUPTED BY A GANGSTA 1-4
BLINDED BY HIS LOVE
THE PRICE YOU PAY FOR LOVE 1-3
DOPE GIRL MAGIC 1-3
By **Destiny Skai**

A KINGPIN'S AMBITION
A KINGPIN'S AMBITION II
I MURDER FOR THE DOUGH
By **Ambitious**

TRUE SAVAGE 1-7
DOPE BOY MAGIC 1-3
MIDNIGHT CARTEL 1-3
CITY OF KINGZ 1&2
NIGHTMARE ON SILENT AVE
THE PLUG OF LIL MEXICO 1&2
CLASSIC CITY
By **Chris Green**

FOR MY ENEMY'S SAKE | IRA B.

A GANGSTER'S REVENGE 1-4
THE BOSS MAN'S DAUGHTERS 1-5
A SAVAGE LOVE 1&2
BAE BELONGS TO ME 1&2
A HUSTLER'S DECEIT 1-3
WHAT BAD BITCHES DO 1-3
SOUL OF A MONSTER 1-3
KILL ZONE
A DOPE BOY'S QUEEN 1-3
TIL DEATH 1-3
IMMA DIE BOUT MINE 1-6
DYING FOR LIKES
By **Aryanna**

A DOPEBOY'S PRAYER
By **Eddie "Wolf" Lee**

THE KING CARTEL 1-3
By **Frank Gresham**

THESE NIGGAS AIN'T LOYAL 1-3
By **Nikki Tee**

GANGSTA SHYT 1-3
By **CATO**

THE ULTIMATE BETRAYAL
By **Phoenix**

BOSS'N UP 1-3
By **Royal Nicole**

I LOVE YOU TO DEATH
By **Destiny J**

I RIDE FOR MY HITTA
I STILL RIDE FOR MY HITTA
By **Misty Holt**

LOVE & CHASIN' PAPER
By **Qay Crockett**

TO DIE IN VAIN
SINS OF A HUSTLA
By **ASAD**

BROOKLYN HUSTLAZ
By **Boogsy Morina**

BROOKLYN ON LOCK 1 & 2
By **Sonovia**

GANGSTA CITY
By **Teddy Duke**

A DRUG KING AND HIS DIAMOND 1-3
A DOPEMAN'S RICHES
HER MAN, MINE'S TOO 1&2
CASH MONEY HO'S
THE WIFEY I USED TO BE 1&2
PRETTY GIRLS DO NASTY THINGS
By **Nicole Goosby**

LIPSTICK KILLAH 1-3
CRIME OF PASSION 1-3
FRIEND OR FOE 1-3
By **Mimi**

TRAPHOUSE KING 1-3
KINGPIN KILLAZ 1-3
STREET KINGS 1&2
PAID IN BLOOD 1&2
CARTEL KILLAZ 1-3
DOPE GODS 1&2
By **Hood Rich**

THE STREETS ARE CALLING
By **Duquie Wilson**

STEADY MOBBN' 1-3
THE STREETS STAINED MY SOUL 1-3
By **Marcellus Allen**

WHO SHOT YA 1-3
SON OF A DOPE FIEND 1-4
HEAVEN GOT A GHETTO 1&2
SKI MASK MONEY 1&2
By **Renta**

GORILLAZ IN THE BAY 1-4
TEARS OF A GANGSTA 1/&2
3X KRAZY 1&2
STRAIGHT BEAST MODE 1&2
By **DE'KARI**

TRIGGADALE 1-3
MURDA WAS THE CASE 1-3
By **Elijah R. Freeman**

SLAUGHTER GANG 1-3
RUTHLESS HEART 1-3
By **Willie Slaughter**

GOD BLESS THE TRAPPERS 1-3
THESE SCANDALOUS STREETS 1-3
FEAR MY GANGSTA 1-5
THESE STREETS DON'T LOVE NOBODY 1-2
BURY ME A G 1-5
A GANGSTA'S EMPIRE 1-4
THE DOPEMAN'S BODYGAURD 1&2
THE REALEST KILLAZ 1-3
THE LAST OF THE OGS 1-3
By **Tranay Adams**

MARRIED TO A BOSS 1-3
By **Destiny Skai & Chris Green**

KINGZ OF THE GAME 1-7
CRIME BOSS 1-4
By **Playa Ray**

FUK SHYT
By **Blakk Diamond**

DON'T F#CK WITH MY HEART 1&2
By **Linnea**

ADDICTED TO THE DRAMA 1-3
IN THE ARM OF HIS BOSS
By **Jamila**

LOYALTY AIN'T PROMISED 1&2
By **Keith Williams**

YAYO 1-4
A SHOOTER'S AMBITION 1&2
BRED IN THE GAME
By **S. Allen**

TRAP GOD 1-3
RICH $AVAGE 1-3
MONEY IN THE GRAVE 1-3
CARTEL MONEY 1&2
By **Martell Troublesome Bolden**

FOREVER GANGSTA 1&2
GLOCKS ON SATIN SHEETS 1&2
By **Adrian Dulan**

TOE TAGZ 1-4
LEVELS TO THIS SHYT 1&2
IT'S JUST ME AND YOU
By **Ah'Million**

FOR MY ENEMY'S SAKE | IRA B.

KINGPIN DREAMS 1-3
RAN OFF ON DA PLUG
By **Paper Boi Rari**

THE STREETS MADE ME 1-3
By **Larry D. Wright**

CONFESSIONS OF A GANGSTA 1-4
CONFESSIONS OF A JACKBOY 1-3
CONFESSIONS OF A HITMAN
CONFESSIONS OF A DOPE BOY
By **Nicholas Lock**

I'M NOTHING WITHOUT HIS LOVE
SINS OF A THUG
TO THE THUG I LOVED BEFORE
A GANGSTA SAVED XMAS
IN A HUSTLER I TRUST
By **Monet Dragun**

QUIET MONEY 1-3
THUG LIFE 1-3
EXTENDED CLIP 1&2
A GANGSTA'S PARADISE
By **Trai'Quan**

CAUGHT UP IN THE LIFE 1-3
THE STREETS NEVER LET GO 1-3
By **Robert Baptiste**

NEW TO THE GAME 1-3
MONEY, MURDER & MEMORIES 1-3
By **Malik D. Rice**

CREAM 2-3
THE STREETS WILL TALK
By **Yolanda Moore**

FOR MY ENEMY'S SAKE | IRA B.

THE STREETS WILL NEVER CLOSE 1-3
By **K'ajji**

LIFE OF A SAVAGE 1-4
A GANGSTA'S QUR'AN 1-4
MURDA SEASON 1-3
GANGLAND CARTEL 1-3
CHI'RAQ GANGSTAS 1-4
KILLERS ON ELM STREET 1-3
JACK BOYZ N DA BRONX 1-3
A DOPEBOY'S DREAM 1-3
JACK BOYS VS DOPE BOYS 1-3
COKE GIRLZ
COKE BOYS
SOSA GANG 1&2
BRONX SAVAGES
BODYMORE KINGPINS
BLOOD OF A GOON
By **Romell Tukes**

CONCRETE KILLA 1-3
VICIOUS LOYALTY 1-3
BLOODY MONEY BAGS
By **Kingpen**

THE ULTIMATE SACRIFICE 1-6
KHADIFI
IF YOU CROSS ME ONCE 1-3
ANGEL 1-4
IN THE BLINK OF AN EYE
By **Anthony Fields**

THE LIFE OF A HOOD STAR
By **Ca$h & Rashia Wilson**

NIGHTMARES OF A HUSTLA 1-3
BLOOD AND GAMES 1&2
By **King Dream**

252

GHOST MOB
By **Stilloan Robinson**

HARD AND RUTHLESS 1&2
MOB TOWN 251
THE BILLIONAIRE BENTLEYS 1-3
REAL G'S MOVE IN SILENCE
By **Von Diesel**

MOB TIES 1-7
SOUL OF A HUSTLER, HEART OF A KILLER 1-3
GORILLAZ IN THE TRENCHES
OOPS CRY TOO 1&2
THE DAUGHTER OF A CARTEL BOSS
By **SayNoMore**

BODYMORE MURDERLAND 1-3
THE BIRTH OF A GANGSTER 1-4
By **Delmont Player**

FOR THE LOVE OF A BOSS 1&2
By **C. D. Blue**

KILLA KOUNTY 1-5
TENDER
By **Khufu**

MOBBED UP 1-4
THE BRICK MAN 1-5
THE COCAINE PRINCESS 1-10
STEPPERS 1-3
SUPER GREMLIN 1-4
A GANGSTA'S SON
By **King Rio**

MONEY GAME 1&2
By **Smoove Dolla**

A GANGSTA'S KARMA 1-5
By **FLAME**

KING OF THE TRENCHES 1-3
By **GHOST & TRANAY ADAMS**

BAD BITCHES WIT GUNZ 1&2
PROBLEM SOLVED
By **"Christopher Diesel" Hornezes**

QUEEN OF THE ZOO 1&2
By **Black Migo**

GRIMEY WAYS 1-3
BETRAYAL OF A G
By **Ray Vinci**

XMAS WITH AN ATL SHOOTER
By **Ca$h & Destiny Skai**

KING KILLA 1&2
By **Vincent "Vitto" Holloway**

BETRAYAL OF A THUG 1&2
By **Fre$h**

COUNTDOWN OF A KILLA 1&2
SEX, MURDER AND GOD 1&2
GUNS DOWN, BOTTOMS UP 1&2
By Lo-Life

THE MURDER QUEENS 1-7
By **Michael Gallon**

FOR THE LOVE OF BLOOD 1-4
By **Jamel Mitchell**

FOR MY ENEMY'S SAKE | IRA B.

HOOD CONSIGLIERE 1&2
NO TIME FOR ERROR
By **Keese**

PROTÉGÉ OF A LEGEND 1,2&3
LOVE IN THE TRENCHES 1&2
By **Corey Robinson**

THE PLUG'S RUTHLESS DAUGHTER 1&2
By **Tony Daniels**

BORN IN THE GRAVE 1-3
CRIME PAYS
By **Self Made Tay**

MOAN IN MY MOUTH
By **XTASY**

TORN BETWEEN A GANGSTER AND A GENTLEMAN
By **J-BLUNT & Miss Kim**

LOYALTY IS EVERYTHING 1-3
CITY OF SMOKE 1-3
By **Molotti**

HERE TODAY GONE TOMORROW 1&2
By **Fly Rock**

WOMEN LIE MEN LIE 1-4
FIFTY SHADES OF SNOW 1-3
STACK BEFORE YOU SPLURGE
GIRLS FALL LIKE DOMINOES
NAÏVE TO THE STREETS
By **ROY MILLIGAN**

PILLOW PRINCESS
By **S. Hawkins**

FOR MY ENEMY'S SAKE | IRA B.

THE BUTTERFLY MAFIA 1-3
SALUTE MY SAVAGERY 1&2
By **Fumiya Payne**

THE LANE 1&2
By Ken-Ken Spence

THE PUSSY TRAP 1-5
By **Nene Capri**

DIRTY DNA
By **Blaque**

SANCTIFIED AND HORNY
by **XTASY**

FOR MY ENEMY'S SAKE | IRA B.

BOOKS BY LDP'S CEO, CA$H

TRUST IN NO MAN
TRUST IN NO MAN 2
TRUST IN NO MAN 3
BONDED BY BLOOD
SHORTY GOT A THUG
THUGS CRY
THUGS CRY 2
THUGS CRY 3
TRUST NO BITCH
TRUST NO BITCH 2
TRUST NO BITCH 3
TIL MY CASKET DROPS
RESTRAINING ORDER
RESTRAINING ORDER 2
IN LOVE WITH A CONVICT
LIFE OF A HOOD STAR
XMAS WITH AN ATL SHOOTER